Sharkland

Sharkland

Morgan & Carissa Goldstein

Dedicated to Joanna and Matt Goldstein for helping us and supporting us so much with this book!

Table of Contents

Flashback (Prologue)

Note: The text in the prologue is in italics to signify that the prologue took place in the past, hence the name Flashback. In future chapters, the text in italics signifies Max's thoughts.

12/31/16 On The Planet Of Wah

It was New Year's Eve of 2016, and my family had attended a celebration with our neighbors, the Istruugabons. In past years that they hosted the neighborhood New Year's Eve party, the Istruugabons had let the kids eat a lot of junk food, so I was not allowed to eat dessert or unhealthy meals during the week leading up to New Year's Eve.

I was very excited. The Istruugabons are rich, yet they are not like stereotypical rich people. At past New Year's Eve parties, they always let me do things my parents did not usually allow.

Dinner was buffet-style beef stew and rice. It was delicious, and there was extra, so Mrs. Istruugabon let me have seconds and even thirds. I ate two slices of cake and two or three caramel chocolates for my first dessert after dinner.

When I finished my cake and chocolates, I went to the basement. The basement had an extra-wide movie screen and five movie theater-style chairs. I watched a two-hour movie called A Shark's World in the basement with a few friends and a can of root beer. After the movie, I went back upstairs to get my second round of dessert, which was ice cream, when the time was around 10:00 at night.

In the Istruugabon's basement, I played Ping-Pong with my mom when I finished my second dessert (and a conversation with a neighbor). After I won twice and she won once, she went upstairs to chat with the other parents, who sat around the dining room table near the door. I went upstairs again and crashed on the couch.

I watched a show called 'Funny Animals' on TV. The Istruugabon's dog, Leo, and two cats, Milo and Willow, cuddled on the sectional with me.

My dad entered the room and told me the time a few minutes later. It was 10:59, so it was almost time for the New Year celebration! The Istruugabons never want to celebrate the new year at midnight because many young kids with early bedtimes come to their party. Instead, they celebrate it at 11:00 P.M.

I looked behind me and saw a crowd walking through the doors to the patio and backyard. Since it was wintertime and the Istruugabons didn't want the snow to rust their outdoor furniture, most of the furniture was covered with large blue tarps. Most people outside grabbed a sparkler or two, and Mr. Istruugabon found the giant outdoor clock and plugged it in. I was full, yet I managed to get off the sectional and go outside with everyone else.

Mrs. Istruugabon helped the younger people light their sparklers. She also passed around lighters to the adults. The outdoor clock's display now showed there were thirty seconds until 'midnight.'

Mr. Istruugabon ran down the stairs while holding the handrail with his right hand. He was going to start the fireworks show. 'Let's get this party started!' he said.

He ran back up the stairs so he could watch the show. The fireworks started, creating a beautiful contrast with colors against the pitch-black winter sky.

'Don't you want to light a sparkler, too?' my mom asked.

'No, thanks,' I remember saying. Deep down, I wanted to, but a terrible thing happened last July 4th, which stopped me from lighting a sparkler. One of my family members had left a hot sparkler on the ground, and I accidentally stepped on it. It hurt terribly for hours until it finally felt better. Nowadays, for the Fourth of July, my family drops used sparklers into a bucket of water to cool them off, but I still didn't want to light one.

'5...,' the crowd said. There were five seconds until 11:00 ("midnight").

'4...'

'3...'

'2...'

'1...'

'HAPPY NEW YEAR!' Everyone shouted at the same time.

After all the fireworks were over and the big moment had passed, everybody headed inside, and the adults talked to each other for a few minutes. The party was over. I slipped my neon blue sneakers onto my feet and pulled my puffer jacket over my arms and torso. When my parents did the same, I said goodbye to all my neighborhood friends and walked out the door into the frigid weather.

My mom got to the front door first because she had the key to unlock it.

I took my coat and shoes off when I was inside the house. My feet were tired, so I went upstairs and collapsed on my bed. When my mom noticed I wasn't doing anything, she asked me to get ready for bed, so I walked into the bathroom to brush and floss my teeth, knowing I could have a good night's rest after I finished my bedtime routine. When I completed my bathroom things, I returned to my room to get my pajamas on.

Once my pajamas were on, I turned my light off and tucked myself into bed. I was tired, so it only took me a few minutes to fall asleep.

Part 1

Max And The Sqwgamugurtz

1
Sharkland

Where am I?

I woke up in the morning. I was sweating from the body part I thought was my arm to the body part I thought was my foot. *Mom must have turned the heat up because it is not normally this hot in winter,* I thought. *Everything's normal.*

Yet part of me knew something was different. My mattress was harder than usual and my room was bright. *Why is my room so bright?* I wondered. *It's the beginning of January!* I tried to stay calm. Although I was still too tired to open my eyes, I reassured myself that I was in my own bedroom in my own house. I didn't remember going to a sleepover yesterday night; I was at a New Year's Eve party.

I rolled over onto my right side, but a sharp pain shot down my spine.

I touched my back and felt something pointy, triangular, slimy, and slightly wet. I was confused, worried, and scared. *Why is a triangular thing attached to my back? How did it get there?*

I gained the courage to open my eyes and looked around my room. It was a completely different room, with a dresser in one corner and a desk in the other. A bay window was placed directly across the bed, which touched the back wall's center. My bed was also higher up off the ground.

I sat up and checked my clock. *6:22? Wow, I woke up early today.* The sky was bright, even though I assumed it would be dark because of the hour. *That's strange. The room's brightness reminds me of summertime, but I don't think sleeping for five months straight is possible. Even if I did sleep for five months straight, that wouldn't explain the room I woke up in. It's as if I didn't wake up in my bedroom, but someone else's.*

With what I thought was my left arm, I reached over to the light switch and flicked it on, which made the entire room even brighter. Strangely, the body part I thought was my arm was now pointy, triangular, slimy, and slightly wet, just like my back.

2

Still experiencing morning grogginess, I got out of bed. I nearly tripped when I tried to stand up. I looked down at what I thought were my feet and realized they weren't feet at all! Instead, something that reminded me of a shark's caudal fin (tail fin) replaced my feet.

Shocked, I wobbled to my mirror once I steadied myself. I slowly moved so I could see myself in the mirror, and nearly jumped in surprise. Instead of seeing a human, I saw something that resembled a shark. *This can't be real. From my knowledge, this isn't possible. I must be dreaming.* I stumbled back to my bed, nearly tripping, and buried myself under the covers. I tried to fall back asleep, but I had almost completely woken myself up by looking in the mirror.

I got out of bed again and walked back to my mirror since I knew I would waste time trying to fall back asleep. I crouched beneath the mirror and slowly rose. I saw more of what I thought was myself, a pale blue-colored human-shark hybrid wearing comfortable shark-print pajamas. Something was attached to my back, which appeared to be a fin. I did not know what happened.

I decided that if I was awake, it would be good to get dressed. I looked around to find the dresser, which touched the left wall. Once I spotted it, I opened the middle drawer, where I expected to find my normal set of clothes, but the contents of the drawer were not what I expected. The only things in the drawer were a T-shirt and one pair of shorts. A pair of underwear and two clean triangular-shaped socks rested in the top drawer. I checked the other drawers, but the rest of the dresser was empty. I did not recognize any clothes in the drawer, which was strange.

Why are summer clothes in my drawer? It's winter! Or, at least I think it's winter. Also, where did all of my clothes go?! I used to have an entire closet of clothes. These shorts also have a fairly big waistline. Even though I was confused, I knew I couldn't wear my pajamas all day, so I dressed myself using the clothes in the drawer.

I wanted to see what was outside the bedroom once I had gotten dressed. The door was a simple dark brown-colored piece of wood. A simple knob was stuck on the right side of the door.

I tried opening the door like I had done every day before with one of my hands, which was now a large, thick pectoral fin[1]. I had two of them! *Why won't it work? Perhaps I should try a different approach if I want to get this door open.* I grabbed the doorknob with my other fin and turned it using both of my fins. I used my body weight to push the door open when the

---

[1] Pectoral fins are the largest fins on the bottom of a shark's body. Both Sharkland sharks and Earth sharks have two. To learn more, turn to the 'Complete Glossary of Sharkland Terms' section at the end of the book.

doorknob turned. A set of stairs with a railing was outside. A small bathroom with a shower was to the right of the stairs.

I stumbled down the stairs while gripping the railing tightly. Three other human-shark hybrids were talking to each other. One of them looked older than the other two. One of the younger sharks wore a pink shirt, and the other was wearing a bright blue one. One of the younger sharks seemed to notice me.

"Hi! I'm Max," I said. "I'm nine-and-a-half years old. I woke up in a strange room and I don't know where I am."

The older shark nodded. "Hello, Max! You're in a place called Sharkland. My full name is Josephene Brime, but I would prefer it if you called me Jo. I just turned twelve years old! To my right is Mary Calida-Yif. She's the one wearing the bright blue shirt. Next to her is Anny, her sister. She's wearing a pink shirt. Both twins are nine years old."

Oh, so this is Sharkland. I was not too surprised. *It makes sense because I somehow turned into a human-shark hybrid overnight. Everybody else in this tiny house is also a shark. I think it's so amazing how I'm in Sharkland! I've always wanted to go to a place like this!* "Hi, Jo! Hello, Mary and Anny!"

"You must be the shark I heard about in the news. I never imagined I'd get to meet you! Mary, Anny, and I won this house in a contest a few weeks ago, and now I get to be your caretaker!" the oldest shark said, who I now knew was named Jo.

"You seem like you will be a great caretaker, from what I've seen so far," I said.

"She really is!" Anny said.

"I agree," Mary agreed.

Jo thought for a moment, then spoke. "When I read about you in the news the other day, the news claimed that sharks... err, humans... who come here for Go Anywhere Day can stay here for up to five months. Does that sound about right?"

"Yes, I did come here from Go Anywhere Day! You're right! I will stay here for five months before I will have to sadly return home. I have a question. What day is it?"

"It's June 2nd, 2017," Anny replied. "School was let out yesterday." *Oh. That date makes sense because it would explain why it was so bright in my room when I woke up. It would also explain the room's temperature. I must have time-traveled five months forward because it is still 2017, but if I were on Wah, my home planet right now, it would be January 2nd. Or maybe I did not time-travel, but the time zones are different here, so it is summer.* "Could you tell me more about Sharkland?" I asked.

Anny responded to my request for knowledge. "Sure! Sharkland is one of the ten countries on a planet called Dennisatroy, plus the North and South points. I'm assuming you didn't know about Dennisatroy before you came here because you can only get here through teleportation. Dennisatroy has many countries[2], but here's a few: Achebail, Fikasi, Genevail, Hacoshof, Hile-Backa, Impood, Quinsiching, Sharkland, The Scar, and Wilderbang. plus the North and South points, which are not countries. Sharkland, Impood, and Hile-Backa are the three main countries."

---

[2] To learn the pronunciations of the following countries, turn to the "Pronunciations of Names in Sharkland" page at the end of the book. To learn more about these countries, turn to the "Complete Glossary of Sharkland Terms" section at the end of the book.

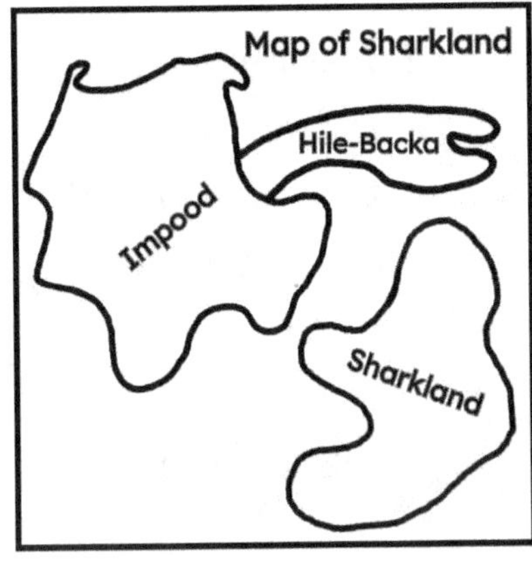

Dennisatroy

- Sharkland is a country on a planet called Dennisatroy.
- The map only shows part of Dennisatroy; there are other countries not shown on the map.
- On Dennisatroy, the smallest country is Hile-Backa and the biggest is Hacoshof. Sharkland is only a bit smaller than Impood.
- Sharkland, Hile-Backa, and Impood are known as the "main countries".
- The only way to get to Dennisatroy is teleporting.

Sharkland

- Sharkland has a temperate climate, with warm, humid summers and very cold winters.
- Shark-human hybrids live on Sharkland, not humans.
- Sharkland is approximately 1,000,000 square miles, and it has a population of approximately 900,000.

Jo started talking. "Also, Max, I'm not sure I told you earlier, but I found some sort of treasure map yesterday in a closet on the main level of this house. It was kind of old, but not too old, and it mentioned gold. We started following the route yesterday, but we got bored and came back here. Do you want to join?"

"I would love to join!" I exclaimed. I was surprised I had gotten such an offer only a few minutes after meeting Jo, Anny, and Mary.

"Thank you! One of the reasons we came back here was because it is hard to find gold with only three sharks. Your help is appreciated!"

"Yay! Sorry to change the topic, but I'm hungry. Do you have anything to eat?" I asked.

"Yes, we do!" Anny replied. She opened a cabinet next to her and grabbed a box labeled 'SharkTadlets.' She opened the box, grabbed two SharkTadlets, and put them on a plate. *These smell so much like fish. I wonder if that's the only thing they're made with.* I carefully took a bite out of one of the SharkTadlets. It tasted like fish as I had assumed. There were a few other flavors, but it was mostly fish. They were good. Anny poured herself a bowl of SharkBites cereal, which also smelled like fish. She carefully put her bowl, plate, and spoon in the sink after she finished.

I walked to the window and looked outside after I ate my breakfast. The area was mainly rural. I could see three or four houses, but they were all off in the distance. A road in the middle divided the open hills and fields in half, and only one car drove down that road.

I should ask Jo to go outside. I want to see what it is like in the backyard and if there are any more strange things. "Jo, can I go outside?" I asked.

"Sure, Max," said Jo. "Although we're thinking of going on our gold-hunting adventure soon, so we'll come and get you when we are ready to start packing."

"Thanks!" I replied. After pausing, I added, "Where's the door to the backyard?"

"It's past the couch and to the right," Jo stated. I slipped on my shoes—which were shaped like my caudal fin—and walked out the door to the spacious backyard.

Nothing but grass was in sight. I looked straight ahead, hoping to find another house, but it was only grass. The backyard seemed to have no end. Compared to its vastness, the house looked tiny. The only thing I could find between me and the horizon was a shed a little over half a mile away. I did not know why a shed would be so far away from its house, but I was curious as to what was inside, so I ran over to it.

The shed looked much, much larger than it did back at the house. Inside was every backyard toy imaginable. I grabbed a blue ball near the front.

I kicked it back to the house and played the kick-and-chase game for a little while until Mary stuck her head out of the door and asked me to come inside because she, Jo, and Anny were getting ready for the gold hunt.

"Max, we're going on our trip soon! Do you want to help pack?" Mary asked.

"Sure," I said. "What do we need?"

"Come inside, and I'll show you the list," Mary replied. I went inside the house, took my shoes off, placed them by the front door, then walked over to the kitchen table where Mary had placed the list.

2
Preparation

"We will need a few things. First, we will need diving suits. The map suggests there will be some sort of underwater cave somewhere during our journey, and even though sharks can swim without diving suits, we could swim faster with diving suits. We will also need four water bottles in case we get thirsty," Mary suggested. Anny wrote "diving suits" and "water bottles" on the list.

"Next, we will need a few boxes of SharkTadlets in case we get hungry. This trip might be energy-consuming, so it's better to have too many rather than not enough, as long as the car has space. The last thing we will need is a pocket knife in case we need it to survive." Anny wrote these things on the list.

"I'll grab the diving suits!" Jo said and disappeared upstairs.

"While you're doing that, I'll grab the water bottles!" Mary disappeared into the first-floor bathroom.

"While you're grabbing the filter, I'll grab the SharkTadlets and pocket knife!" Anny disappeared into another room on the first floor.

Jo came down the stairs again about a minute later with many rubber-like garments in her fins. Mary returned shortly after with four water bottles. Anny was still in the other room on the first floor, rummaging through something.

She came out of the room, though, a bit later, holding a *very* large bin, a much smaller storage container with a lid, and a pocket knife. "Anny, what's the bin for?" I asked.

"It's an extra bin," Anny replied.

"Why do we have an extra bin? Do we *actually* need it?" Jo wondered.

"Why not? We might need it for some reason. We probably—hopefully—have enough room in the car to hold it. Let's put everything into a backpack or bag or something. Jo, you have a backpack, right?"

"Yes, I do," Jo informed everybody. "I use it for school. I'll go grab it and take my things out."

Jo went to the closest to grab her backpack. She took her school supplies out, then set the backpack on the table. Everybody put the supplies in the backpack's various pockets.

"Yay, we're finished packing! Let's go to the car!" exclaimed an excited Anny.

"Okay!" Jo replied. She zipped the backpack and put it back on the table, then she grabbed the large plastic bin and walked to the door to open it for Anny, Mary, and me. Jo's shoes were already on, so she didn't need to stop to put them on."I can wear the backpack," I volunteered.

"Thanks, Max!" Anny commented. I grabbed the backpack and slung it over my shoulders. "Geez. That's heavy." Mary giggled before walking out the door. I followed.

I couldn't help wondering who would drive while Anny and Mary got situated in the back seat and Jo set up the trunk for the large plastic bin. *Who's going to drive the car? There's no licensed grown-up anywhere around here!* Although I wanted to ask, I decided I would wait since Mary and Anny, both giggling, were involved in a conversation, and Jo was focusing on something pesky in the trunk. I opened the door to the back seat and climbed inside. I closed the door behind me and buckled my seatbelt.

"Max, if you like , you may sit in the front seat," Jo stated.

"But I'm not old enough," I replied, very confused.

"Maybe that was the case on the planet you came from, but sharks your age are allowed to sit in the passenger seat on Sharkland."

"Okay," I said, trusting that Jo wasn't lying. I had never sat in the front before! I was excited.

Suddenly, I remembered we needed a driver. "Who's going to drive?"

"Me!" Jo said. "I'll drive! I always do."

"You're driving? Aren't you not allowed to drive?" I asked.

Jo sighed. "You're right, Max. In terms of age, I'm not, but I got my license because the government knew I was responsible enough to drive. When I was a baby, my mom abandoned me, and I learned how to live on my own. I needed to get around, so I took the test for a driver's license a year or so ago. That's why I can drive."

I paused. "Oh." I did not say anything more.

"It's fine. Maybe my mom will come back someday. Besides, it's awesome being able to drive!" Jo said, showing me her driver's license. "Anyways, let's get in the car!"

Jo turned the engine on, and the car started to move. We were going to the first destination on the map, which was unknown to me, but I knew I would learn soon. Jo turned the steering wheel abruptly to the left, which caused the car to drive up the curb and into the house's front yard. "Jo! What are you doing?" I asked bluntly. "Err, sorry. I don't mean to be rude."

"To start our journey, we first need to get to the house's backyard. We will drive a while from the house to get to the roads we need. The only route to the gold is off-road through the forest."

3
The Adventure Starts

"I know I forgot to ask, but everyone's seat belts are buckled, right?" Jo asked after we had gotten to the house's backyard.

"Duh. I don't want to fly out the window," Mary replied with a hint of sarcasm.

"Yep," I replied.

"Of course," Anny said.

"Good. Let's move!" Jo exclaimed. She was ready for this journey.

About fifteen minutes had passed, yet there was no sign of anything that resembled a road. We had been driving across what looked like somebody's backyard for a long time. I closed my eyes.

I think I fell asleep, because the next thing I knew, Mary was shouting. "STOP THE CAR!"

I opened my eyes to see a few trees and many rocks. We were now driving on a dirt road. The road led into a forest-like area, but a series of roads had cut through it, and they appeared to be barely wide enough for the car. Many trees hung over the road.

"What? Why?" Jo asked Mary. Jo pulled over onto the side of the dirt road.

"Look at that rock," Mary replied, pointing.

"What about it?" Jo asked, clearly confused.

"No, not that one. *That* one. Right there," Mary answered. "It's lumpy and has many cracks."

Jo understood which rock Mary meant. "Oh, that one! Wow, that is strange. Would you like to get out of the car and investigate?"

"Yes, please."

Everybody unbuckled their seatbelts, exited the car, and crowded around the rock. Anny pushed on the rock's side. "Anny, why are you doing that?" I asked.

"I don't know," was her reply. She continued pushing on the rock.

Much to our surprise, the rock flipped over. The rock's bottom was dirty and wet, so it was hard to be sure, but it appeared to have a carving.

"Woah, what's that?" I asked. I brushed the dirt off the rock with my pectoral fin.

"It looks like some sort of treasure map," I said. "See, here's water, and here's a road. And there's an X over here on the right in the middle of nowhere."

Jo compared the carved map with the paper one in her fins. "Judging from the fact that there is a lake on both of these maps in the same spot, it looks like the map on the rock is a zoomed-in portion of this section of the paper map," she said. "Let's draw it onto the back of the paper map so we can save it. We might need it later."

"I see that!" Anny replied. Jo grabbed a pencil from the backpack's side pocket and started drawing the rock's map onto the back of the paper map.

"Okay, I've now drawn it onto the back of the map," Jo stated. "I'm ready to continue."

Everybody got back in the car and buckled their seatbelts. "Max, may you hold the map and direct me where to go?" Jo asked.

"Sure," I replied. Jo handed me the map, and I looked it over. There were a series of very short roads ahead of us. Most roads were no longer than two of Jo's cars put together.

Jo turned the car back on and turned it onto North Street. Before Jo's caudal fin had been on the gas pedal for only half a second, the car was at the end of

North Street. The roads in this forest-like area were the shortest I had ever seen.

"Okay, now turn onto Pencil Way," I said as soon as Jo had turned onto North Street, which she did. Once it ended, I added, "Turn onto Star Boulevard," which was not short like most other roads. I could not see where it ended.

I closed my eyes again, but did not fall asleep. About a minute later, the car drove over a bump, and I sat straight up. "Sorry," Jo told everybody. "Ooh, a clearing! Do you all think we could stop, look around, and get some fresh air?"

"I like that idea!" Anny enthusiastically agreed.

"Okay," Jo said. She parked the car in a clearing next to a body of water, and everybody exited the car. The body of water looked like a pool because it was rectangular, but I knew it was a lake because the sign next to it read 'Closest Lake.' "That's strange," I replied. "Why does the sign say 'Closest Lake'? Closest to what? And how can they even call this a lake? It's rectangular, and it has no shores!"

"I don't know," Jo replied. "To both questions."

Another *very* short road led into the edge of the "lake", and it was called Chip Drive. It seemed that anybody who drove on that road was supposed to drive off and fall into the river.

I shuddered and thought to myself. *Wow, I sure am thankful that Jo won't be driving off the road and*

*making us fall into the river! Well, I hope she won't
drive off; she's too cautious to do that.*

    "Max!" Anny interrupted my thoughts by shouting
into my ear. "Do you know what this is?" She handed me
a piece of paper. I shrugged.
    "I'm sorry, I don't know, but I would like to look
at it, please." Anny handed me the strange thing she
found on the ground.

It was hard to read. The paper was dirty, ripped, and faded. The clue had probably been on the ground for a long time. It also looked like somebody had crumpled it into a ball and flattened it back out, but dropped it and forgot about it. There were two sets of words on the clue: large text in the middle and small text near the bottom. Near the bottom, some text looked to be in a different language.

"Can anybody tell what this says?" I asked.

"Let me see it," Mary said. I handed her the paper. "It's extremely dirty, so it's hard to tell, but it looks like it says 'Clue #1: Half shark half sqwuh-guh-muh-gurtz.'" Mary tried her best to pronounce the strange word with the strange spelling. "So it's supposed to be a clue."

"What's a sqwuh-guh-muh-gurtz?" Anny asked, also trying her best to pronounce the word on the clue.

"I don't know," Mary responded. She handed the clue back to me. "Does anybody else know?"

"No, I'm sorry, I don't," Jo replied. "I think I've heard the word before, though. I just can't remember what the word means."

"I don't know what it means either," I said. "I just got here this morning, and I don't know. I wish I did, though."

I turned the clue over to see if there was any information about what a sqwgamugurtz was. Instead, a tiny slip of paper was affixed to the back of the clue. Like the front side of the clue, it was dirty and took work to read.

"Mary, what does this say?" I asked.

"That's really small," Mary replied, moving her eyes closer. "It says something like, 'Go to closest lime?'"

"Go to closest lime?" I asked.

"What?" Anny mentioned, pretending to brag that she knew what the word read when nobody else did. "No, it says, 'Go to closest lake.' Jo, I think you should look at it." Anny handed Jo the clue, and she examined it.

"Can I have the clue again?" Anny asked once the clue had cycled around the rest of the group.

"Sure, why not?" I replied. I handed Anny the clue, and she gladly grabbed it from my fin, only to drop it.

"Don't drop it!" Jo exclaimed.

"Oh, I'm sorry," said Anny. She picked the clue up from the ground, but the taped paper had fallen off of the clue. It made sense because the clue was probably old. "Woah, it looks like there was something under the tiny scrap of paper!" she said.

"Cool!" Mary replied.

"Nice!" Jo said.

"What do you mean?" I asked. Sure enough, the scrap of paper was taped over something else. Somehow, I could read the words, which read 'Turn onto Chip Drive'. "Everybody! I think the words under the scrap read 'Turn onto Chip Drive'."

Jo looked at her map and realized that Chip Drive was the small road leading into the lake. She realized something. "Well, now we know that this was meant to be here. It wasn't forgotten by accident. But why are we so focused on this paper, anyway?"

Everybody thought for a moment. Jo had a good point. "Well, it seems like the clue also says to go off Chip Drive like the map, so I see no reason why not," Anny mentioned.

"That makes sense," Mary agreed. "Everybody, find everything that should not get wet and put it in the spare tire compartment in the trunk." *Do we seriously have to drive off that scary road? Perhaps we can find another way around.* Everybody started finding something that should not get wet, including me.

"Okay, is everybody ready for the very big fall?" Jo asked, shivering.

"I'm scared, but I am," Anny answered.

"I'm even more scared, but yes, I am too," Mary added.

"Max, what about you?" Jo asked me.

"Well, I guess I'm ready..." I murmured. I sighed. *I've been outvoted. We have to drive off Chip Drive.*

"Okay. Everyone, buckle your seatbelts much tighter than you normally do. And I would suggest holding your breath so you don't breathe in water by accident."

"Got it," Mary replied.

"Okay," I said.

"Understood," Anny stated.

"If everybody is ready, I'm going to start the car and drive it off the cliff," Jo said without a hint of fear in her voice. She started the car, turned it around, positioned it, and pressed the gas pedal. I closed my eyes. On Wah, cars weren't meant to be driven off cliffs, and I assumed it was the same on Sharkland.

I could not help thinking that we were going to drown, even though I knew sharks had gills and could breathe underwater.

4

Across the River

We were falling.

Jo had driven the car off the cliff. I wanted to close my eyes, but for some reason, I also wanted to watch the fall, so I kept them open. I held my breath.

The car flipped midair before hitting the cold, clear water with a loud splash. A chill went down my spine. I closed my eyes.

A few seconds later, Jo pressed a button. She started speaking a moment after. "Is everybody okay? That was a hard landing."

"I'm okay," Mary replied, opening the car door and climbing out.

"Me too," Anny said, following her twin sister's lead and exiting the car.

"Max, what about you?" Jo asked. I was holding my breath. "Remember, you may have only had lungs on your other planet, which meant you couldn't breathe underwater, but you now have both gills *and* lungs, remember?

"Oh, right," I said. I knew it would take time to adjust to my new shark body. I had only been here for less than half a day. "I'm fine. It was just a little scary." Jo nodded in agreement.

I carefully breathed in through my gills. Oxygen entered my body. I cautiously took another breath. *It's amazing how I'm able to breathe underwater! Back on Wah, I had to use a snorkel if I wanted to breathe underwater. I do have a question, though: how is the car floating?*

"Jo, how is the car floating so well? I thought the car was too heavy and would sink instead of float." I climbed out of the car, and Jo did the same.

"Your assumption is anything but wrong, Max. If the car had normal tires, it would have sunk to the bottom of the lake and we would not have a car anymore. It is floating because I took the car to the auto service shop yesterday. I bought the tires that claimed to float on water because they were cheaper." Jo paused, probably expecting a response. When she did not get one, she turned to Anny and added, "Also, did you notice the clue got wet?"

Anny's facial expression turned horrified. "Wait, what? Oh no. Really?" Since Anny was the one holding the clue, she had assigned herself the job of Clue Keep-Dryer. She looked down at the clue, which was wet but hadn't ripped. The water showed the clue's reflection.

The reflection showed the words written on the clue. The large words looked like they were facing backward, but the small words looked like they were facing the right way. *Those words on the bottom of the clue looked like they were in a different language, but now they look like they are in English. They must have been written backward because now they read something.* "Jo! Mary! Anny! The words at the bottom are backward!" I said.

"What makes you think that?" Jo asked.

"Well, if you look at the clue's reflection, the big letters look backward and wrong, but the small letters don't. I can read the words clearly in the reflection of the clue!"

"Cool! What does it say?" Anny asked.

"It looks like it says 'cave emerald,'" Mary offered.

"What do you think that means?" I wondered.

"I don't know, but that big gray thing on the other side of the lake looks a bit like a cave. Do you all agree?" Jo asked.

I squinted. "I can't quite tell, but I think it looks like a cave."

"That makes sense," Mary agreed.

"I think that too," Anny said.

Jo examined her map, then continued. "After we fell from Chip Drive, we landed in a lake. An island in the lake's middle divides Chip Drive and the other side of the lake. A bridge connects the island to the other side of the lake, which has a cave. It is to the left of the bridge's ending. Should we try to get there?"

"Yes, I think we should," I offered. "But how? Jo probably paid a lot of SBucks for the new tires on the car, so we have to get it to the island."

"You're right, Max. I *did* pay a lot of SBucks for the tires." Jo started thinking of a way to get all four of us *and* the car to the island safely, but Mary interrupted Jo's thoughts by sharing her idea.

"We could try getting in the car and starting the engine," she stated.

"We could try that, even though it might not work," Jo replied. Everybody got in the car and buckled their seat belts. Jo started the engine.

A few minutes had passed, yet the car had not moved much. It was still floating on the water's surface, but it hadn't appeared to move much. "The car's not moving," Anny stated.

"I agree," Jo replied. "Gas is also being wasted. Does anybody have any other ideas?"

"Jo, do you have a rope in the trunk?" I asked. "I have an idea."

"Actually, I do! What's your idea?"

"My idea involves tying the rope to the front of the car and one of us pulling that rope. Somebody else can push from the back, and the other two sharks can help by assisting the car from the side."

"Great idea!" Mary commented.

"I can swim to the front of the car and pull," I offered.

"I will push from the back of the car," Jo stated. She swam behind the car and opened the trunk to find a rope she thought was in the back. She noticed the rope a few seconds later.

Jo grabbed the rope with her fins and swam to the front of the car. She attached one of the loops to the car's tow hook, which was screwed to the back bumper. "Max, would you like to pull?" Jo asked. "Perhaps you could swim through the loop and grab it with your fins."

"Sure," I replied. "I like that idea."

I opened the loop with my fins. I swam through it and grabbed the loop. I pulled it as hard as I could, hoping to move the car. Jo, who was in the back, pushed as hard as possible. Anny and Mary assisted the car from the sides. The car moved forward about ten feet or so. "Great work, everybody!" I said.

"Thank you!" Anny and Mary replied at the same time. Jo and I nodded in agreement.

"Let's do it again!" I suggested.

"Okay!" Jo answered. "Is everybody ready?"

"I am!" Anny exclaimed.

"Me too!" Mary offered.

"Okay. 3... 2... 1... Do your thing!" I exclaimed.

I pulled. Jo, Mary, and Anny pushed. The car moved again and the car was now closer to the island. Jo, Mary, Anny, and I continued until the car touched the island's shore.

Once the car touched the shore, I wiggled out of the rope's loop and detached it from the front of Jo's car. The island's diameter looked much smaller than it did from Chip Drive. It was only the width of two or three school buses.

A bridge connected the other side of the lake to the far side of the island. It was much easier to see what was on the other side of the lake, and I could make out a rock formation that looked like a cave. I assumed it was the emerald cave the clue talked about. "It looks like that bridge leads to the other side, where the emerald cave is," I observed.

"I see something sparking in that rock formation over there. It looks like it has a defined entrance, and the sparking thing inside is green, so I think you're right, Max," Mary replied.

"If the only way we can get to the emerald cave is by driving across the bridge, then we should probably get the car out of the water and onto the shore," I stated. "Here's the rope."

Jo grabbed the rope out of my fin and attached it to the front of the car once more. "Alright. It would work best if two sharks pull this rope and the other two push from the back."

"I can push," I replied. "I pulled last time."

"I would like to push," Anny stated. "Mary, what about you?"

"I feel a little sick to my stomach, and I don't know why. I feel pain, but I also have that strange gut feeling you get sometimes when you know something bad is about to happen. I think I'll sit down," Mary replied.

"You may do that, Mary. I'll pull extra hard," Anny offered. She loved her sister.

Jo and I moved to the back of the car while Anny walked onto the sand and grabbed the rope. "Is everybody ready?"

"Yes!" Jo and I said at the same time.

"All right! 3, 2, 1, go!" Jo and I started pushing as hard as we could. Anny pulled as hard as she could. Even with our efforts, the car's weight seemed heavier on land than in the water. It took five more tries until the entire car touched the sand.

Once it was on the sand, we decided what to do next. Everybody thought in silence.

"I have an idea," Anny stated. "What if we go inside the car and start the engine? It probably won't work, but it might."

"We can try that! It didn't work in the water, but that was different." Jo pressed the 'unlock' button on the car keys, which unlocked the car. Anny opened the door to the driver's seat and sat in the wet leather cushion. "Can I drive?" she asked.

"I thought you didn't know how," Jo mentioned.

"I don't, but I want to learn!" Anny exclaimed.

"I would love to teach you, but now isn't the best time. Please move over," Jo replied with a smile. "Maybe I can teach you after we find the gold."

"Okay, fine," Anny replied. She moved out of the driver's seat and into the back. Jo moved into the driver's seat and held the button for a few seconds to start the car.

The car tried to start but failed. Jo tried again, but the car did not start. After the 7th try, the car still hadn't started. "This isn't working," Jo said, looking at the gas meter's arrow, which pointed to text that read 'Empty.' Jo sighed. "The gas tank is empty, but I like this car because it can turn into a solar car, which is helpful for times like this." Jo pressed a button, and solar panels came out of the car's roof.

"What just happened?" I asked.

"It's now a solar car," Jo replied. "Instead of running off of gas, it converts the Sun's energy to electricity. Now the car doesn't need gas. Let's let it charge for a little while so we can go across the bridge."

"Okay," I replied. I sat on the sand and waited.

About ten minutes had passed, and I was bored. "Is the car charged yet?" I asked.

"I'll go inside and see," Jo replied. She opened the car door and checked the 'charge meter.' "The car's charged," Jo said. "Let's go!"

"Yay!" Anny exclaimed.

"I agree!" Mary agreed.

"Let's drive!" I said.

"We have to make sure the car starts before we can drive it," Jo reminded us. "I'll try starting it." She opened the driver's door to the car for the second time and pushed the green 'Change Fuel' button. Next, she tapped the 'Push to Start' button. The car did not rev up like I expected, but instead, it sounded a little like a cross between a human voice and a flute. "Wow, the car sounds a lot different," I said.

"It does," Mary noticed.

"It's because the car now moves with electricity," Jo commented. "It's strange, though. I see why you think that."

"Anyway, let's move!" Mary exclaimed. She had gotten off the sand and was in the car already.

"Can we drive with the car's solar panels revealed? Don't we need to press a button or something that will hide them?" Anny asked.

"Surprisingly, we don't. That's one of the things I love about this car," Jo replied. "The solar panels can be out even when the car is moving. The car can charge while it is running."

"Wow!" I said.

"I'll get in the driver's seat," Jo told us. "We can start driving."

"Yay!" Anny exclaimed.

"Woohoo!" Mary commented.

"Everybody, buckle your seatbelts," Jo told us. "We're going to the other side of the lake."

5
The Underwater Cave

Jo, Mary, Anny, and I had driven across the bridge. It was a bumpy ride.

Jo parked her car to the cave's left. "We're here!" she exclaimed. Everybody exited the car and walked to the cave's entrance.

"What's that?" Anny asked. A boulder blocked the entrance, meaning we couldn't get inside the cave.

"The entrance is completely blocked," Jo said with a hint of disappointment. "Either we came here for nothing or took a wrong turn." I leaned against the cave wall but noticed my fin touching something other than stone. *Woah, what's this?*

"Jo! Mary! Anny! Look what I found!" I observed. It was a keypad, and it was small. A red light was above it.

"Where?" Mary asked, but she learned the answer when she looked behind me.

"What does it do?" Jo asked.

"Do you think something inside the cave walls pushes the rock aside if we type the right code?" Anny wondered.

"I think we should try," I replied.

"Good idea," Jo responded. "What do you all think the code is?"

"What about 1234? 1234 is a very common password," Mary suggested.

I examined the keypad to find the buttons labeled 1, 2, 3, and 4, but the keypad had only letter buttons. "The keypad only has letter buttons," I said.

"Oh. What about c-a-v-e?"

I spelled the word on the keypad. The buzzer made a loud noise, which caused Mary and I to jump.

"Wow. That's loud," I whispered for no reason.

"What about 'S-h-a-r-k-l-a-n-d'?" Jo suggested. "I know it won't be right, but we should try in case I'm wrong." Before typing s-h-a-r-k-l-a-n-d on the keypad, I spelled the word inside my head. I pressed the buttons on the keypad that spelled the word once I thought I spelled it right. A loud beep came out of the speaker again. I winced.

"What about m-a-x?" Anny wondered.

"No, you should try m-a-x-a-m-i-l. Max is a common name, but Maxamil is not," Jo suggested.

"That's a good idea." I mentally spelled my name and typed it into the keypad. Surprisingly, the buzzer did not make the loud noise like it had done every time before. Instead, it beeped and the red light turned green. The boulder started moving to the left with a track a few seconds later. *Why did the boulder move with a track? Boulders don't do that. And why was my name used as the passcode?*

I could not see much inside the cave because it was dark. The entrance to the cave was higher than the rest of the cave because the rest of it was flooded with water. *The reason the entrance is high must be so the water doesn't drown the rest of the island.* "Can someone grab the diving suits? I know sharks can swim, but diving suits will help us move faster through the water. Moving faster is necessary if we're unknowingly competing against others for the gold," Mary suggested.

"That's why I brought the diving suits," Jo replied. "I'll go back to the car and grab them."

Jo swam back to the car and opened the trunk. She grabbed her backpack, which was where all the supplies were. She started handing the diving suits to the sharks that would wear them.

"Thank you!" Mary said when she received her suit.

"Thanks," Anny said in a monotone voice.

"*Gracias!*" I thanked in Spanish. Everybody laughed.

Mary, Anny, Jo, and I scattered so we could change without fearing somebody was watching. I grabbed my diving suit and ran to the car so I could change inside it, Anny went behind a thick tree, and Jo commuted to a tall pile of leaves. Mary traveled to the space behind a tall rock next to the cave, but she emerged from the rock before she had her suit on. She ran to a muddy patch next to the cave's left. Next, she bent forward and opened her mouth as if she was about to vomit.

"Mary! Are you okay?" Anny asked. She ran to Mary to see if she was hurt though Anny was still taking off her day clothes.

"I've had this strange feeling lately and I don't know why. It occasionally takes the form of a headache, but other times, it is butterflies in my stomach. Sometimes it makes me feel like I need to vomit," Mary replied.

Anny facial expression changed from sad to surprised. "Oh no, not you too! I've also had that feeling," Anny informed her struggling sister. I stepped out of my shorts and into the diving suit's bottoms.

"Can I sit down?" Mary asked the group.

"Of course," Jo replied. "We'll wait. When you feel better, please change into your diving suit. We're going to leave soon."

"Okay, thank you," Mary said. She walked to the car and opened the door to the driver's seat. She rested on the roomy seat.

Later

Mary no longer felt like she needed to vomit. She had gone back behind the rock and changed into her diving suit. The rest of the group had also finished changing.

"My suit is too tight," Mary complained.

"They are supposed to be tight," Anny informed her.

"But it's so tight that it hurts. I think I've grown since we wore these last and the suit is too small."

"I'm sorry, but you'll have to deal with it. You won't wear it for long," Jo replied. "We don't have any bigger sizes, sadly."

Mary sighed, looking dejected. "Okay."

"Everybody, please fold your day clothes and put them into the bag with your name on it. If I remember right, your diving suits came in those bags," Jo instructed. Everybody nodded. "Alright, is everybody ready to enter the cave?"

"I am," Anny mentioned.

"Me too," Mary offered.

"I think so," I said.

"All right. I'm ready, so let's go!"

Everybody formed a line. Since Jo was the oldest, she was at the front. I was behind Jo, and Mary and Anny were behind me. We walked down the thirty or forty steps and into the water. It was not as cold as I expected.

Four tunnels were inside the cave. By instinct, I knew only one would lead to the gold, wherever it was.

Jo shined her flashlight into the tunnels so we could see them. According to the flashlight, the first two tunnels were dead ends.

Two tunnels were left to choose from. I shone the flashlight into the fourth tunnel, and a large animal, maybe a stingray, looked back at me. "There's a stingray in that one. Let's not go in there."

"Great idea," Jo replied. "I feel that our experience with Chip Drive was the closest I have ever been to dying. I don't want to do that again." Everybody swam into the third tunnel, which seemed like the best option.

Will this tunnel ever end? We had been swimming for about five minutes, but the tunnel had not changed direction. The only thing that was changing was Mary's pain.

"My suit is making it hard to breathe," she said. "I'm using my gills, but it still hurts."

"Uh oh. That's bad. It's probably not worth wearing a diving suit if you struggle to breathe. Let's keep swimming for just a little longer until we find an air pocket," Jo answered.

"Thanks," Mary said, barely audible.

An air pocket appeared in the tunnel only a short while later. I saw a rock wall preventing the water from getting through. Mary noticed it before Jo, Anny, or I did. I followed her into it because I was curious.

It was warm and dry inside the air pocket. It was small and a rock divided it into two parts. I could just barely stand up inside it.

"All right, Max. My suit is off. Should we head back and continue with our journey?" Mary asked.

"I kind of want to see what's on the other side of that rock," I stated.

"Now that you mention it, I'm curious, too," she replied.

"Jo! Anny! Come up here, please!" I shouted.

"Okay!" Jo shouted back.

"We're coming!" Anny replied.

"Why did you call us here? There's nothing wrong with it, but I would like to know why," Jo asked.

"Do you see that large rock? I got curious and wanted to climb over it," Mary replied. "I also wondered if you wanted to climb over and see what's on the other side."

"We can do that, but we should get back to the main tunnel when we're finished exploring," Jo answered.

"Okay." Mary nodded. She poked her head through the space and squeezed her body through. I heard a loud 'thunk' from the other side. "Ow! That hurt!"

"What's it like over there?" I asked.

"It's weird. You, Anny, and Jo have to see it," she replied.

"Okay. I'm coming," I stated. *What does Mary want us to see so badly? Is it cool? I* have *to know.*

"Holy sharks, what is that?" Anny said once she climbed over the rock.

"Woah, that's so cool!" Jo exclaimed once she also had climbed over the rock.

"Ow," I said once I had gotten over the rock.

I looked around. This half of the air pocket was darker than the other half, and a large emerald shone in the distance. It looked fake, but the angle I saw it from was strange, so I was not sure. I wanted to say something, but it was hard to do so.

"Hi everybody!" Mary exclaimed. Jo adjusted the flashlight's brightness so it lit the space more. *Why is this emerald here in a random air pocket in an underwater cave in the middle of nowhere? Who put it here? Why?*

"Woah," Mary said. "I want that emerald." Mary ran toward the emerald, but she never got to it. Her body faded away as she approached the emerald. *How is that even possible? Sharks' bodies don't fade away as they run or swim.*

"Mary?" Anny asked. "Where did you go?" Mary did not respond. "Mary!"

"Mary!"

The emerald continued to be perched on a rock, but it was not like it was before. It had split in two. "What happened to the emerald?" Jo asked.

"Woah! You're right," Anny replied. "I thought it was intact before."

"It was," I said. "It must have split in half when Mary tried to grab it."

"It looks like a piece of paper was inside," Jo observed. "Perhaps the emerald split in half to reveal it."

"Yeah, Mary may be missing, but we have this really cool emerald in front of us, and we'll find her later, so it doesn't matter," Anny stated bluntly.

Everybody was shocked by Anny's statement. "ANNY! Your great friend and sister is MISSING! We should be freaking out!" I revolted.

Anny sighed. "Hmm. Now that I think about it, you're right, Max. My gut feeling tells me we'll find her later, but I can't remember a time when I was without Mary. Wait... what if she... DIED?"

Hearing this, Anny and Jo started running around screaming.

"It's okay," I told Jo. "We can look for Mary when we escape this place."

"That's a great idea," Jo replied. I examined the emerald closer.

"Woah, what's this paper in the emerald?" I asked.

"It also looks like another clue," Anny observed. "How should we grab it without fading away like Mary did?"

"I'm not sure. Wait. did Mary even *touch* the emerald, or did she just get too close?" I asked.

"You have a point, Max! I don't think so," Jo replied.

"I'll try grabbing the paper without touching the emerald," I stated. "My body shouldn't disappear as long as I don't touch the emerald."

"I think you're right, but please please please *please* don't touch that emerald. We need you. I mean, I love Mary more than anybody else because she's my sister, but she's gone, at least for now. We can't lose you, too." Anny sighed.

"Okay. I will be extra careful and I won't touch the emerald," I said.

I slowly started walking toward the emerald. When I was above it, I grabbed the paper. I was still careful, but I must have not been careful enough, because I knocked the emerald over with my left fin. *Oh no.* I screamed.

I closed my eyes and prepared to disappear like Mary did. I held my breath. I was going to bid my farewells to the people I loved, but Anny suddenly interrupted me.

"What are you doing?" she asked. I opened my eyes. *Huh? I'm not going to die? I thought touching the emerald would transport me into the spirit world.* "Oh. I was preparing to die, but it seems that wasn't necessary," I said in an ironically cheery voice. Nobody responded.

After what felt like an eternity of silence, Jo spoke. "What does the clue read?"

I read the clue in my fins. "Teamwork equals 'blank.' Does anybody know what could go in the blank?"

Everybody thought for a moment. "No, I'm not sure," Anny answered. *What word could go in the blank?*

Suddenly, a different noise could be heard. "Ow." Jo had accidentally shone the flashlight in Anny's eyes.

"Sorry," Jo apologized. She moved the flashlight beam out of Anny's eyes. "Woah, what's that?"

"It looks like somebody carved text into the wall," I noticed.

"What's it say?" Anny asked.

I read the paper I held. "'Desert.' What does that mean? Do either of you think the word 'desert' goes in the clue's blank?"

"Teamwork equals desert," Anny thought out loud. She could not finish because Jo interrupted her.

"Ow!" Jo exclaimed. When Anny filled 'desert' in for the clue's blank, a green button appeared behind Jo. *I'm confused. A boulder moved when I typed in the password, which was my name. Mary's tight diving suit led us here. We only swam into this air pocket, not another, because it was closer than any other one. This air pocket must have been special because a fake emerald with a clue inside it was in this one. When Mary swam toward the emerald, she started disappearing, which is impossible. Something about this trip does not feel right.*

"Woah, a button!" Jo exclaimed, like a first grader. A button had appeared behind her.

"Should we press it?" Anny asked.

"I don't see why not. If we don't, we might be trapped here. I think that rock we climbed over just got taller," Anny said, pointing to the rock. It appeared to have come out of the ground, so there was no way Jo, Anny, or I could return.

The button turned red once Anny's fin touched it. The rock wall in front of us moved to the left, which revealed a large room with no windows and a very high ceiling.

A set of metal doors were on the right wall. The doors' handles had many padlocks and chains. The only other thing in the room besides the doors was a small wooden table in the room's center. It looked like it was about to fall over.

What is this place? I walked inside. *And how are we going to find Mary?*

6

Max's First Encounter

Shaking from fear, everybody entered the room. The rock wall slid shut with a loud "BOOM!", as if by magic.

The room looked as tall and wide as a warehouse, but its style looked most similar to a commercial kitchen because the walls, floor, and ceiling were made of a shiny metal that looked like steel. It was very different from the dark, wet cave we had just been in.

"Where... are... we??" Anny asked with a shaking voice, pausing between words.

Neither Jo nor I responded. We didn't know any more about where we were than Anny did.

Attempting to set her fears aside and be brave, Jo walked around the room, trying to find a way out. Suddenly, she stopped. "Guys," she said with a hint of confidence in her voice. "Come over here."

Hesitantly, Anny and I walked to Jo. We noticed what she was looking at almost instantly. "It's some sort of secret door," I observed.

"It must be," Jo added. The metal door was the same color and material as the surrounding walls, but it was separate from the rest of the wall. It was almost like someone had taken a knife to the wall and cut out a rectangular outline. It had no handle, but it was the same size as most doors I had seen. "How do we open it?"

Jo and Anny felt around the door, looking for a way to open it. Meanwhile, I walked over to a small wooden table roughly in the middle of the room. On the table, a stand supported a tablet. "Jo and Anny, you should come. This looks a bit like a button to open the door," I said with more confidence than I actually had.

Jo and Anny came. Anny walked by the tablet to look at the screen, and it changed. *Suspicious*, I thought. Now a large neon green play button was in the center of the screen. Underneath the button was some thick black text that read "Math Game".

I could not explain why, but I had strange feelings about that tablet. *Why is this table giving me such weird feelings? No, it's not only the tablet. The entire adventure has made me feel like this, but why? Well, it* is *kind of suspicious. We were exploring the cave in hopes of finding the gold, and that led us to an emerald that magically split in half and made Mary disappear. That led us to here, a large, in-the-middle-of-nowhere room with no windows and a freaky tablet.*

"Does anybody else feel this trip is suspicious, even if it's only a little?" I asked the group.

"Well, my beloved sister went MISSING, and now we're trapped in a metal room with no way out, so of course!" Anny said with a half-angry, half-scared tone of voice. "But just out of curiosity, why do you ask?"

"Think about it this way. A map carved on the bottom of a particular rock near the entrance to a forest filled with tiny roads led us to near death, also known as Chip Drive. A boulder moved when we typed in the password, which was *my name.* The consequence of Mary wearing a tight diving suit was having to find an air pocket so she could take it off. We continued exploring the air pocket, only to find a fake emerald that appeared to capture her somehow and led us into this strange metal room with no windows. Do you all remember that word written on the wall behind the emerald? A message was complete when that word was filled into the clue's blank. When Anny read the clue out loud, a button appeared on the stone wall. It makes no sense, but at the same time, it makes complete sense."

Everybody considered my opinion. Jo shook her head in strong agreement. Anny stayed silent, but we both knew how she felt: scared, worried, angry, hopeful, and used.

She did get curious about the button, though. "Should I press the button on the screen?"

I didn't think that was a good idea. I told Anny why in the silliest way I could, trying to lower the tension in the air. "I don't think you should. What if instead of the button triggering a math game, it sends flying elves to come and kidnap us?" Jo laughed a bit at my joke. "Hey, it could happen. I mean, I'm a talking shark who's walking somehow."

Anny didn't seem to hear me. "What? May you repeat?" Instead of waiting for my response, she pressed the button on the screen.

Jo and I exchanged sympathetic glances. "I said that I don't think it's a good idea to press the button, but it's just a button. I mean, what's the worst that can happen?"

"Oh, sorry. Hopefully it's just a math game that's suspiciously placed in a room that we're trapped inside..." Anny apologized with a voice full of fear.

Another screen appeared that showed the rules of the game. I read the instructions out loud.

"Rule number 1 says if we win the game, we can escape. Rule number 2 says playing the math game is forbidden. But why would you create a math game if nobody was allowed to play it? And why are there no instructions for the game's play?"

Everybody thought for a moment. When Jo could not think of anything to say, she settled on, "I'm not sure." Which might have also happened to be the truest thing she could have possibly said.

Anny's tone suddenly switched from scared and worried to optimistic and hopeful. "Well, what's the worst that can happen? If we win, we get to escape. That's what the screen says, at least. Max, do you want to play it with me?"

"Sure," I replied. "Anny, can I press the start button?"

"Of course," she said.

I pressed the button to start the game. What appeared on the screen next was not a game like everybody expected. Rather, it was a message, which read, 'You Won!'

"We won? Already? We haven't even played the game yet!" Jo exclaimed.

"Perhaps the game knows who we are and is letting us win," Anny mentioned.

"Or maybe it's a trap," I uttered, my mind running in a circle of anxiety. I couldn't help it, but my brain started generating a list of as many bad things that could happen as it could think of. I felt little happiness, even though the rules told me I would get to escape if I won the math game.

Suddenly, the doors behind the tablet unlocked and slid open, revealing a long glass hallway leading to a tall spaceship enclosed in a tall cylindrical metal enclosure with no roof. The only ways out of the glass hallway were the door Jo, Anny, and I came through and a small hole in the see-through ceiling. The hole did not seem large enough for a shark to fit through. *This adventure is getting weirder and weirder,* I thought.

It almost went without thinking that Jo, Anny, and I would have to enter the hallway if we wanted to have any chance of escaping, so that is what we did. The doors locked behind us. "What is it with us and closing doors?" Jo asked jokingly, trying to lighten the mood. I laughed as much as I could manage.

The door to the spaceship opened when Jo, Anny, and I were roughly in the middle of the hallway. A comfortable interior was visible, with a soda machine, television, and couch. Every second, I was getting more and more scared that we had fallen into a trap.

From what she said next, it seemed as if Anny had been put under a spell. Had she forgotten that this ship was located in the freakiest place ever, and that her sister was *missing*? "Wow! That looks amazing!" Anny exclaimed excitedly. She ran onto the spaceship before I could stop her and tell her boarding it might not be the best idea. Suddenly, an ultra-loud noise filled my eardrums, and gasoline and smoke filled my nostrils.

"ANNY! COME BACK!" I screamed at the top of my lungs, but it was no use. The sound of the rocket lifting off the ground drowned my voice out.

"There goes Anny," Jo said, not needing to say it with emotion. I already knew how she felt.

Jo and I both stared in shock at where the spaceship used to be. The spaceship was now no more than a dot in the sky. Suddenly, Jo screamed. "Ow! Where did *this* come from?"

A rope ladder had suddenly dropped out the hole in the glass hallway's ceiling and hit Jo on the head. She looked up and noticed the ladder was attached to a high-up platform.

"A ladder. Interesting," I observed.

I was correct. A rope ladder was attached to a platform about 100 or so feet up. I thought I saw a door on the platform, though I couldn't see it well from where I was standing.

I ran to the steel doors that let us into the "spaceship room", but they were still locked. "Well, if we want to escape this strange place, we should climb the ladder. It might be our only way out."

"Let's do that," Jo agreed.

"How should we get through the hole?" I wondered. If the hole was only a bit smaller, it would have been too small for the ladder, and it wouldn't have hit Jo on the head. I was almost sure we wouldn't be able to fit through.

Jo reached into her backpack and pulled out a hammer. "Woah, where did you get that?" I questioned.

"I grabbed it on our way out the door earlier today. I didn't know if we would need it, but I hoped I did because this is *heavy*."

I laughed. "I feel your pain," I replied, holding the hammer in my fins to feel its weight. "May I go first?"

"Of course," she said. "Just be careful."

"Thanks. Now, please stand back, because this is going to be messy," I told Jo with newfound confidence.

"Okay, I will move out of the way." Jo backed up. She paused. "If the glass doesn't break after you go, can I try?" she added a moment later.

"Yes," I replied. After pausing, I added, "But only if I don't break the glass."

"Well, duh," she replied. We laughed.

I grasped the hammer with my left fin, grabbed right above with my right fin, and positioned it above my head. I swung the hammer up at the hole where the ladder came down, hoping it would break and the glass would fall to the ground. The glass cracked, but it did not shatter. I repeated this process three times after, and each swing added one crack, but not much more.

I was slightly disappointed, but I handed the hammer to Jo anyway. "Here you go."

"Thank you." Like me, she grabbed the hammer with her right fin and held it over her head. She swung it like I did, but something about her swing must have not been the same because it caused the glass to shatter and fall to the ground.

I stared at her, impressed. "You first?"

"Thank you," Jo replied. She placed the hammer back inside her backpack, grabbed the first rung of the rope ladder, and pulled herself up. I followed behind.

A tiny platform with an area of only a few feet was at the top of the ladder. To the right of the ladder, the yellow-brown of a wooden door contrasted against the silver of the corrugated steel walls of the "spaceship room". "I'll climb down a few rungs of the ladder so you can open the door," I offered to Jo, who opened the door to reveal a dark space. I followed her inside, and the wooden door mysteriously swung shut and locked itself.

The room was damp and smelled of cement, and our voices echoed when we talked. If it was even a room at all. From where we were standing, it looked more like a never-ending ultra-wide hallway.

Jo reached into her bag and looked around until she felt a cylinder-shaped device that was the flashlight. She pressed the button to turn it on, which lit up the space a bit.

"Woah, this place is big," I commented.

"Yeah, a bit too big," Jo stated, unable to hide her fear. She started walking, but suddenly— "AAAAAH!"

"ARE YOU OKAY???" I shouted much louder than what was probably necessary. Jo had started walking, but she must have tripped on something; I heard a scream and a twig breaking. Jo's scream was so bloodcurdling that it sounded more like a shark getting stabbed with a knife than Jo tripping on a small stick. It echoed loudly, making it even more startling.

"Sorry, Max. I'm fine. I just tripped on a stick. And I *almost* fell into here—" Jo pointed to a place that should have been part of the floor, but the floor had ended, leaving what looked like a deep chasm.

"Oh, gosh," I muttered, still very startled by Jo's overly dramatic scream. I looked where Jo was pointing, and I saw it too. The floor had suddenly ended. "That's a problem," I stated, as if it wasn't obvious. "We think the way out of here is on the other side of this hallway, but if we can't cross this somehow, we'll be trapped." Jo nodded in agreement.

"Wait, what's this?" She grabbed something that looked like a chain, which must have been connected to the ceiling somehow, because it didn't fall when Jo grabbed it.

"I think it's a chain," I stated the obvious. I pulled on the chain to test how much it was secured to the ceiling; it was secure. "Should we swing across with this chain?"

"Sure. I just don't want to go first," Jo said with obvious fear in her voice. As I had learned over the past few hours, it was not normal for Jo to be scared, or at least to show she was scared, but that seemed untrue now.

"Okay. I'll go first." I wiped my fins on my shirt to remove unnecessary sweat, reached for the chain, and gripped it tightly. I counted down from 3 in my head: *3. 2. 1. Jump.* Hesitantly, I pushed off the platform, my stomach dropping. I almost felt nauseous for a moment as I swung through the air, but I painfully landed on the cold stone floor after letting go once I reached the other side. "I did it!" I swung the chain to Jo.

Jo took the chain but did not move. "Max, I'm scared!"

"Whatever you do, don't look down," I advised her. "The jump is easier than it looks. Trust me. And if you hold on really tightly, everything will be okay."

Jo didn't seem to trust me at first, but she convinced herself to jump and stepped forward after a few moments of pep-talking to herself. She gripped the chain as tightly as her fins could manage and pushed off the damp concrete. She had a safe landing afterward. "You did it!" I exclaimed.

"I did!" We both congratulated each other for a minute or so, but then we realized we still had to escape the hallway. "What should we do next?" Jo asked me.

"I think we should keep walking until we can hopefully see natural light," I replied. "There's no guarantee that we will find an exit over there, but it's our only option."

We started walking further away from the door, hoping it was the right decision.

"Jo, I'm tired," I complained. Jo and I had been walking for an amount of time that felt like an eternity. "How long have we been walking?"

"I know. I'm tired too, especially with this huge backpack." Jo did not look tired, but I trusted her. She pulled her watch out of her backpack, which she had taken off before we entered the underwater cave so it wouldn't get wet.

"It looks like about ten minutes," Jo replied.

"Wow," I commented. It seemed like hours had passed since we had started walking.

Finally, I noticed daylight. According to Jo's watch, about twenty minutes had passed since we checked last. "Jo! I see daylight!"

"No way!" Jo looked up and noticed I was right. She started running, and I followed her lead and did the same. The tunnel got brighter as we reached the cement hallway's end. The room connected to the tunnel also 'got bigger.'

An open gunmetal-colored metal double door led into the room. The room had a ceiling as tall as the room was wide, and the walls as well as the ceiling were primarily made of huge windows. Across the room was another double door that looked the same as the first one, but it was closed.

The world outside the room looked more like a desert than anything else; I could not see anything besides sand.

I stopped before entering the room. Another clue was on the ground in the door's threshold area.

"Jo, wait!" I shouted, even though Jo was standing right next to me.

"What?" she asked with a hint of curiosity.

"There's another clue on the ground."

"Oh, cool! Let's read it."

I picked up the clue and started reading it. "It reads, 'Clue 3: Royal Palace.'"

"What does that mean?" Jo asked.

"I don't know. But I *do* know we should put it in the backpack in case we need it again."

"Great idea," Jo added, slipping her backpack off, unzipping it, and dropping the clue inside.

"Woah! Jo, look at that!" I exclaimed, pointing to something in the distance. It looked a lot like a fairy-tale castle, and it was bright pink and sparkly with white towers.

"What? Where?" Jo was confused.

"It's the building that looks like a fairy-tale castle," I bluntly stated.

"Oh. That one. Do you think it's the royal palace the clue reads?" Jo asked. I thought for a moment.

"It's worth a try," Jo replied. "We don't have many other options."

We walked through the "window room", both sets of doors closing as we crossed their thresholds, into the sand outside. It was hot and dry.

"Gosh, it's hot," Jo complained. "It's like a desert!"

"Very true..." I trailed off. "Wait! What if this is the desert the second clue from the underwater cave meant?"

"Maybe! Actually, yeah, I think so!" Jo noted.

We stood at the castle's entrance after about ten minutes of walking through the sand. With every step I took, the castle appeared even larger and more grand.

"Should we enter?" I asked. "It could be a really rich shark's house, for all I know."

"Nah. I doubt it. I don't think much real estate is sold in places like these," Jo joked. I laughed.

Jo opened the doors to the castle. I closed my eyes; I did not know if we would get in trouble. When I opened them, though, I did not see anything except noisy animals standing behind laser bars. One of them was pink and one of them was bright blue.

A piece of paper was taped to a post close to us. It was stained on the edges, and it appeared like it had been there for a long time. It was printed with a drawing that mimicked what the animals inside the cages looked like. Hoping I wouldn't get in trouble, I sneakily ripped the paper from the post, folded it in half, and placed it in my shorts pocket.

"What does this paper mean? Also, what are those animals over there? I've never seen them before," I asked Jo.

Jo thought for a moment. "I don't know. Wait! Actually, I do! They're called sqwgamugurtz," she replied. "I don't know why they're here. It's a weird place for two sqwgamugurtz to be. Some sharks are born as sharks, but might turn into sqwgamugurtz if somebody possesses them. I'm not sure why. I didn't think Mary and Anny were born with sqwgamugurtz traits. At least, they didn't tell me if they *were* born that way."

An enlarged version of the drawing on the paper.

"Oh. I understand." I ran to the laser beams, making sure to not touch them. Now that I was closer to the sqwgamugurtz, I noticed a strange thing: They had pieces of paper taped to their bellies, which read "Mary" and "Anny." "Jo!" I exclaimed.

"What?" she asked.

"Come over here!" Jo came. She also noticed the papers taped to Mary and Anny.

"Oh," Jo said. "That's strange. Do you think they're actually Mary and Anny?"

"It would make sense if they were. Both of them disappeared during the journey after feeling bad things would happen. When I arrived at Sharkland this morning, Mary wore a bright blue shirt, and Anny wore a pink one. The bright blue sqwgamugurtz's paper reads 'Mary', and the pink's reads 'Anny'."

"That makes sense," Jo replied.

"Why do you think Mary and Anny are sqwgamugurtz? You said sqwgamugurtz are sharks that are possessed. And why are they in a laser cage?" I asked.

"I don't know," Jo replied truthfully. "But perhaps we could stop thinking about the sqwgamugurtz and start thinking about the gold. The gold is the whole reason why we're here, remember?"

"Oh, right. I admit, I forgot about the gold," I admitted. "I also feel sort of betrayed. I'm not sure if Mary and Anny did it on purpose, but we ended up having to hunt for the gold with only the two of us because they disappeared and turned into sqwgamugurtz. I miss my new friends."

Jo sighed. "I miss Mary and Anny too, even though I don't think they turned into sqwgamugurtz on purpose." A tear rolled down Jo's cheek for the first time.

Suddenly, I felt like tearing up too. I wrapped my short fins around Jo as much as I could and squeezed her tightly.

I released Jo eventually, though. "Thank you, Max," she told me.

I nodded and said, "Anytime."

Jo pulled the map out of her backpack and pointed to various places. "Well, we know *this* is the "spaceship room", so *that* has to be the dark hallway, and *this* is the room after the hallway. If *that's* the room after the hallway, *this* shape has to be the castle we're in now. There is a big X in the corner of the castle, which probably means the gold is *there*."

"Should we go that way?" I asked.

I heard Jo respond, but I could not hear what she said. All of a sudden, all my senses seemed to become dulled and my thoughts became hazy. A force pulled me upward and into the air. It was like a higher power was controlling my body. Jo screamed in a similarly spine-chilling way.

This scream didn't scare me as much as before, but it still terrified me nonetheless. It shocked me out of my dream-like state and I fell to the ground with a *thud*. "Gah!! Jo, are you okay??"

Jo replied in an ironically calm and chill way. "Oh yeah, Max, I'm fine. Just seeing you levitate like that made me scream. *And your face!* You looked like you were in a trance or something. It just scared me a bit, that's all. I'm fine." Jo laughed. I sighed; Jo could be a *bit* dramatic with her screams sometimes.

But the moment I became calm and relieved that Jo's scream was nothing to be worried of, I saw something that scared me for real.

Something was standing behind Jo. It was big and blue and looked exactly like the sqwgamugurtz in the drawing taped to the post. "Jo—! Look behind you—!!!"

Jo slowly turned around. A look of horror spread across what would have been her face if she were completely human. I covered the holes that would have been my ears if I were completely human, anticipating another scream. But Jo did not scream; she was so scared that she could not make a single sound.

Out of instinct, I ran over and punched the sqwgamugurtz. But when I did that, I suddenly felt slightly woozy again. *"Why would you dare mess with my precious sqwgamugurtz?"* said an angry voice inside my head.

"Who said that?" I asked out loud—or I thought I asked it out loud. I felt brave.

"Those sqwgamugurtz you call Mary and Anny are now my servants. You shall not mess with them," the voice said again.

I froze. But after a few moments of gathering my thoughts, I found the courage to speak. "But how did they turn into sqwgamugurtz?" I asked with an attitude.

"Mary and Anny weren't born with sqwgamugurtz traits. They were my friends!"

"The Changer-Animals 2000," the voice said. *"And now they follow every command I give. Works like magic."*

I thought to myself. *Where is this voice even coming from? It doesn't sound like a shark talking. It's different. And what is the Changer-Animals 2000?*

I was going to say something more, but then I dropped to the ground again and snapped back to reality. I felt dizzy. When I opened my eyes, I saw Jo leaning over me and checking to make sure I was breathing.

"Max, I think we should leave," Jo told me. "Gosh, you looked *so* possessed when you were in the air like that."

"Yeah, that voice was *scary*," I added. "Forget about the gold. Let's get out of here." I grabbed Jo's right fin with my left and started running, pushing the door open with my other fin.

We ran back the way we came and got in the car when we saw it. The car ride home was long and quiet since we had experienced the crazy trip together, so there was not much to discuss and help each other understand. We did not get home until much later.

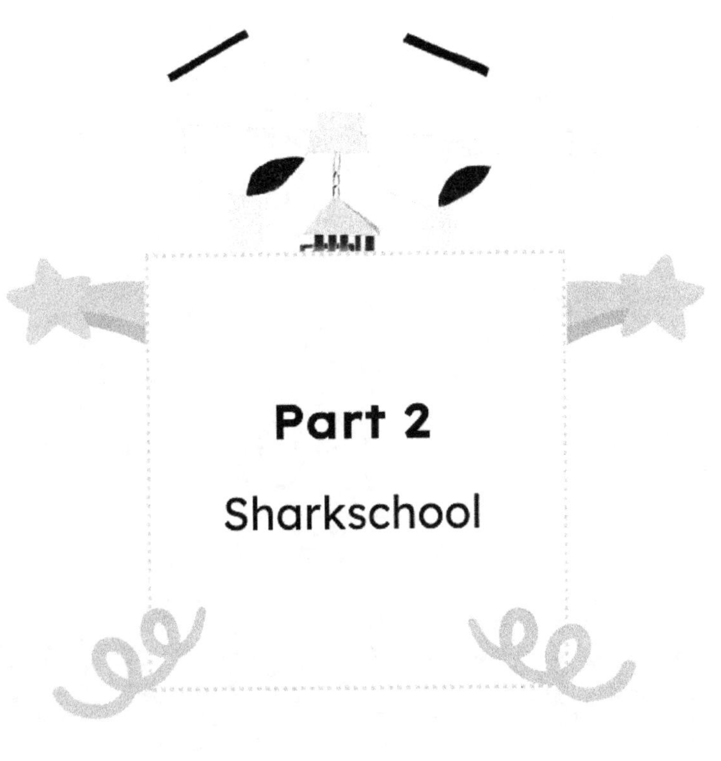

Part 2

Sharkschool

7

A Big Change

Sometime around the end of June

I woke up around 7:30 one day a few weeks later and sat straight up in bed. I had an idea.

My heart racing from a surge of adrenaline, I ran downstairs before the idea of getting dressed even crossed my mind. "Hi! Jo! How are you?" I rapidly asked in one breath.

Jo seemed surprised by the energy I had so early in the morning. "Good morning, Max! I slept well. I woke up hot, but that's okay. Thanks for asking!"

"You're welcome!" I paused. "May I ask you a question? Well, another question?"

"Of course!" Jo exclaimed.

I sighed. Although I was slightly nervous to say what I was going to say because I was afraid Jo would say no, I gathered my confidence and shared my idea anyway. "Do you agree that this house is too small for both of us?"

"CERTAINLY. It is SO hard to live in a house this small with four sharks. Although Mary and Anny are no longer with us. Gosh, I really miss them. Why do you ask?"

Now it was time for the million-dollar question. I took a deep breath. "How do you feel about moving into a bigger house with me?"

Jo paused. My heart forgot a beat. In a calm yet excited tone, Jo said, "You are one of the nicest sharks I have ever met, Max. I'm unsure if we can afford a house, but if we can find a cheap one, that would be so awesome!!"

I felt a wide grin spread across my face—or what would have been my face if I were completely human. "Thank you SO much!" I ran to Jo and hugged her very tightly.

"You're welcome!!" After looking out the window, Jo added, "Should we get in the car and drive around the neighborhood to see the houses for sale?"

"I love that idea. I'll get dressed and eat breakfast."

Later, after dressing and eating breakfast with Jo, we were ready to look for houses. Jo and I walked to the door where our shoes were.

Jo pulled on her golden yellow-and-blue canvas high tops decorated with sharks she painted on, grunting because she said they were hard to put on. I slipped on my neon blue running sneakers. We were ready to leave, but then Jo's facial expression—or what would be her facial expression if she were completely human—turned nervous. "Uh oh. Max, have you seen my car keys?"

I scanned the room, only to notice Jo holding the keys in her right fin. "They're in your hands, Jo."

"Oh, thanks." Jo blushed in embarrassment. We walked outside to Jo's car, got in, and started the engine.

During the first minutes of the ride, all the houses labeled 'for sale' were too expensive and/or wouldn't work for us. Ten minutes later, though, we noticed one that would have worked. Its walls were pinkish-red, and it had a porch. "This looks like a nice house to live in! It's a good size, and it's cheap, too. Let's park the car to check it out."

Jo parked the car across the street. We waited until no cars passed by, and then we excitedly ran across. But Jo suddenly looked disappointed. "Wow. I couldn't see it from the street, but *so many other sharks* are trying to see the house, too. I think we should try a different house. What do you think, Max?"

I nodded in agreement. "That sounds like a good idea. This house is just *way too* popular."

Later, we found another house that was for sale. It was large and painted yellow, and I smelled chlorine, which probably meant it had a pool. It appeared to have two floors but may have also had a basement; I couldn't tell from the curb. It had a porch, just like the other house. A wide smile spread across Jo's face (or what would have been Jo's face if she were completely human). "It would be lovely to live in a house like this! What do you think, Max?"

"I agree with you, Jo. It looks like we would enjoy this house a lot!"

Jo looked at the sign in the front yard. The shark-human hybrid equivalent of her facial expression turned disappointed again. "Oh, no. This house is expensive. It costs a whopping one million dollars! The amount of money we have is nowhere near that. Let's try a different house."

"I agree."

Later, we found yet another house marketed as "for sale." It was a modern black house with wood accents and a white roof to keep it cool, and it was so big it probably could have comfortably housed four sharks.

There was a sign in the front yard, which I read out loud. "'Only ₿50,000 SBucks! Reason: There are three bedrooms in this spacious 4-shark house, but only two bathrooms. Having fewer bathrooms than bedrooms was common a long time ago but is no longer popular today[3]. There are no other problems with the house. Schedule a showing and see!'"

"Only ₿50,000 SBucks? I could buy a new car for a price that cheap! Also, it's huge! I say we sign up for a showing time."

"I agree. That's the sign-up sheet over there."

The sign-up sheet was next to the door. A shark wearing a badge that read "Moe the Realtor" stood on the other side of the door. Many rows stating available times were on the showing sign-up sheet, as well as three columns: full name or names, date, and optional comments.

Many times were still available. One time was available five minutes from the current time, so Jo and I only had to wait five minutes. Jo and I filled the sheet out together and started waiting.

Jo and I walked inside the house after waiting. It was not staged, which meant no furniture was inside

____

[3] On Earth, having fewer bedrooms than bathrooms is still common for cost-related reasons.

showing how the house would look if somebody lived in it.

I noticed the main floor was in a loop shape. When Jo and I walked inside the kitchen, we noticed the kitchen came with new appliances, including a double oven. Two bedrooms and two bathrooms were upstairs, with one of the bathrooms being in the primary bedroom. Both bathrooms had showers and two sinks. Also, the basement was spacious, with a laundry room with two windows, a huge family room, and a bedroom that looked bigger than both the other bedrooms in the house. I tried to envision where furniture would go if Jo and I lived here.

We had seen all the rooms, so we exited the house. Moe, the realtor, said hello to us. "I love this house. I think we should buy it. Do we have enough money?"

"Not right now; I only have a few dollars physically with me. But I read a sign outside the bank that said if you open an account with them today only, you will get ₿100,000 SBucks simply because you opened an account. I think we should see if that would work for us," Jo requested.

"Good idea!" I agreed. "Should we get back in the car and drive to the bank?"

"Yeah. The bank closes in only a half hour. If we want to open an account today, we should leave now," Jo said.

"Holy sharks! Let's get in the car!"

"I agree."

After Jo and I arrived at the bank, we opened the doors and walked inside.

"Hello, may I help you?" a shark at the front desk asked.

"We would like to start a checking account," Jo said.

"Okay, come with me." The shark at the front desk stood up and motioned for us to follow. She led us into a room behind the front desk. "Stay here, please. Our account-creating specialist will be here shortly," the female shark said.

"Okay," I agreed.

"We'll stay here," Jo promised.

Two minutes later, another female shark walked in. She wore a badge that read 'Account Specialist.' She started asking us questions.

After about forty-five minutes of answering questions, the Account Specialist informed us she had created our bank account. "Okay, Maxamil Alderin and Josephene Brime, your checking account has been officially opened!"

"Yay!" Jo exclaimed.

"Do we still get the bonus for opening the account, even though the bank's closed?" I wondered.

"Yes, there is still a bonus since you started opening the account when we were open. How would you like the money? Would you like it deposited into your new checking account?" the Account Specialist asked.

"Yes, please. But we would like a check for ℬ50,000 SBucks, please," I replied politely.

"I can do that," she said. After a short wait while she wrote the check, she handed us the rectangular paper and said, "Here's your check receipt."

"Thank you!" Jo exclaimed.

"Thank you!" I added.

"Have a great day!" the helper exclaimed.

"Thank you! You too!" I replied. Jo held the bank's large doors open for me. We walked to the car, climbed inside, and drove back to the home we were buying.[4]

Moe was still there. Jo held the check in her fin.

"Did you open your account at the bank?" Moe asked. After noticing how Jo and I were confused, he added, "Sorry, I overheard you speaking, so now I know you went to the bank."

"Yes, we did. Now we have the money," I said.

"Could we put an offer on the house?" Jo asked.

---

[4] Please note this does not mimic the bank account creation process on Earth.

"That sounds great!" Moe replied. "I'll submit the offer into the system. I'm not sure if the seller, Shan, will accept it, but so few people have scheduled showings that I think Shan will accept it and you'll get the house."

"Yay!" Jo and I said in unison.

Moe saw a new notification on his computer only a few minutes later. "Shan accepted your offer!!"

"Wow, that was quick!!" I noticed.

"Yay!" Jo said.

"How do you feel about closing tomorrow?" Moe suggested.

"That sounds great!" Jo said.

Later, at the closing the next day

Shan, the closing agent, and the realtor were already at the house's closing the next day when we arrived. Jo and I had our checkbook with us in case we needed it, even though we already had the $75,000 check. A very tall stack of paper was on the kitchen counter. "Hello, Jo and Max! First, I need identification from one of you. And then you can start signing the forms."

My heart started racing. I did not have any Sharkland identification because I had come here only a few weeks ago. "Jo, do you have any identification?" I whispered to Jo.

"Actually, I do," Jo replied. "It's my driver's license." She pulled her wallet out of the pocket of her cargo shorts and grabbed a small piece of plastic printed with ink. It had her photo, date of birth, address, Sharkland Security Number, and more. "Here you go," Jo said and gave her driver's license to the closing agent. The closing agent looked over the license carefully.

It was time to sign papers once Jo got her ID back from the closing agent.

Shan informed, "Since you're paying for the house with a check instead of with a loan from the bank, you don't have to sign the forms required when paying with a loan. Most of those papers are agreements that promise to pay the loan back. So that's nice, right?"

"Yeah! I understand," Jo said. I nodded.

"I will hand you the forms one at a time," Moe added. "When you finish reading and signing one, you will hand it to me, and I will give you the next one." Moe handed me the first form, which made Jo and I promise to pay the house's entire price.

I started reading the form out loud to Jo. "The undersigned borrowers..."

"I don't think it is necessary to read the entire form, personally," Moe interrupted. "There are many forms, and reading every form from top to bottom would take hours. Aim to understand the general idea of the form, sign it, and continue to the next one."

"That makes sense," Jo replied. "There is *too much* text on here. We know this form's about paying the house's entire price."

"We have the SBucks, so we'll pay the price," I stated. I grabbed a pen and signed the first form. Jo did the same.

We continued in this manner throughout the rest of the forms. There were about ten or fifteen. We skimmed through each, discussed them, and signed them. Each one was printed on thick paper.

We finished not too long later. "We've signed all the forms. What should we do next?" I asked.

Moe answered my question. "I'm reading through all the papers to check that you signed all of them. If you did..."

"You pay. After you do that, you get the keys!" Shan interrupted.

"Yay!!" Jo exclaimed for what felt like the millionth time in the past two days.

"Thank you!" I told Moe.

"You're welcome!" he replied. I handed the check to Shan.

A few minutes later, Moe finished checking all the forms and verifying with the closing agent. "Would you like the good news or the bad news first?" Shan asked.

"Oh. Good news." Jo became worried.

"You signed all the forms and paid! You get the house!" Shan exclaimed. "The bad news is that we need to leave because this is no longer our house!" Jo and I were speechless. We had bought a house, and the transaction was successful. I hugged Shan.

"Oh, thank you…?" she said. She did not expect me to hug her.

Shan, the closing agent, and Moe put their shoes on and walked out the door.

"That was one of the best house closings I've taken part in for a very long time," I overheard Moe say.

"Agreed. Both sharks were polite and patient, and Max hugged me," Shan added. All three sharks went into their cars and pulled out of the driveway.

"Max, we did it!!" Jo exclaimed.

"I know!!" I added. I paused. "Wait, what about the other house?"

"We still own it. We bought a new house, but that doesn't mean we don't own the other one. Perhaps we could remodel it and maybe build an addition. It is an amazing area in the middle of nowhere, and we could use it like a cabin to visit in the summer or over Winter Break."

"I love that idea!" I paused. "Err, sorry to bring that topic up. Let's finish moving into this house first. We can think about the other one later."

"I agree." After pausing, Jo added, "Let's pack up all of the furniture there for now. We'll be spending most of our time here."

I nodded. "Good idea."

"Should we get in the car and go back to the house? We can't exactly start moving in without our furniture, personal belongings, and food," Jo mentioned.

"Definitely," I replied. "Let's get in the car."

"Okay." Jo pressed the 'unlock' button on her car keys. We pulled our shoes on and tied them. I held the door open for Jo, and we got into the car. We drove back to our old house and started moving out.

We came back to the house about two hours later after packing all our furniture and going to the moving store.

We unloaded the seven or eight boxes and eleven or twelve bubble wrap-covered pieces of furniture into the living room of our new house. The items in the boxes were organized and packed neatly into boxes of the correct size, which were labeled things like "Max's Clothes", "Bathroom 1", "Board Games", and "Katrina's Stuff"—I didn't know who Katrina was, but I decided not to question it. Jo and I discussed where to put everything once all the furniture was in the living room.

"Where should we put all this furniture?" I asked.

"Let's think. We have a lot of furniture, such as the dining room table and your ugly desk. We don't have any furniture that could go in the basement except for the foldable chairs, which we'll probably store in the laundry room," Jo answered. "The beds and identical nightstands will probably go in the bedrooms."

I added to Jo's response. "First, let's make a list of rooms in this house. Once we do that, let's divide this furniture by room," I said. "We can make a shopping list once we figure out what we need and what we already have. Our old house was small, so let's expect to add many things to that list."

"Awesome idea." Jo grabbed a notebook and pen from her backpack.

"And do you think we should share the primary bedroom, Jo?" I asked.

"I think we should," she suggested. "It's unfair for one of us to claim the small bedroom while the other claims the large one."

"I love that idea. Let's place the bedroom furniture over here."

8

Sharkschool

Panting, I grabbed a heavy lamp from its base and heaved it onto the dresser in what would eventually become my and Jo's bedroom. Now that all the boxes were empty, Jo and I had officially moved in.

"Gosh, that was a *workout*," I stated, collapsing onto my twin-size bed. "Great job moving in, Jo!"

"Thanks, Max!" Jo agreed, who was sitting next to me on the bed. "And it's only 5:30! So it only took us the afternoon to move in."

Jo was correct. In the past few hours, Jo and I had finished moving in, which included moving the furniture, whether from the other house or new from the furniture store, and unpacking all the boxes. Even though we were exhausted, our new house felt more like our new home.

But suddenly, I heard a noise. It was super quiet and I didn't think Jo could hear it, but it sounded like an engine. Along with brakes squealing and a door opening, it sounded like the mail truck. I jumped up and ran to the closest window. "Jo! Did you hear that??"

Jo looked at me like I was crazy. "Huh? I don't hear anything."

"It's the mail truck!!" It *was*, in fact, the mail truck. Through the window, I saw a shark in a white vehicle putting something in our house's mailbox. The mailshark closed the mailbox and drove away.

Jo noticed, too. "You're right, Max. The mail truck came!!" But suddenly she added, whispering, "Wait, why are you getting so excited about the mail truck?"

"I don't know, honestly," I admitted. "But I'll go get the mail anyway." I slipped my shoes on, walked downstairs, and retrieved the mail from outside. One piece of mail was inside the mailbox.

"What's this?" I asked Jo when I came back inside.

Jo examined the paper carefully like she was worried it would blow up. And then her smile grew and her eyes widened. "OMG, Max! It's an advertisement for Sharkschool!! Sharkschool is a private school I've gone to since preschool, and I've loved going there! My teacher even threw a dance party on the last day of sixth grade! Well, anyway…" Jo flipped the advertisement over. "…it says here that registration starts today! Also, Meet Your Teacher Day is in the middle of August for enrolled sharks, and Sharkschool starts at the beginning of September."

I tried to absorb all the information I had just learned. "Oh, wow!" I paused and added, "Can I attend Sharkschool, too?"

"I see no reason why not. We have the money to pay for tuition…" Jo pulled a few crisp one-SBuck bills out of her pocket… "…and I'll be attending Sharkschool for seventh grade, so you can come with me for fourth grade or whatever grade you're in." I laughed.

"Yes, I *am* in fourth grade. Thanks so much, Jo!!" I grabbed Jo by the waist and hugged her.

"You're welcome!! I think it's the right decision to continue with school while you're here!!"

"Can we fill out the registration form?" I asked, pointing to the folded paper that came with the flyer.

Jo sighed and shook her head—or what would be her head if she were completely human. "I've had enough of filling out forms for one day."

"So no?"

"No, sure. If we want to attend Sharkschool, we should fill the form out now!"

"Thank you, Jo!"

August 5

I was chilling on my bed reading a book when I suddenly sat straight up.

Adrenaline rushing through my nerves, I jumped up and ran to my window. I peeked out the glass and almost started jumping up and down in excitement. "Jo!"

Suddenly, I heard frantic caudal fin-steps running from the kitchen and up the stairs. The door flung open to reveal Jo. "Hi, Max! What do you need me for?"

I replied in an ironically excited tone for something so seemingly simple. "I just heard the mail truck!! Do you think— do you think we got mail from Sharkschool?"

Jo sighed. "I'm sorry to ruin your excitement, Max, but I don't think it is. At least ten mail trucks have come since the enrollment form came, and none of those have given us anything from Sharkschool."

Jo's claim made sense to me, but I wouldn't let it ruin my mood. "You're probably right, but you could be wrong, so I'm going to check," I stated in a jokingly stubborn voice. I slipped my shoes on and ran down the stairs.

When I opened the mailbox, I was surprised Jo was wrong. The new paper from Sharkschool told us we were enrolled! It also stated that Sharkschool's Meet Your Teacher Day was in ten days. I brought the form back inside.

"Jo! Jo! Guess what! Guess what! Guess what!" I
exclaimed while practically jumping up and down in
excitement.

Jo sighed. "What, Max?" she asked, clearly
annoyed. But when I unfolded the flyer and showed it to
her, she started jumping up and down in excitement too.
"OMG! OMG! OMG! We got in, Max!! Now all we have to
do is wait for Meet Your Teacher Day to arrive!!"

August 15, at Sharkschool's main entrance

"Wow!" I said as I walked into one of
Sharkschool's four buildings. When I saw the building,
my mouth dropped open in awe. It looked so big and
new, as if a remodel had just been completed.

"Welcome to Sharkschool's Low Building, also
known as the building the kindergarteners–6th graders
go to," Jo informed me with an ironically blank tone.

"Wow. It's huge," I stated.

"Yeah!! It's awesome," Jo agreed.

A staff member in the hallway approached us
shortly after we entered the building and asked us a
question. "Hey, young sharks. Where are your parents?"

Jo and I exchanged glances, neither of us knowing
what to say. Finally, I thought of something:

"I came here from another planet called Wah on a
day called Go Anywhere Day. I left my parents behind

and came here by myself," I told the staff member, my sad words yet cheery tone reminding me of Anny.

Jo seemed to get ideas from what I said, but she didn't share as much as I did, and I assumed that was because it was personal. "To put it shortly, my mom left me when I was little. And my dad died."

"Oh." The staff member walked away. He had probably never heard stories like that.

I felt despair on Jo's behalf. I never knew her mom had left her! I looked her in the eyes and said, "I'm so sorry your mom left you when you were little."

"Thank you, Max." After pausing, Jo added, "When I was four years old, my single mom abandoned me. Or, at least, I think that's what she did. The whole thing is a mystery; she left without her things, and I still have to figure out why. That's why you've seen me living by myself; I have been since then." Jo paused again and completely changed her tone to almost cheerful. "Anyway, should we meet your teacher?"

Jo's tone change was a bit awkward, but it was okay. "I would love that! What does the schedule say?"

"You don't have a schedule like I do, but your fourth-grade teacher will be Ms. Hagger. I've heard she's nice." Jo's teacher was in the Middle Building.

"Let's go see her. There's a map here," I said. The map was a piece of paper protected by a thick plastic protector.

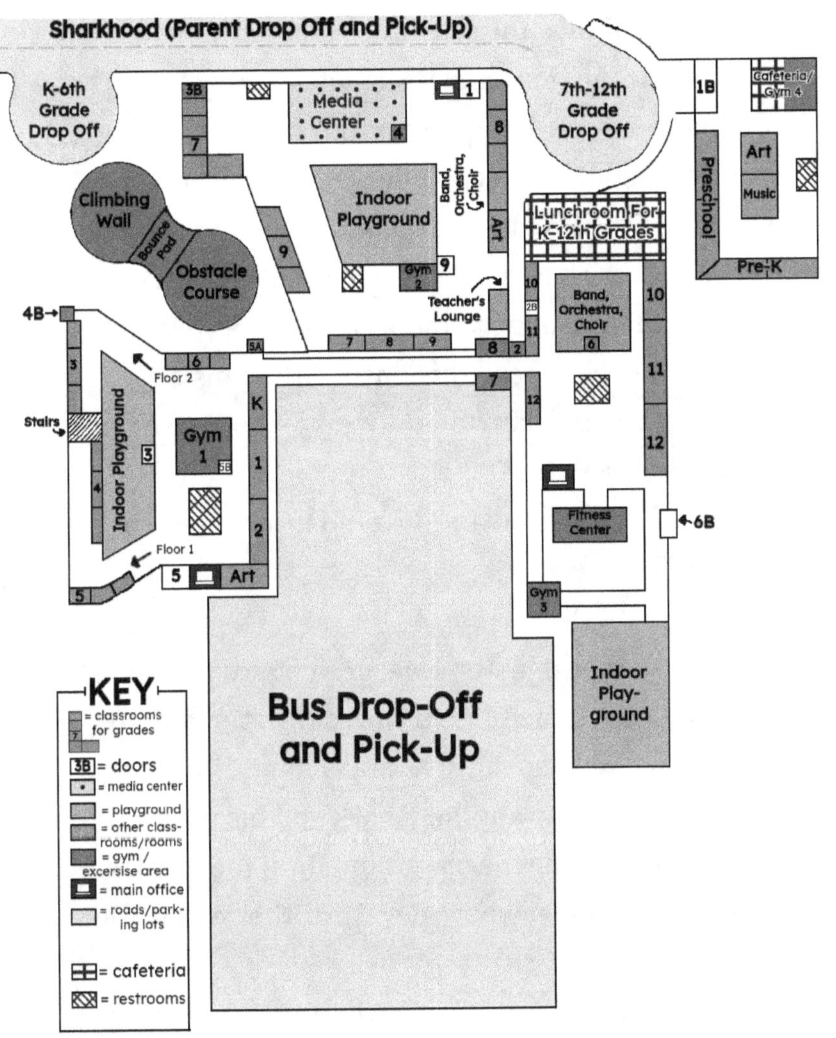

Sharkhood (Parent Drop Off and Pick-Up)
K-6th Grade Drop Off
7th-12th Grade Drop Off
3B
1
1B
Cafeteria/ Gym 4
Media Center
8
Art
Music
7
4
Band, Orchestra, Choir
Indoor Playground
Art
Preschool
Climbing Wall
Bounce Pad
Obstacle Course
9
Gym 2
9
Lunchroom For K-12th Grades
Pre-K
Teacher's Lounge
10
2B
Band, Orchestra, Choir
10
4B
5A
6
7
8
9
8
2
6
11
3
Floor 2
11
11
Stairs
Indoor Playground
K
7
12
12
Gym 1
5E
1
Fitness Center
6B
4
3
2
Floor 1
5
Art
5
Gym 3
Indoor Play-ground
Bus Drop-Off and Pick-Up
KEY
= classrooms for grades
7
3B = doors
= media center
= playground
= other class-rooms/rooms
= gym / excersise area
= main office
= roads/park-ing lots
= cafeteria
= restrooms

I examined the schedule and Sharkschool map. I realized for the first time Sharkschool was bigger than I originally assumed. "Wow. Sharkschool is even bigger than I thought." The schedule was complicated, but I was excited for the first day of school.

"Yeah. Sharkschool is big, but it 'shrinks' as you get used to it. Suddenly, it doesn't seem as big," Jo replied. "I experienced this during my transition from preschool to kindergarten. Anyways, should we find Ms. Hagger's classroom?"

"Please," I told Jo. "I would love to meet my teacher!"

We arrived in Ms. Hagger's classroom after a short walk. Jo remembered where the fourth-grade classrooms were, so it did not take long. Ms. Hagger was finishing talking to another shark and his parents. Jo and I waited inside the classroom until the shark and his parents were done; when they were, they exited the room.

"Hi! Which one of you will be in my class this year?" Ms. Hagger was sitting at her desk. She wore a floral print dress and a bonnet. I did not like her outfit very much—but that was my problem.

"Me!" I said. "My name is Max Alderin. I'm new here."

"A new student?" Ms. Hagger asked. "Yay! I always love new students! Nice to meet you, Max!"

Gosh, I'm bored. Jo and I had talked with Ms. Hagger for about ten minutes, but it was mostly a conversation between Jo and her; I did not say much. I stood up.

I remembered hearing something about "every shark getting their own computer", so I walked to the back of the room, where the computer cart was stored. I opened the door, grabbed the computer that was assigned to me, and loaded games like Tig Tang, Robosha, and Virtual Hide Starter. I gamed until Jo finished talking with Ms. Hagger.

"Hi, Max!" Jo said. "Sorry it took so long! Ms. Hagger had a lot to say. We can go home, if you would like, or I can give you a tour of Sharkschool's property so you know the campus better."

I thought for a moment. "I want a tour of Sharkschool. When the first day comes, I should know the rooms a bit more than I do now," I explained. "Uh, please."

Jo nodded. "I think that's a good idea. See you later, Ms. Hagger!"

Ms. Hagger suddenly stood up out of her chair and grabbed a cooler. "Oh, wait, Max! Do you want a popsicle?"

I was surprised by the offer. "Sure, Ms. Hagger!" I grabbed a lime green one. "I'll see you on the first day!"

Jo and I left the classroom. Next, we walked around and explored Sharkschool's campus until Sharkschool closed. After that, we went home.

95

The first day came less than fifteen days later.

9

First Day Drama

September 1st

I felt a strong yet light tapping on my shoulder one morning. *What's that?* Somebody was whispering, too, but I couldn't tell who or what it was.

Slowly, I opened my eyes and realized it was Jo trying to wake me up. "Max, it's 6:45 in the morning and time to wake up. Remember, today's the first day of school! How did you sleep? I made peanut butter pancakes for breakfast!"

I sat up, yawned, and stretched, still trying to wake up. And I *loved* Jo's peanut butter pancakes! I could almost taste their creamy nuttiness in my mouth just by thinking about them. "Thanks, Jo! You know how much I love those!"

"Well, Max, I'll see you later! Please put your pajamas away and make your bed before coming down," Jo reminded me before exiting the room.

I was going to put my pajamas away like Jo told me, but I saw my book lying on my bookshelf with the bookmark at the climax. Not able to resist, I opened the book and started reading, my brain soaking up all the exciting action. I laid down on my bed and did this for what I thought was only a few minutes.

But I felt the need to check the clock. I leaned over and looked at the timepiece hanging on my wall, and I was so surprised by what it read that I screamed out loud. "7:00? Oh no!!"

My heart racing from a sudden surge of adrenaline, I quickly grabbed clothes from my drawer and rapidly dressed myself in them. I made my bed in record time, then I flung my door open and raced down the stairs. Jo was at the sink downstairs washing her dirty dishes. "What took you so long, Max? Your pancakes are getting cold."

"Sorry, Jo! I guess I read for a bit too long." I laughed nervously, then I cut off a large chunk of butter and spread it on my pancakes.

When I finished eating my breakfast, Jo instructed me to wash my dishes like I had always done and check I had all my necessary items for school. But there was one thing I did not have: my book, which was upstairs in my room. I ran up the stairs to my room, grabbed the book, and threw it into my backpack.

Now I was almost ready for school; I zipped up the backpack and started tying my shoes. "Jo, I'm ready to go to school. What about you?"

"Yeah!" Jo responded excitedly. "Let's go!"

It went without saying that Jo and I would walk to school, since neither of us liked using the car unless that was necessary. I followed Jo's lead as she put her backpack on and exited the house through the front door.

We arrived at Door 4B of Sharkschool later just minutes before the morning bell.

Jo let go of my fin and looked into my eyes. "Well, Max, I guess I'll see you after school."

I didn't want her to leave! "No, Jo! Don't leave me!!" I grabbed Jo and wrapped her into a hug.

"Sorry, Max, but I've gotta go, or else I'm going to be late," Jo stated matter-of-factly. "Don't worry, I'll see you later."

It took a while, but I eventually let Jo go to class. "Alright. Fine. I'll see you later!" I waved goodbye to Jo and walked on the path to the Low Building, the building

Ms. Hagger's classroom was in. Jo left for the Middle Building, where her classes were.

I ran into my classroom, panting, just moments before the bell rang. Judging by the "name tent" I assumed Ms. Hagger had put on my desk earlier, I found my desk at the front of the classroom and set my supplies down.

I was going to sit down, but I saw something out of the corner of my eye that looked serious enough to make me turn around to see what was happening. I watched as a male shark ran over to the recycling bin near the door and, for a reason I could not understand, crumpled many sheets of paper from inside into balls and threw them at another male shark who looked like his friend. Wincing from what looked like a painful hit, the shark who was the target picked up a piece resting on the table and threw it back at the shark who threw it first.

On Wah, I didn't like seeing people—and same here with sharks—bully each other, and I knew I had to do something about it. Feeling brave, I stated "Hey, what's your name? And why are you throwing trash at that shark?" to the shark who first threw the recycling.

He made a fake "I don't know what you're talking about" face. "I'm Vhreho, and that's Guhyeo." Grabbing the fin of the shark standing next to him and pulling him over, Vhreho added, "But what do you mean? I'm innocent! *He* started it!" The *real* innocent shark suddenly looked surprised and angry, mad that Vhreho was scapegoating him.

Okay, *now* I was angry. "No, I watched you do it," I stated. I knew what I had seen. "*You*, Vhreho, threw the recycling at him—Guhyeo."

"What do you mean? I'm just an innocent shark!" the troublemaker re-stated.

"I'm just trying to state what I saw, and I know it's the truth," I said bluntly. I felt my whole face—or what would have been my face if I were completely human—reddening in anger. Gosh, this Vhreho was a troublemaker!

But I never expected what Guhyeo would say next. His comment was extremely random, yet it confirmed that he was taking Vhreho's side. "Your grandma is dead! What are you talking about?" he shot back.

Now I felt tears coming to my eyes. How DARE he say such a thing! Not only was my grandma still alive, but she was the coolest 80-year-old ever. Infuriated, I said the first thing that came to mind. "My grandma is still very much alive. I was at her house a few months ago."

But Guhyeo wouldn't give up. "You would only think that if you were stupid!"

I was going to respond, but something distracted me from doing that: suddenly, out of the corner of my eye, I saw a male shark slap a female shark with amazing emerald eyes. He whispered something in her ear, and she uttered a few words to me. "Yeah, Max. Maybe you *are* stupid."

Now my feelings were really hurt. Choosing not to answer, I walked to my desk and laid my head down on the table so nobody would see me cry. I was not used to such mean classmates, and although I assumed it would take some time to get used to them, it still hurt. But when Ms. Hagger arrived and told everyone to go to their desks, I sat up and became alert as if nothing ever happened.

Later, after morning meeting and math class

I glanced at the last problem of my homework assignment, which read, "What is 596 times 198?". And then I picked up my pencil again and completed the entire problem in under twenty seconds. I knew how to do this kind of long multiplication—it was almost all I did in math class at my old school on Wah!

But suddenly, the bell signaling the end of class and the beginning of lunch rang, surprising me and making me jump a bit.

"RING!!!"

Everybody started racing to pack up their things and leave the classroom. I jumped out of my seat and put my things away as quickly as possible, then I followed everybody else to the locker area outside.

By the time I got to lunch, which was a few minutes late because I got lost in the huge school, everybody was already seated. Looking around the large room, I noticed the only seat not dirty or taken was at a table where Vhreho and Guhyeo sat. And it was next to the shark who had called me stupid earlier.

I didn't want to sit next to her; why would I? But it was the only seat available, so I had no choice. I hesitantly approached the table nervously and asked to sit. "May I sit here? There's nowhere else to sit."

Much to my surprise, she didn't say no or try to insult me. Instead, she seemed strangely friendly—and although she didn't say anything about permission for me to sit, her easygoing tone of voice gave me all I needed. So I sat down and set my lunchbox on the table. "Hi! My name is Kay. Are you Max?" she politely asked.

Oh, so that's her name! I tried to match Kay's voice's warmness with my response. "Yeah! I'm Max."

I thought Kay was going to apologize for what she said earlier, but she did nothing of the sort. Judging by her tone of voice she had when she let me sit, I expected her to be sorry. Instead, she jumped into a topic I didn't expect her to jump into at all. "Where are you from? I didn't see you at the school last year, and new students don't come often."

I didn't know how to answer, but I tried to explain. "Well, to put it in the shortest way possible, I lived on a planet called Wah three months ago. On Wah, on New Year's Day, me and all kids—err, I mean, young humans—who are nine years old can wish to go to any place they can dream up, real or fake. I wanted to go to Sharkland."

Kay's response was even more unexpected. "Me too!"

"Wait, what?" That was *not* how I expected Kay to respond!

"On my day, I chose to go to Sharkland too!"

"No way!!" I exclaimed. I couldn't tell whether Kay was lying or not. But I assumed I would be able to see it in her eyes if she was, and her eyes didn't say anything about lying. "Also, would you like to be friends?"

Yay, my first friend at Sharkschool! "That would be amazing!"

"Okay, another strange question. Did you come here three months earlier like I did?"

Now I was surprised. And I was getting a bit suspicious, too, but I tried to ignore that doubt. "OMG, yes! That is *so* cool! I wonder how rare it is to meet somebody on one planet who came from the same planet as you. That's awesome!" I sighed. I was starting to feel a bit homesick since I had now been in Sharkland for over two-and-a-half months.

"Probably not a lot," Kay suggested. It's cool how we found each other, though!" She paused. "Would you like to... hang out at... the gingashlucka— err, my house after school today?"

This was exciting! "That sounds awesome!" I exclaimed. "Nah, I think we should hang out at *my* house. Jo and I just bought a new house, and I'm really proud of it." My response came off a bit rude, but I hoped Kay wouldn't mind.

"We can do that, I guess...?" She didn't even sound confused about how a fourth-grader and somebody named Jo bought a house; just sounded disappointed that I suggested my house instead of hers.

Not long after I finished my lunch, the teachers dismissed us. Next up was recess, which was indoors today because it was raining heavily outside. I knew we were supposed to go to Ms. Hagger's classroom in the Low Building for the next half-hour of indoor recess, though I wanted to look cool in front of Kay. Therefore, I pushed the door at the end of the hallway open when none of the teachers were looking. A paper sign with the words "**Outside Door**" in black marker was taped to the door.

Little did I know that the door would make a sound when I pushed it open. A loud "*BZZT, BZZT!*" came from a speaker above the door. Some teachers in the lunchroom came running. I stumbled outside, only to almost slip and fall because of the rain.

The teachers came outside and surrounded me. Kay watched from the other side of the door through the window. Suddenly, I remembered a candy bar I did not have time to eat during lunch was still in my lunchbox, so I popped it in my mouth. I heard one teacher quietly curse about not remembering to lock the door.

"Hey, you! What are you doing here? You're supposed to go back to your classroom for indoor recess!" another teacher exclaimed.

A third teacher followed the lead of the second teacher and instructed me, too. "Go back inside! It's raining, and recess is indoors today!"

"You're not allowed out here!" a fourth teacher reminded me.

I felt a spark of rebelliousness light in me. "What do you mean? I'm still eating my lunch!" I opened my mouth and showed the teachers the chewed-up candy bar.

"Eww!" the first teacher exclaimed.

"Gross!" the second teacher added.

The third teacher made a face. "Disgusting!"

"It's rude to behave like that in front of a grown-up shark," the fourth teacher said.

I turned around and saw Kay give me a fins-up from inside the building. I burped as loudly as I could, which caused all the teachers to start talking at once.

"Go back to Ms. Hagger's classroom!" one of the teachers said while pulling a sheet of paper out of her pocket. "Never mind. I'm going to send you to the office! Nah. I'm going to call the office so they can contact your parents or guardian instead."

The teacher used her walkie-talkie to contact the Low Building's main office. The teachers ushered me inside the building, locked the door behind them, and walked away.

"That was extremely naughty, Max," Kay, who was still hiding behind the door, informed me. I turned red with embarrassment, and I felt a wave of guilt rush through me. "But it was awesome! I want to do it, too!"

I smirked. "Well, good thing my caretaker doesn't have a phone number. The office won't be able to contact her." *Not that Jo would probably care much if she found out what I did. She's the best.*

Most sharks were playing games on their laptops when Kay and I walked back to the classroom. Ms. Hagger called me over.

"Max. I know you went outside when you weren't supposed to, so you have lost your laptop during indoor recess," she said. "I know that you are new here, but we went over the rules earlier today." *Oh well. Losing my laptop isn't too bad.*

Next, I commuted to my desk and sat down in the chair. I opened my independent reading book and immersed myself in the world that was in its pages.

But I had not read a single page before I heard somebody say my name. I spun around. Vhreho and Guhyeo were standing behind me, and Guhyeo held a box. Both sharks had slightly mischievous expressions for some reason.

"Max! We're playing a game, and we need one more player! We need you to join!" Vhreho commanded.

Hesitantly, I replied, "Sure, I guess. What's it called?"

"It's called 'Be Mean: When Hurt Feelings Mean Winning!'"

I stepped back in shock. Why did I say yes to playing *before* I knew what the game was called? "Actually, I don't really want to play anymore, no thanks. I don't like being mean," I said without hesitation.

"No. You have to join, Max," Guhyeo demanded. "You already said you would." I did not dare ask why *I* was the one they wanted to play with.

The game had a colorful box, and the lid had a blob-like creature colored a bit like a shadow on a red background. Guhyeo opened the box, revealing many silver coins and a "How To Play" guide.

Now I was starting to feel even more resentful towards the game. Embarrassed with my decision, I ran and hid behind the rolling storage unit, hoping that neither Vhreho nor Guhyeo would see me. Sadly, Vhreho noticed me and threatened to tell the teacher if I didn't play—this made no sense because I shouldn't have to play if I didn't want to, but I didn't want to risk getting in trouble. Guhyeo emptied the box's contents onto the table without waiting for a response.

"These coins are called Nuggings," Guhyeo stated, capturing my attention. "Here's how to play. There are 100 Nuggings. You have to start being mean to another shark, and if the other shark starts crying, you get ten. When all the Nuggings are out of the box, everybody counts how many they have. If you're the shark with the most Nuggings, well, 'winner winner, chicken dinner'!. Okay, now that you know how to play, let's start!"

Vhreho made five sharks cry, so he earned fifty Nuggings, and Guhyeo made four sharks cry, so he earned forty. I made no sharks cry, so I earned zero Nuggings. And instead of making sharks cry, I was comforting the sharks who were crying. But Guhyeo noticed this. "Max! You can't comfort the crying sharks! You have to play with us!"

Now I was in a dilemma. *I don't want to fight with Vhreho and Guhyeo because they probably have entire mental scripts of insults, but innocent sharks don't deserve to cry because of them. I know Vhreho and Guhyeo will continue to bully other sharks if I don't do anything about it. What should I do? Perhaps I could continue comforting the sharks Vhreho and Guhyeo have hurt. That would mean I do not have to fight with Vhreho and Guhyeo, but it would still help the problem because fewer sharks have hurt feelings.*

But I was suddenly pulled out of my thoughts by Kay's whispering from across the room, barely loud enough for me to hear but not so loud that Vhreho or Guhyeo heard her. "Max! Over here!"

I turned around. "What?"

Kay came to where I was sitting. "I know you don't like being mean, which I think is strange, but I respect your lack of ability to cause hurt feelings. I can help you complete the last challenge, though."

"How?" I was intrigued now. *What* did she mean?

"I have this *amazing* ability to make myself start crying on command. If I can make tears come out of my *beautiful* green eyes, Vhreho and Guhyeo will think you made me cry. That way, the game'll end, and you won't have to play for any longer."

I was impressed. But was she serious? I decided to find out. "Okay." Kay took a sip from her water bottle and made a noise with her mouth. Suddenly, tears welled in her eyes, and she looked like she would cry. It worked; Kay was now fake-sobbing hard.

Guhyeo heard Kay and turned around. "Great work, Max! Here's your reward." He handed me ten shiny silver Nuggings.

I couldn't take my eyes off the Nuggings. Was I supposed to like having these? *Now the game might finally end, but was earning the Nuggings worth it? I earned them by pretending to be mean to Kay, and even though I wasn't actually mean, being mean SUCKS, and now my classmates might think of me as a bully.*

You know what? I don't want these. Goodbye, Nuggings. I threw the Nuggings to the ground and stomped on them with my caudal fin for good measure. But I was still dissatisfied. *What would happen if I did that to Vhreho and Guhyeo's Nuggings, too? It probably wouldn't do much because it's just a game, and the Nuggings aren't money, but it's worth a try.* I positioned my right fin underneath Vhreho's fins, which held his fifty Nuggings, and hit them out of his fins. The Nuggings fell to the ground.

I did the same to Guhyeo. Suddenly, both sharks started crying, which was *not* what I expected! "Why are you crying?" I asked. "I'm sorry, I didn't intend to make you cry!"

What Guhyeo said next was far from what I thought he would say. "We *want* to be bullied!" It didn't even make sense!

But I took advantage of my sudden dominance over the two male sharks. "Being mean is awful for any reason. Promise you will never play this game again."

"We promise!" both sharks said without hesitation. They fell to the body part that would be their knees if they were completely human and pleaded.

While they did that, I walked the hundred Nuggings back to the box and closed the box. I would never say it out loud, but Vhreho and Guhyeo seemed a bit dim-witted.

After indoor recess, Ms. Hagger announced we were going to gym class. "Everybody, we're going to gym class!" A chorus of groans came from my classmates, but we still made a single-file line by the door. Ms. Hagger opened the door, and everybody followed her to the gymnasium.

The teacher, named Mr. Kennager, stood outside the doors to the gymnasium when we arrived. He was a muscular shark with a deep voice. "How's everybody's first day of school going?"

Everybody else knew what to do: they sat down in grids on the gym floor. Since I had never attended this school before and had no idea what they were doing, I just followed their lead. I tried to sit down far away from everybody else, but Kay came and sat next to me. She laughed.

"The way you're sitting makes you look like a fat pig, Max," Kay said. She laughed again.

I felt my back to make sure I hadn't sprouted wings suddenly. What did she mean by "flying wig"? "I look like a flying wig? Huh?"

But apparently this is not what Kay *actually* said. "No, I said, 'fat pig,' but it's okay."

Before Kay or I could say more, Mr. Kennager shared the rules of the game we would play. The way I understood it, everybody would split into two teams, and one team would stand in the outer circle in the middle of the gym while the other would stand in the inner circle. The object of the game was to swat the ball back and forth between the two teams without catching or dropping the "hot potato". Sharks did not get to choose teams.

When Mr. Kennager was not looking, sharks who were friends cleverly moved away from each other so a shark separated them and they could be on the same team. Kay wanted to be with me, so she moved away from me with a shark named Linda separating us. Mr. Kennager assigned either a 1 or a 2 to every shark in the class; Vhreho and Guhyeo were on team 2, and I was on team 1 with Kay.

Vhreho was the first shark with the Hot Potato. He balanced it on his left fin and used his right to launch the Hot Potato into the air, right towards me.

The round object was now soaring toward me at high speed. *Uh-oh. I felt I would be the first to receive the hot potato, but I did not think it would move this fast.* Recalling the game's rules, I decided to swat it away. I intended to hit it so it would be below the head and easy for somebody to hit back, but the way I hit it made it soar high into the air, above everybody's heads.

But the Hot Potato did not go where I planned it to. Instead, it flew a few feet over everybody and towards Guhyeo's head. It hit him, and he burst into tears. I felt a surge of shame. *Why* did the "hot potato" have to hit him?

I didn't know whether to be sorry for him or not; I could tell Guhyeo did not get hurt because I saw him side-eye me. I was removed from the game, Mr. Kennager's assistant took Guhyeo to the nurse, and he told me to sit in the corner of the gym.

Kay and another shark named ZY were eliminated after two rounds, and that's when Ms. Hagger came back. I assumed class was over, but when the first thing Ms. Hagger did was start talking to Mr. Kennager, I got a bit nervous.

My confusion was cleared up, though. "Max?" Ms. Hagger asked once the two teachers finished talking.

Uh-oh. "What?"

Ms. Hagger did *not* look happy. "I heard you purposely hit Guhyeo in the head with the ball—err, 'hot potato'."

I wanted to say that it was an accident, but I
didn't want to seem defensive and risk losing my
reputation as a shark Ms. Hagger liked. But I decided the
truth was more important. "Sorry, Ms. Hagger. It wasn't
on purpose."

Ms. Hagger didn't know whether to believe me or
not. "I'll ask Guhyeo and see what he says." And this
worried me since I knew Guhyeo would lie and say I hit
him on purpose—his expression from earlier told me he
knew it was accidental.

Ms. Hagger spotted Guhyeo, who had been
eliminated, and walked over to him. The two talked for a
while. Guhyeo made crazy fin motions that made him
seem angry. A wave of nervousness flushed through my
body.

*Wow, this is my first day at a new school on a
new planet, and it's going GREAT,* I thought
sarcastically as I sat down in a chair, waiting to meet
with the principal.

"Max?" somebody at the front desk said. "Can you
come in here, please?"

Shaking from fear, I stood up and followed the
secretary to an empty room with no furniture inside
except for three folding chairs. When I sat down in one
of the chairs, the secretary left, and the principal came
in. He sat down in one of the two chairs left.

"I heard you threw a playground ball, also known as a Hot Potato, at your classmate Guhyeo on purpose," he stated.

I didn't know what to say to this. Would it be better to sound professional or be defensive? "I didn't mean to. The Hot Potato was coming toward me, and I tried to hit it over Guhyeo, but it ended up hitting Guhyeo on the head."

The principal seemed to consider this. "Okay, I'll think about that. Do you have any evidence to prove that you didn't hit Guhyeo on purpose?"

Now I was *really* at a loss for words. How was I supposed to have *evidence*? I didn't want to look guilty, but I couldn't think of any evidence.

Turns out, I didn't need to. A familiar shark's voice suddenly screamed "Wait!". It was Kay, who was running into the room.

The principal looked extremely surprised to see Kay. "Aren't you supposed to be in class right now?"

"Yes," Kay answered. "But I wanted to tell you this shark didn't do anything. I saw what happened, and he never intended for the ball to hit the other shark in the face."

This was my evidence!! But the principal didn't totally buy it. "Are you telling the truth, Kay, or are you just saying that because you two are friends?"

"We're not friends," Kay lied. "I don't even know his name. I don't like it when innocent sharks get in trouble, though."

Kay and I walked back to the classroom together when I was done meeting with the principal. The principal decided I was innocent, and therefore, I did not get in trouble.

"Kay, thanks for saving me from getting in trouble!!" I said to Kay, who was walking next to me.

"You're welcome," she said slyly. She made a devilish grin.

When Kay and I were in the classroom, I remembered something I had wanted to ask her. "Kay?"

"Yes?"

"I've started noticing how Vhreho and Guhyeo seem kind of dim-witted. Have they always been like this?" I asked. Vhreho and Guhyeo kept being naughty and getting in trouble.

"What?" Vhreho, who sat at the table group next to me, responded. *Oh no. He must have heard me.* "Max, relax. You just need to get to know us a little bit more."

But Guhyeo seemed to disagree with this statement. "Actually, Max, you're not wrong. We ARE a bit stupid. But it's not because we don't have brains. It's because we don't have hearts."

This was slightly surprising because I assumed every shark needed a heart to survive, but then I remembered that he could just mean "hearts" figuratively.

"There is a story, though. Everybody is born with a heart. Do you want to hear it?" Vhreho asked me.

Now I knew that Vhreho meant "hearts" literally. I didn't know what to think about that. "Um, sure, I guess."

Guhyeo continued to tell the story. When he was finished, I was speechless for at least a minute, if not more.

9½

Guhyeo's Flashback

New Year's Day That Year, Guhyeo's Point Of View

"RING!! RING!!" the doorbell rang.

Who was at the door? Curious, I stood up and walked to the window. But when I learned who was there, I quickened my pace and ran down the stairs. I pulled my right snow boot onto my right caudal fin and opened the door to meet the sharks outside.

My best friend Vhreho and partial friend Lachenz were outside my door holding a playground ball. They had come to play a game we loved called Skicks in my backyard. It was winter break and we were bored, so I had asked if they could come over and play.

"Hi, Guhyeo!" Vhreho greeted me. "Are you ready to go DOWN??" I laughed.

We all ran across the snow-covered grass to get to the backyard, where we would play the game. When we got to the spot we wanted, everybody moved so we formed a triangle.

Lachenz, who held the ball, set the large, round object on the snow. Skicks was harder to play in the wintertime but still possible. He kicked the ball, sending it flying over the white powder. I caught it, meaning I wasn't eliminated.

We continued playing this way for a while. By now, everybody was getting tired, but we were still having fun.

It was Vhreho's turn to kick. He stood up, positioned his caudal fin, and kicked. But this kick was unlike the rest—instead of going to me, it soared over everybody and rolled into the forest-like area behind my backyard.

"Oops," Vhreho apologized. "Sorry, guys." He knew the ball wasn't supposed to go there.

Out of instinct, I automatically darted towards the rapidly moving rubber object. "Guhyeo! Don't go in there! You might never come back!" Lachenz shouted.

But it was too late. I had already committed to retrieving the ball, and that is what I had to do.

I suddenly heard fast-paced caudal fin-steps coming in my direction. Shaking with fear, I jolted around. But it was just Vhreho coming to help look for the ball. Phew.

Vhreho and I continued running into the expansive forest, looking for the ball. But it was nowhere to be found, even after five minutes or more of running around and searching for the yellow, round object. But I needed to stop.

"Vhreho, wait," I informed Vhreho. "I'm sweating."

"Okay," Vhreho agreed. I took my coat off. We were going to keep searching for the ball, but what happened next stopped us from doing that, something I never would have expected.

Suddenly, I felt a very strong punch land in my back, sort of near my heart. It felt as if somebody had kicked a burning soccer ball as hard as they could, and it hit me. Wincing, I leaned over in pain, the full force of the attack still radiating throughout my bones. Running over to help me, Vhreho worriedly asked, "Guhyeo, are you okay??"

"Vhreho, how could you—" I started. But somewhere inside, I didn't think Vhreho did it. It was hard to believe a punch that painful could have been caused by a shark.

But then I heard another forceful slap. Clutching his stomach, Vhreho leaned forward just like I did and winced in pain. And then his eyes widened.

"What?" I wondered.

"Guhyeo, look..." Still clutching his stomach, Vhreho pointed to the air. Woozy from the impact, I looked up, and almost jumped back in shock. I saw two slimy, red objects—hearts—seeming to levitate in the air as if gravity didn't exist. Judging by the hole that had appeared in my chest, they were shark hearts, Vhreho and I's hearts. I jumped up, scrambling to bring our hearts back down to Earth, but I wasn't able to catch them. They rose farther and farther into the sky until I could not see them anymore.

My eyes met Vhreho's, both of us suddenly realizing that somebody else had to have punched us. But who? Who punched us so hard that our hearts came out of our bodies? How was that even possible?

Overflowing with questions, I turned around to see if anybody besides Vhreho was there.

Nobody was there except for us, on the verge between dead and alive.

10
The First Week

A lot happened during gym class on the second day of school.

First, our class played another game, called Sharkball, which reminded me a bit of a game called kickball that I played on Wah. I was in line and next to kick. But first, the shark in front of me had to take her turn.

She kicked, and I stepped up to the front of the line. My body was shaking; I did not like this game, and I was nervous. But I reminded myself that if my kick was bad, it would be no big deal.

Next, the pitcher on the second team retrieved the ball from somebody else on that team and rolled the ball toward me at top speed.

I suddenly felt my heart jump and my breathing speed up. I was terrible at the fielding position of kickball on Wah and even worse at kicking, so I feared the worst. As the ball came closer and closer, I prepared to kick.

When the ball came close enough, I kicked it as hard as possible. Hoping no shark would catch it and I wouldn't be eliminated, I bolted to first base. Thankfully, my caudal fin touched just *before* the shark caught the ball. I was safe!

The next shark in line stepped up to the front—he was known to be a weaker kicker. When the ball rolled toward him, he lightly kicked it just enough so it moved forward but not hard enough for it to lift off the ground.

I started running as soon as he kicked the ball. The whistle blew just as my caudal fin touched the next base. I was safe again! Or so I thought. I waited for the shark who caught the ball to throw the ball back to the pitcher, but for some reason, everybody seemed to be staring at me.

"Max, you have to go back," Guhyeo finally stated after what felt like an eternity of silence.

"Why? I made it in time." Didn't I?

"Uh, no, you didn't! Mr. Kennager blew the whistle *before* your caudal fin touched."

Unlike Ms. Hagger, because this was Guhyeo, who I could tell would probably become my worst enemy in the future, I felt no reason to *not* be defensive. "I know what my fins are doing. My caudal fin touched the base before the whistle blew."

Mr. Kennager took Guhyeo's side, to my surprise. "Go back to the end of the line, Max. I did not see your fin touch the base, and cheating is not allowed," he said coldly.

Fuming, I walked back to the end of the kicking line. How embarrassing! But at least Kay was there to comfort me. "Don't worry, Max. Life is unfair sometimes." Her beautiful green eyes sparkled.

After class ended, I saw Guhyeo high-finning Vhreho. "Great work, Guhyeo," I overheard Vhreho whisper.

"Thanks," Guhyeo whispered back. "Remember what you're doing tomorrow?"

Third day of school

It was our class's turn to be in the music room the next day, and the teacher, Mrs. Gingashnugger, had just finished assigning seats. I was seated in the second-to-last row, and Vhreho was right behind me.

Next, she started instruction. "Class, repeat after me. We're singing camp songs today. I've got this great big hunk of tin..." Mrs. Gingashnugger sang.

Everybody in the class sang back, except for Vhreho. "I've got this great big hunk of tin..." Vhreho screamed instead. "I'VE GOT THIS GREAT BIG HUNK OF TIN..."

Mrs. Gingashnugger thought it was me, though. "Max? Is that you? Please stop screaming. It's distracting, and let's not forget there are classes around here with their doors open who can hear you. If you do that again, you get a time-out in the hallway."

Uh, oh. "Uh... that wasn't me, but okay," I said.

Ms. Gingashnugger seemed to ignore me. "Class, repeat after me again. Nobody knows what shape it's in..."

Everybody in the class repeated the phrase. Vhreho screamed. I tried to keep my mouth closed; if I didn't sing at all, nobody would think *I* was the one screaming. But I felt like I needed to yawn just before everybody sang the sentence, which may have made me look screaming.

Sadly, this is what Ms. Gingashnugger thought, and man, she was *angry.* "Max, you cannot scream in this classroom. Do you see the rules sign up there? It *clearly* reads, 'No screaming in the classroom.' Go into the hallway. You obviously cannot be inside the classroom; unlike you, other sharks here want to learn."

I knew she didn't mean it, but wow, those words struck me like a sword.

Confused, embarrassed, and furious, I slowly stood and walked to the door. I pulled out the cold chair and sat at the desk in the hallway; I knew teachers commonly did this for sharks who wanted to take their tests without the distraction of the loud classroom. Feeling miserable, I rested my head in my arms, listening to the noise inside the room.

"Let's retry those two verses without Max in here," I heard Ms. Gingashnugger say from inside the classroom. "I've got this great big hunk of tin..."

Everybody in the class repeated the first verse of the song. Vhreho did not scream.

I also heard Kay's voice from inside the classroom. "Excuse me, Ms. Gingashnugger, may I go into the hallway and talk to Max?" she requested with a sweet, innocent voice.

Now Ms. Gingashnugger's tone was much calmer and nicer than it was before. "Sure, Kay. Just come back inside quickly, and don't go anywhere with Max. The last thing I want is you two running around the school, a janitor finding you, and me getting in trouble for something I didn't do."

I sighed. *If only she knew.*

Suddenly, I heard the door click and saw it open; Kay came out and sat on top of the table. "Don't worry, Max. Life is unfair sometimes." Her green eyes sparkled.

Fourth day of school

If the day after was a normal day, our class would have gym class, but Ms. Hagger wanted to do something else instead. That 'instead' was a presentation about being nice to others. When I learned this, I couldn't help wondering, *did yesterday's music class influence this?*

But about halfway through the presentation, the landline phone on Ms. Hagger's desk started ringing.

Running to the phone and picking it up, Ms. Hagger delicately said, "Hello. Katarine here…"

She was on the phone for a while. But suddenly, she set the handheld device back down and speed-walked to the door. Opening the door, she informed the class, "I need to go pick up my computer that the technicians at the media center fixed. I'll be right back." She ran out the door.

I was prepared. I pulled my video camera out of my backpack—it was on the school supply list, so I had brought it to school today—and was ready if Vhreho or Guhyeo did anything naughty.

Turns out, I was right.

"Vhreho, let's trash this classroom!" Guhyeo exclaimed to Vhreho. I clicked 'record'.

"Yeah!" Vhreho replied, completely unaware that he was being recorded. He ran over to Ms. Hagger's desk and reached into her recycling bin, grabbing a fin-ful or so of the crisp graphite-covered "tree sheets". Vhreho crumpled them into balls and threw them around the room.

Meanwhile, Guhyeo's eyes darted around the room. Suddenly, his eyes lit up—he had an idea. Strolling over to a table group in the back of the room, he grabbed somebody's supplies bag. Shaking the contents onto the table, all the pencils, pens, and papers fell onto the floor, and the neatness of the shark's bag was destroyed. He did the same for the other bags of that group.

I was sure to record both Vhreho and Guhyeo.

Suddenly, I heard the door mechanisms click, and an adult shark wearing a floral-print dress stepped into the room. Vhreho and Guhyeo—who knew they would get caught if they didn't act quickly—darted to their seats and pretended to talk to each other before Ms. Hagger saw them. But once she saw the room's mess, she was utterly shocked. "Who did this?!" Ms. Hagger screamed.

Vhreho and Guhyeo stared blankly at each other for a moment. Then Guhyeo, who was a master of the poker face, lied, "It was Max. Everybody watched him chuck paper balls across the room and shake everything in everybody's bags onto the floor. Everybody knew that Vhreho and Guhyeo were too powerful to stand up to, so they remained silent.

I was speechless; I knew Vhreho and Guhyeo would lie to the teacher, but the way they said it made it sound like I really *was* the culprit. My mind went blank, struggling with things to say. Thankfully, though, it didn't last long. Gathering the courage to stand up to the bullies, I declared, "No! I didn't do it! I have proof!"

"What do you mean by 'I have proof', Max?" Ms. Hagger wondered. I couldn't tell if she was curious or not, but her eyes widened. I grabbed my video camera and played the video for her.

Ms. Hagger didn't know what to think—she had previously thought the friends were the best students in the class, but the video proved her wrong. She was silent for a moment. Vhreho and Guhyeo exchanged worried glances.

As if an angel had whispered in her ear, Ms. Hagger suddenly thought of the best thing to say: "To the office. Both of you." She scribbled on the top sheet of a pad of office referral forms; Vhreho and Guhyeo quietly muttered curse words to each other. "Here is your office referral form for lying, making a mess of the classroom, disrespecting me, and cursing. Show it to the office staff when you get there."

As my class walked into the art room, the teacher, Mr. Klongei, could be heard giving instructions. "Alright, class! Go to your assigned seats. I'm going to the art supply storage room to pick up some more paper."

When the adult shark was out of sight, I noticed Vhreho and Guhyeo out of the corner of my eye looking around the room mischievously. But both of them had their eyes set on something—three open, large jars of washable tempera paint the previous class had used. I sighed. *Here we go again.*

Next, the two troublemakers did exactly what I was afraid of: they walked to the back counter and grabbed the largest brushes in the paintbrush jar and dipped them into the paint. Creating bright streaks on their ratty, holey black T-shirts, Vhreho and Guhyeo used those to paint their clothing.

I knew what to do, though. Feeling smart, I rifled through my bag, looking for my video camera. And a wave of panic washed through me when I realized the expensive device wasn't there. But when I noticed Guhyeo toying with a small, silver object attached to his belt, he shot me a sly look.

That's when the door opened again. Mr. Klongei came in, holding stacks of large watercolor paper.

Vhreho and Guhyeo raced to close the paint jars and run across the room back to their seats before the teacher noticed. They pretended to be shocked. When Mr. Klongei *did* notice, his expression became horrified. "Vhreho...?! Guhyeo...!? What happened!?"

Pretending to cry, Vhreho was the one who answered this time, his voice sweet and innocent. "Mr. Klongei, Max painted all over our clothes. We tried to stop him, but he just wouldn't. And we're wearing black shirts, so the streaks are more visible."

Mr. Klongei looked at me in shock; like Ms. Hagger, he previously thought I wasn't that naughty. A few sharks in the class rolled their eyes—the majority of my classmates knew I was innocent. I didn't know how to respond.

Thankfully, I didn't need to; Kay nearly saved my life by standing up for me. "Max didn't do it. I was watching, and Vhreho and Guhyeo painted on themselves but chose to blame Max for it. *They're* actually the guilty ones."

Everybody started talking at once. "Kay is right."

"Yeah! Max never did anything."

"Vhreho and Guhyeo are *so* busted!!"

"You should send them to the office!"

Mr. Klongei agreed, and when the troublemakers got their office referral form, they hesitantly placed my video camera on the table and walked out the door. I smiled, feeling victorious for winning against Vhreho and Guhyeo.

A few hours had passed, and it was now break time. I knew exactly what I would do for break today: I would meet with the principal, Mr. Schakss. But first, I needed to ask Ms. Hagger if that was okay. "Ms. Hagger?"

"Yes, Max?" She was at her desk.

"May I meet with Mr. Schakss for break today?"

"Sure. What about?"

"Vhreho and Guhyeo."

"Oh, right. I remember you talking about this earlier. Yes, you may." Ms. Hagger dialed Mr. Schakss' number on the phone. She gave me a pass slip once she confirmed the principal knew I was coming.

Once I had received my pass slip, I grabbed my video camera and walked to the office.

When I got there, I noticed Mr. Schakss waiting for me in the main area. "Hello, Max! Feel free to come with me to my office to talk about Vhreho and Guhyeo."

I sat down at the large, circular table in his office and described my struggles. Mr. Schakss gave me his thoughts on why I was being bullied, and I thought of an idea to stop it.

"Oh! I have an idea. How about we add cages around the school? If a teacher or staff member notices somebody is misbehaving, they can send them into a cage, where they will stay for the rest of the day and learn their lesson."

Mr. Schakss liked my idea. "I like that idea! I'll ask the janitors to install the old security cameras and build cages around the school."

I got back to the classroom just moments before the bell. When it did ring, I rapidly grabbed all my things and headed out into the hallway. But I couldn't quite get to my locker; two sharks were blocking it! A shark named Zing-Yang, who went by ZY, was talking to another shark named Lindang, who preferred the nickname Linda.

I did not know what they were saying; I was focusing on waiting for a pause in their conversation so I could jump in and ask them to move. But Ms. Hagger did. "ZY! You know potty talk is not allowed here!

"Sorry, Ms. Hagger. Linda and I-" ZY started.

Ms. Hagger cut him off. "Go to the office, ZY! No, wait; school's over and there's nothing I can do!" She thought for a moment. "No, there *is* something I can do! I can lock you in one of these new cages!"

I knew ZY did not intend to use potty words. I didn't know much of what they said, but I knew Linda was talking that way, and ZY was just trying to get her to stop, but he had to use an example. *Oops. I mentioned the cage to punish Vhreho and Guhyeo, not an innocent classmate!*

As much as I wanted to tell Ms. Hagger that ZY wasn't to be blamed, I decided going home should be prioritized. I opened up my now-unblocked locker and put my things into my backpack—I was one of the first sharks to finish.

I slung my backpack over my shoulders and walked to Kay's locker. "Are you coming over today?"

"Yeah, that's the plan. I just need to go home first to drop off my things and tell my guardian."

"Okay, thanks! I'll meet you at the main door!"

I started walking to the door I entered before school. I saw Ms. Hagger locking ZY in the cube-shaped cage down the hall; I turned around and gave Ms. Hagger the side eye. "Ms. Hagger, ZY didn't do anything!"

"Sorry, Max, but he was talking potty talk. He deserves to be in the cage."

"But-"

"Don't backtalk, Max, or I'll lock you in a cage too. Now, it's way past the bell. You need to go. ZY will be okay."

"Fine." I groaned.

I turned around and continued walking to the outside doors. Another shark named Lachenz and I were the only ones outside, except for Linda. But Linda disappeared around the corner of the building. Everybody was silent for a few minutes while the buses pulled into the parking lot.

Suddenly, I saw Jo—she had come from another door. I ran to Jo and hugged her.

"Hi, Max!" she said.

"Hi!"

"Are you walking home with me today?"

"Actually, Jo... do you mind if I walk home with my new friend Kay?"

"Of course! It's great how you're already making friends! I'll start walking home."

But I didn't get a chance to respond, because suddenly, Lachenz started screaming. "MONSTER! MONSTER! THERE'S A MONSTER OUTSIDE!"

11

The HifftYiz, Part 1

Jo halted and turned around. I did too.

"What? Where?" I didn't see a monster, but the air was suddenly tinted purple.

But I had no time to stop and think about if the purple air was associated with the monster because I saw Kay exit through the main doors. "Kay!" I yelled. "Come here!"

"Okay, I'm coming!" she shouted and ran towards me. When she saw the purple air, she screamed.

"Oh no. Oh no, Max, we're in *trouble*," Kay worried.

Trouble? What was so troublesome about purple air? "What? Is it about the air?" I asked.

"Yeah. There's this one type of monster that leaves acid puddles on the ground as it walks. The acid makes the air purple. So, basically, that monster is really close. I forgot what it's called, though."

Thankfully, Lachenz knew what it was called—he had heard me whisper to Kay, and he had an open book in his fins. "It's called a HifttYiz—it can also be called a HifftYuez, but it depends on where you live in Sharkland. It's a wide monster with short legs and a claw for a nose with great hearing. Acid comes out the ends of its legs when it is scared or angry." Lachenz showed us the image. The caption read, "Drawing created by the authors of this book."

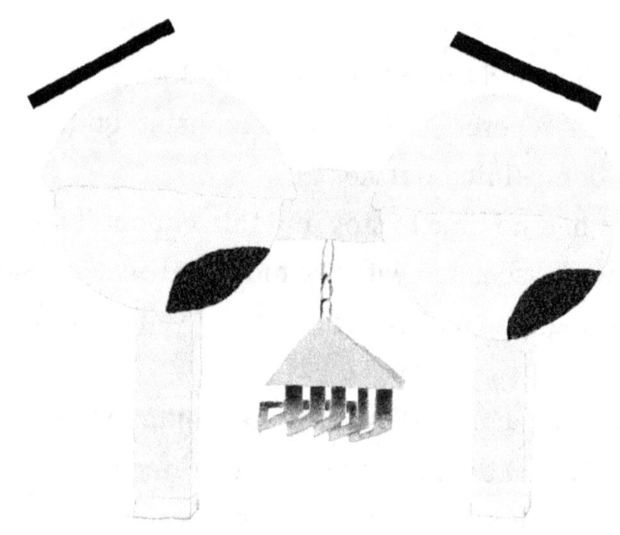

"HifftYizes attack sharks sometimes, but it depends whether the HifftYiz thinks sharks deserve to live or not," Lachenz continued reading. He closed the book and added, "Sharks *definitely* deserve to live."

I tried to absorb all the information from the book. "Even though we haven't seen the monster yet, I think it might try to attack us," I stated. "We don't know if the HifftYiz is a shark-attacker or not." Everybody around me nodded in agreement.

"Should we create a plan to make it go away when it sees us, in case it does try to attack?" Kay added.

"Yeah," Lachenz stated.

"I have an idea," I whispered to Kay, Lachenz, and Jo. Jo had not said anything, but she was listening. "I will first unlock ZY from the cage just to be nice. Next, I'll..." I thought for a moment. "Well, I'm not sure what to do next. Does anybody else have suggestions?"

Lachenz, who had opened the book again, had one.

"I have an idea. The books says most of Sharkland's monsters were originally sharks but because monsters with some sort of spell or possession. It also states that a bottle of monster changer is needed. For the HifftYiz, the Monster-Bottle 2000 is the most effective option. Somebody could try finding a bottle of one of these and using it on the HifftYiz."

Suddenly, I heard screams from sharks standing close to the back of the building.

A large monster emerged from behind the building, dripping acid as it walked. It had two large eyes the size of car tires, two short legs coming down from the eyes, and a claw-like object coming from between its eyes. It was the HifftYiz, and it was moving toward *me*. *Oh no. This HifftYiz must like attaching sharks.*

Out of instinct, I sprinted past the HifftYiz to reach the door and pulled it shut before the HifftYiz got inside. I guess I would be the one to find the Monster-Bottle 2000 and unlock ZY from his cage.

Thankfully, the HifftYiz was left outside. I was safe. I noticed ZY not far away, in the cage next to Ms. Hagger's classroom. I ran to him.

"ZY! How are you doing? Can I help release you?" Even though we weren't friends, I still felt bad for ZY.

"Hi! You're name's Max, right? I think Ms. Hagger put the key inside her jacket pocket. If you want to help get the key, you should probably wait until she comes down from her office on the second floor." He checked his watch. "I think Ms. Hagger left her jacket on the desk chair in her classroom."

"Thanks, ZY! I'll find the key and unlock the cage. Also, you were right. My name *is* Max."

"No, thank *you*!" was ZY's response.

"You're welcome!" I replied.

I entered Ms. Hagger's classroom and searched for her coat—it was on the back of her desk chair like ZY said it was. I ran to the chair and started searching for her coat.

I checked the left pocket. No keys. I checked the right. No keys. I panicked.

My anxiety worsened when I heard caudal fin-steps coming toward me. Thinking fast, I pulled the chair out from under the desk, crawled into the small space under the writing surface, and pushed the chair back in so I would not be seen.

Ms. Hagger came into the room and grabbed her coat. She rummaged through a pocket I did not check, grabbed a keychain with three keys on it, and exited, not remembering to unlock ZY from his cage. *Uh oh; I didn't look hard enough, and now Ms. Hagger has the key to the cage.*

A few minutes later

It was a few minutes after Ms. Hagger locked me in the room, yet I remained under the chair, not knowing if anybody else would come in. At least, that was my plan until the pain in my torso from the position I was in became too much to handle. So, I pushed the chair away from me and crawled out from under the desk.

Walking to the classroom's door and looking out the window, I tested the handle to see if it was locked. It was. "Max! Are you okay?" ZY shouted from inside his cage on the other side of the door.

"I'm not hurt, but Ms. Hagger locked the door when she grabbed her coat and left, and now I'm trapped in here."

ZY's facial expression turned blank. "Oh. That's problematic," he confessed. He was silent for a few moments while he thought of ways to get me out. "Max! I have an idea!"

Now I was curious. "What is it?"

"When Ms. Hagger was out of the room the other day, I opened that drawer at her desk because I was curious. And I found what looked like spare keys there. If the classroom key is in the drawer, the copy of the cage key might be too." ZY seemed proud of his idea.

"Yeah! That's a great idea! I'll check the drawer."

I ran back towards the desk. Once I got there, I opened the drawer underneath the desk.

No key was inside from what I could see. The only vaguely helpful thing I found was a small piece of paper that read, "Monster changers are in the janitor's closet in the High Building." I was disappointed I couldn't find the key, but I didn't know if the paper would be helpful, so I put it in my pocket.

I thought about possible ways to free myself and ZY without keys, but before I could think of anything, I had a different idea. I could check the drawer again in case the key was there and I missed it.

Thankfully, I did not need to search for long. *What's that? Is it one of the keys?* I moved some things aside to "examine my findings". *It is the key!* I didn't know what it unlocked, but I could find out with trial and error. Grabbing the key, I ran to the door and shared the good news with ZY. "ZY! I think I found the keys!"

He was so excited, he would have been jumping up and down had he not been in a cage. "No way!"

I examined the door, looking for a keyhole. The handle did not have a keyhole. I thought that was one of the worst design ideas I had ever thought of, but I decided not to think about it.

"There's no keyhole here," I told ZY.

ZY did not seem surprised. "Oh, right. I forgot about that. Sharkschool bought doors that lock on one side, not both, to save money. Perhaps you can send the key under the door so I can unlock the cage?"

"Great idea!" I passed the key under the door.

"Hey, Max!" ZY called only a few seconds later.

"What?" I was right there.

"The key you gave me worked!"

No way! "Wait, really?"

"Yeah!" He made a joke. "I wonder if this key works for the classroom door, too." He placed the tip of the key into the lock, expecting the key to not fit. Surprisingly, it did!

ZY turned the key and opened the door. I was so relieved I was finally freed and ZY was no longer in the cage!

"Woah! That was just a joke, but it worked!"

"Haha." I was going to say more, but I suddenly heard a loud snort from the end of the hallway, louder than any shark could manage. "Woah, *what was that*?"

ZY looked down the hallway. He screamed. "*Oh no*. It's the HifftYiz. It got inside somehow."

I looked down the hallway too and screamed too. "What? Uh oh. That's a big problem. We need to get the HifftYiz out of the school before it does any damage. Look, it's dripping acid."

I looked down at my pocket, at ZY, then at the HifftYiz. Thinking at lightning speed, I started running. But I stopped suddenly. "Max, where are you going?"

That was a good question; where *was* I going? "To wherever this product called Monster-Bottle 2000 is," I replied. "Could you lead the HifftYiz outside? That would make my job much easier."

ZY laughed. "I can do that. I think all the monster changers are in the janitor's room, by the way." I said thanks, then started running to the hallway connecting three of Sharkland's four buildings.

Now I was at one end of Sharkschool's connecting hallway. I was going to continue, but a shark's voice stopped me from doing that. "Young shark! Why are you still here? Sharkschool ended almost a half hour ago."

My mind started racing to think of excuses quickly, but the only one I came up with was strange and unrealistic. "Um... at the end of the day today, I realized the left half of my caudal fin was growing green hair. My mom's finally here to take me to the doctor."

The adult shark's response was strange, and even more unexpected than my answer. "Oh. That makes sense. I once had green caudal fin hair in sixth grade."

"Uh... alright, I guess?" I was surprised. I did not think the teacher would believe me, but they did. *I should keep going, though. I don't want anybody to get hurt because I was too slow to save them.* I continued running through the highway until I was in the High Building.

The connecting hallway brought me to the west side of the High Building, near the eleventh-and-twelfth-grade classrooms.

Looking around, I noticed a door with a sign next to it labeled "Janitor". This is when I started to realize the text on the paper would be helpful. Next, I walked to the door and tested the handle to see if it was locked, and thankfully, it wasn't. Not wanting to be caught in case anybody was there, I opened the door slowly.

A staircase leading to a large room was on the other side of the door. The whole place was made of cement, and a strong "wet mop" smell hung in the air. I crept down the stairs until I reached the bottom.

When I got there, I noticed a single, large, L-shaped room with many dangerous-looking tools, cleaning supplies, large garbage bins, and a few couches, plus an old television in the corner. Two shelves touching the north wall held chemical sprays and powders. I knew I had to be quiet. Walking on the tips of my caudal fin, I made my way over to the shelf on the north wall.

The bottles of monster changer were on the third shelf up from the bottom. *Alright. I'm looking for Monster-Bottle 2000*, I thought.

There was one bottle of Monster-Bottle 2000 on the shelf behind what looked like a few other brands of monster changer. Carefully, I tried to grab the bottle's handle, but my fin hit another bottle and knocked it over in the process. It fell to the ground with a *crash*. I winced.

"What was that?" a shark with a low voice hissed. The voice sounded far away, but also close. *Too* close.

"I think somebody else might be down here," another shark guessed.

A surge of adrenaline rushed through my body and I started sweating all over. Trying to keep my fin steady, I quietly rested the dropped bottle back on the shelf and carefully grabbed the Monster-Bottle 2000. I then ran back up the stairs, not stopping until I reached the all-gender bathroom, which was surprisingly close to the janitor's room. If I went into the all-gender bathroom instead of the binary restrooms, nobody would be able to find me.

"Who's down here?" he replied. "Bryan, are you sure you're not just hearing things again?"

"No, I actually heard somebody this time," Bryan replied.

"Well, if you did hear somebody, they probably ran towards the door."

"Okay." The janitors walked to Door 6B. "Hey, can we go outside? I want fresh air," Bryan wondered.

"Of course. Both of us have been inside all week." I heard a door open and shut after a few seconds. *Phew.* I exhaled. Almost instantly, I exited the restroom and sprinted down the connecting hallway, letting my adrenaline rush help me run faster.

It didn't take me long to reach the outside door in the Low Building. I exerted all my body weight on the door, causing it to open so fast it bounced off the wall and nearly hit me. "Max!" everybody exclaimed in unison.

"What are you holding?" Kay asked.

"Monster-Bottle 2000," I stated, panting heavily. "We can use it on the HifftYiz. Please don't ask me how; I have no idea."

Kay's expression lit up. "Yay!"

"Awesome job, Max!" Jo exclaimed.

Showing two fins-ups, "Great work!" ZY commented.

"Amazing!" Lachenz cheered. "Max, I agree. I don't know if it will work, but let's hope it will!"

The HifftYiz stood at the highest part of the hill, close to the edge. Meanwhile, Lachenz dug around in the shed used to store equipment for recess. "Hey, Max! I found a tarp in the recess shed!"

"Great!" I paused. "Wait what for?"

"We don't want to ruin the grass with chemicals," Lachenz stated matter-of-factly.

"Oh. That's smart!" I replied. Lachenz placed the tarp on the grass. "Does anybody know how we could do this?"

Jo did! Her breath heavy, she made a 'come here' notion. ZY, Lachenz, Kay, and I gathered in a circle, and Jo whispered her idea. "Does everybody notice how the HifftYiz is standing at the top of the hill? We could pour some of the Change-Your-Animals 2000 onto the tarp and push the HifftYiz off the hill, which would send it rolling into the puddle of Change-Your-Animals 2000."

I liked this idea. "I think that's a great idea. Does everybody agree?"

"I agree!" ZY claimed.

"Me too!" Kay agreed.

"Me three!" Lachenz said.

ZY volunteered to help. "I'll pour the Monster-Bottle 2000 onto the tarp."

And that is what he did. ZY poured half the bottle of Monster-Bottle 2000 onto the tarp. "I did that. Jo, what did you say to do next?"

"We push the HifftYiz off the hill," Jo reminded.

"Yay!" Kay exclaimed. "May I do the honors?"

"Of course," I added. Everybody nodded in agreement. "Can I help?"

"Sure," Kay agreed. Kay and I silently walked to the top of the hill so the HifftYiz wouldn't notice us. When we reached the top, we placed our fins on the HifftYiz's back and pushed with all our might. Even though it wasn't much force, it was enough, and the HifftYiz started rolling down the hill.

The HifftYiz did not roll very fast because of its odd shape, but I knew it would reach the bottom eventually. Suddenly, though, the HifftYiz stopped in the middle of the hill—it sat upright and spread its legs out so it could not roll any farther down the hill.

"You cannot make me roll into that puddle!" the HifftYiz hissed with a relatively familiar shark-like voice.

We were all surprised. "Woah, you can talk?"

"Of *course* I can. Most monsters on Sharkland can—

we just choose not to most of the time. Anyway, now it's time to destroy you all."

ZY's facial expression turned horrified. I felt a sense of hopelessness. Lachenz looked confused. Jo became furious. Kay did not seem to care.

Driven by her fear of being destroyed by the HifftYiz, Jo snuck up behind the HifftYiz and positioned her fins when it wasn't looking. She landed a few large uppercut punches, strong enough to make the HifftYiz roll out of its sitting position down the hill and into the puddle. At first, when the HifftYiz touched the puddle, nothing seemed to happen, but after a few seconds, white fog surrounded the monster.

"What's happening?" I asked.

Lachenz answered. "If the Monster-Bottle 2000 is working correctly, the HifftYiz is turning back into a shark."

The fog took a while to clear, but when it did, we saw a shark none of us had expected to see.

It was Linda, my classmate.

"Linda?" I asked.

"Linda?" Lachenz wondered.

"Linda?" asked a surprised Kay.

"Linda?" ZY gaped.

Jo did not know who Linda was since she was older than everybody else, so she was silent.

"Yep, that's me," Linda said. I thought to myself. I had many questions, but I decided to ignore them for now and just be happy I was alive.

Everybody except for me—I was still wearing mine—
grabbed their backpacks, which were leaning against a wall. Kay came over to me and reminded me of something very important. "Now the adventure's over, so let's hang out."

"Oh, I almost forgot!" I exclaimed. "Yay!"

"I wonder if my parents— err, caregiver— are looking for me," Kay wondered. "Sharkschool ended, like, a *really* long time ago."

Kay wasn't wrong—forty-five minutes ago, to be exact. "Probably. But we should check in with our guardians just in case. Let me ask Jo, my caregiver. She's over here." I walked to where Jo stood. "Jo, can Kay come over?"

"Of course," Jo replied. "I'll stay here for a bit to help clean up."

"Thanks! Kay, you can come over!"

"Yay! Let's go!"

We arrived at Kay's house a short while later to tell her parents we were going to my house—her house was only a few blocks away, so it was not a long walk.

The house was small but good-looking, and from what it looked like, it seemed that Kay had parents instead of caregivers, which surprised me—didn't Kay come here from Wah?

She knocked on the front door, and a male shark in his thirties or forties opened the door. His face turned angry when he noticed Kay was standing there.

"WHERE WERE YOU?"

Kay bragged to him. "Fighting a monster. Me and Max did the honors. But it was mostly me." I sighed. I should've known Kay would say something like that! "Please don't tell me you weren't watching from the window."

"Uh... Yeah, I was watching, but I didn't realize it was you. That's so cool, though!" I assumed he didn't actually watch Kay from the window and was thinking of an excuse to keep her satisfied.

"Thank you. I'm going to Max's house now." Kay did not even ask.

"I'm okay with that. Just be back in time for dinner!"

"Woah! Your house is *huge*!" Kay exclaimed when we reached my house. "It's *sooo* modern, too."

"Thank you," I replied. I was excited.

But before either of us could even open the door, we saw Jo drive into the driveway. I walked to the door, pulling my key out of my backpack's side pocket. "Hey, Max and Kay," Jo called from the car. Her window was rolled down.

"Hi, Jo," I replied.

"Max, would you like to go with Kay to this new store called Awesome Stuff For Less? We don't have a lot to do here, so I think you two would be kind of bored. I've wanted to go for a while now, and I wondered if you would like to come with me," Jo replied. "It's the only store in Sharkland without workers."

Wow, a store without workers! "Even the name is awesome! I think that sounds great. Kay, what do you think?"

"I want to come," Kay demanded. "Let's go to the car."

"Yay! I think you'll like it."

12

The Fall

Kay and I were in the middle of a lively discussion when Jo suddenly interrupted us and shouted, "We're here!"

I snapped my head around and looked out the window. Jo's car was pulling into the store's tiny parking lot. Kay and I discussed what to do when we got inside, and we wondered what the store would be like.

About half of the miniscule parking lot was filled with cars, and two stores shared the lot: Awesome Stuff For Less and another store I didn't recognize. Awesome Stuff For Less was only a bit bigger than the other store.

Both stores had walls crafted of large polished stone panels, making them look very modern. Large glass windows and doors let sharks see into the stores from the parking lot. Big yellow light-up letters labeled 'Awesome Stuff For Less' glowed above the glass door of the store Kay, Jo, and I were about to walk into.

"Can we go inside?" Kay asked, so excited she was almost jumping up and down in her seat.

Jo unbuckled her seatbelt and got out of the car. "Of course!! That's why I brought you two with me!"

Because the front doors were made of heavy glass, Kay struggled to open them since they were so heavy, so I helped her open them. We all ran inside.

The store was completely empty; I didn't see anybody, not even employees! Many large, round tables were inside, and they all displayed random objects divided into vague categories, such as 'Clothing,' 'Home,' 'Toys,' and 'Weapons.' From the inside, Awesome Stuff For Less looked like it had previously been a warehouse, yet it had been remodeled, and it looked *awesome*.

One way I knew Awesome Stuff For Less was a warehouse before was because it had many narrow garage door-looking things on the back wall. They were all decently small, and some of them touched the ground, but others did not. "Jo, do you know what those garage doors are for?" I asked.

Jo thought for a moment. "I'm not sure, but I think they might be so trucks can back up and unload their shipments into the store."

"Oh, thanks! That's cool."

Jo stood on the tips of her caudal fin to look for the clothing racks, and when she found them, she ran to them without hesitation. Kay examined the items on the table next to her labeled 'Weapons: Toy, Real Broken, and Real Working.' I wandered around the store, not finding one section I wanted to visit most. But I turned around when I realized just what Kay was looking at.

"Kay! Don't touch that!" I exclaimed. Kay was picking up a rifle with a neon orange sticker labeled "Real and Working."

Kay ignored my warning. "It's fine. I'm only looking at it; I've never seen a gun in real life before. Besides, it's not even loaded."

I looked more carefully at the gun and noticed another sticker on the back claiming it wasn't loaded. Sighing, I decided to trust Kay and added, "Well, as long as you're not going to try to shoot it, I guess that's okay." I continued wandering around the store.

Later

A long time had passed—maybe ten minutes or so—and not being able to find much, I was becoming bored. And I had an idea that would not only cure my boredom, but also might impress Kay.

I noticed many boxes ordered biggest to smallest were stacked to the left of the garage door furthest on the left. That garage door was one of the two that touched the ground, and a metal bar extending about two feet away from the wall was placed over the garage door. My idea was to climb up the boxes and use my caudal fin to hang on the bar.

After thinking of the idea, now I was excited. Commuting to the bottom box, I climbed up the stack of packages quickly and carefully—I didn't know what was inside the boxes, but they didn't collapse when I stepped on them.

The top box was barely big enough for me to stand on. Slowly, I grabbed the bar to stabilize myself; the bar was directly above the ground with no boxes underneath.

I could see the entire store hanging from that bar. Kay was now observing the clothes rack. I did not see Jo.

"Kay!" I shouted, not considering other sharks in the store or if Jo would see me and I would get in trouble.

Kay looked up. "What? Where are you?"

When she saw me, her expression changed from surprised to worried to horrified to angry to rebellious. Her final expression was a mischievous grin. "Woah. How did you get up there? Can I do that too??"

All I wanted now was to impress Kay. "Watch. I'm going to hang on the bar from my caudal fin."

Becoming excited, Kay's gaze was fixated on me. "Ooh. I'm watching." I prepared to pull myself up off the boxes and hang from the bar with only my fins; I counted backwards from three.

Three!
Two!
One!
GO!

Readjusting my grip on the bar, I let my caudal fin leave the boxes. I hung from my two pectoral fins high above the ground below.

I was doing good so far, but I wasn't done yet! *Alright. Now it's time to hang.* I took one pectoral fin off the bar so my caudal fin could get through, leaving me hanging by only one fin. Then I wrapped my caudal fin around the bar and let go with my pectoral ones.

But hanging on the bar with my caudal fin was nothing like my jungle gym back on Wah; it was too weak. I didn't realize I was slipping until it was too late.

I was falling.

I was sure I would die. The metal bar was at least ten or fifteen feet off the ground, if not more, and the ground was made of concrete. Although my senses were dulled as I fell, I heard fast-paced fin-steps running to somewhere close to where I was.

The next thing I knew, I stood in a lightless black void.

Suddenly, a large shadow-like blob creature lit up in the distance as if somebody had turned its lights on. It had a sucker, but no mouth. What did this creature want?

Suddenly, I heard something coming from somewhere in the distance: *"Come to me, my friend."* It was coming from somewhere inside my head, almost as if somebody was talking to me mentally. "Who said that?"

I got no response, only a repeat of the phrase. *"Come to me, my friend."*

Gathering my strength, I shouted as loud as I could, "Who *are* you?" *Who is speaking to me?* I thought. *I've never heard of it before.*

But suddenly, I had a realization. *Actually, maybe I have heard it before. It reminds me of the gold hunt when I heard the voice speak to me in my head.*

I didn't get to hear the voice again to be sure I had heard the voice before. Instead, I felt somebody shaking me and trying to wake me up. When I got in touch with reality again, I found myself in an uncomfortable position on a comfortable surface, and I heard a familiar voice. "Wake *upppp.*" It was Kay.

When I opened my eyes, I found myself lying on a mattress far from the place I fell. Kay must have scooted it here when she noticed I was falling. "Wow, for somebody who's 10 entire years old, you sure are light," Kay joked, referring to my weight.

I sighed. Kay had saved me!

Suddenly, we both saw Jo emerge from the restroom. *So that's where Jo was. The restroom.* I was going to run to her and see how she was doing, but I remembered that might not have been the best idea—Jo would probably put me in big trouble if she learned what I did. Ignoring my own concerns, I ran to her anyway. When Jo opened her mouth to speak, I held my breath.

"So there you are. Have you two had fun? I sure have. I bought a shirt." Jo held up a shirt, a black cotton tee with a colorful skateboard on the back. "I'm hungry. How about we go home for dinner? I can make pizza! By the way, if you have anything you want me to buy, I can buy it for you as long as it doesn't cost too much." Out of the corner of my eye, I saw Kay eyeing the rifle.

I loved pizza! "Yay. I love pizza. Thanks, Jo!"

Kay took this as an opportunity to compare herself to me. "I love pizza more than you, Max," Kay commented. "Hehe."

Phew. That was a relief.

13

Friday Appointment

I was in my advanced math class during Friday of the third week of school, and I was *bored*.

The teacher—my advanced math class was in another classroom with a different teacher—was giving *another* lesson about fractions, a topic that was basically drilled into me when I was on Wah! Not to mention lunch was in ten minutes. I looked up hungrily at the clock on the wall again.

Suddenly, the door opened before I could think any more about my hunger; a female shark in a marble-print shirt and light blue jeans stepped in. *Uh oh. Did I get in trouble??*

A wave of adrenaline washed through my body for a moment. But it went away after I remembered I hadn't gotten in trouble recently, and therefore, it would be unlikely if she came for *me.*

I was wrong. "Max?" she asked.

My heart started racing even faster. *Did* I get in trouble? "What?" I stood up and walked to the door, where the female shark ushered me outside.

"Don't worry, Max. You're not in trouble. The front desk staff told me you and your caretaker Jo Brime will get excused from school early today. Vhreho Chinkchink and Guhyeo Skigamon have a doctor's appointment, and you and Jo Brime need to come with them."

Appointment? "Oh, okay." Now I knew I had to hurry; if the adult shark wasn't lying and I *did* have an appointment for some reason, I knew Vhreho and Guhyeo well enough to know they would get grumpy if I was slow. I ran back into the classroom to grab my school supplies.

Next, I ran out of the classroom and shoved my things into my backpack. I slung the backpack over my fins and started running to the door I assumed Jo was at already.

I didn't get far, though, because suddenly, a stricter teacher stopped me in the hall. "Hey, why are you running?"

I knew I had to tell the truth. "I have to go to a doctor's appointment."

The teacher did not seem to care about my doctor's appointment. "You will get there if you walk. Stop running."

But because I knew I had to get to the car as soon as possible, I ignored the teacher and broke into an even faster sprint. As I ran, I heard her in the background screaming, "I'll send you to the office if you don't stop running!"

I reached the door a bit later. Jo stood outside next to her car. Neither Vhreho nor Guhyeo were outside yet, which was a relief. Jo waved. "Hi, Max!"

I waved back. "Hi, Jo!" Then I paused. "Do you have any idea why we're going with Vhreho and Guhyeo to their doctor's appointment? Doesn't it seem strange how we need to come to an appointment for two sharks we barely know?"

Jo shook her head, not able to answer my question. "I'm not sure, Max. Apparently, Vhreho and Guhyeo are getting new hearts today—I'm not sure how they lost their hearts in the first place or why we needed to come, but we have to go anyway, so let's get in the car and wait for Vhreho and Guhyeo. Sorry I didn't tell you before. I just learned about this yesterday evening, and I guess I forgot to tell you."

Suddenly, Vhreho and Guhyeo emerged from Door 5, the same door I came out of.

"Vhreho! Guhyeo!" Jo shouted. She waved to the two male sharks so they would see her.

Guhyeo responded in a much ruder way that I never even imagined was possible. "Who *are* you, and *why* do you know my name??"

I could tell Jo was hurt, but she tried not to show it. "I'm Jo," she replied in a much nicer way. "Apparently me and my best friend Max are taking you to a doctor's appointment so you can get new hearts."

Suddenly, Guhyeo's expression changed from utter confusion to understanding. "Oh, right. I forgot you were taking us. Vhreho wanted Max to come with for some reason."

Vhreho looked stunned how Guhyeo was throwing him under the bus like this. "I just wanted Max to come with me, but I think I forgot to ask him," he stated. "Sorry. Guhyeo, I thought you said Max would drive us when my mom registered us for this."

Now Guhyeo was shocked. "No, I did NOT say that!! I said *my mom* would pick us and Max up! I didn't think you meant Max would take us! Besides, he's not old enough to drive! What were you thinking?" His volume was rising to a very angry level.

Vhreho was visibly scared by Guhyeo's angriness. He seemed to almost cower over a bit in fear. "Sorry," he murmured. "I don't know what I was thinking."

Guhyeo didn't respond to Vhreho. Instead, his next comment was directed towards Jo. "Are you even *old* enough to drive?" he demanded.

Jo said nothing. Instead, she pulled a driver's license from her backpack pocket and showed it to Guhyeo. He ignored Jo. *Rude,* I thought. "Anyway… Let's get in the car. We don't want to be late to this appointment."

"Okay," Vhreho replied.

Guhyeo sighed. "Fine."

I only said one last thing before getting in the car. "Vhreho and Guhyeo, If either of you ever want me to take you somewhere, please make sure to ask me first." Although when I got in the car, I leaned over to Jo and assured her, "Jo, I don't know why Guhyeo was so rude to you. He's not usually like this."

Strangely, in the car, I didn't feel as much hunger as fatigue, even though it would be lunchtime if I was at school. I rested my head on the armrest.

"Max! Wake up! We've arrived at the doctor's office!" Jo exclaimed while exiting the car. Vhreho and Guhyeo did the same. "You fell asleep."

I slowly sat up. "What? I fell asleep? Oh, okay." Opening my eyes and looking out the window, I saw a large brown medical complex with many windows. Next, I followed Jo, Vhreho, and Guhyeo into the building.

The building's ground floor was spacious. An elevator across from me connected the six or seven doctor's offices, orthodontists, and surgeons on the ground floor to the two other floors of the building.

Vhreho and Guhyeo raced across the hallway to get to the elevator. Both sharks tried to reach the button, but Guhyeo pressed it first. "Hey!" Vhreho exclaimed.

"You can press the one inside the elevator," Guhyeo assured.

"Okay."

We arrived at the third floor after a short ride. "Dingaklongo Orthodontics and Xynoggi Dental. Is the surgeon's place to the left? What's the surgeon's place called?" I asked.

Jo didn't hesitate to answer. "The surgeon we need is named Dr. Yaincala. He owns a business called Dr. Yaincala's Family Care."

"Oh! There it is!" I pointed to an office labeled *Dr. Yaincala's Family Care* down the hallway. Everybody followed me to the office.

We walked in the office's door.

Inside, we saw a large room with windows on the farthest wall. Two rows of chairs faced a fish tank touching the left wall. The front desk was to our left, and rooms used for operations and normal check-ups were to our right. The carpet was a colorful abstract print with many "blobs".

Jo checked in with the shark at the front desk. "We're here for Vhreho Chinkchink and Guhyeo Skigamon's doctor's appointment to get new hearts. We are not their parents. I'm not exactly sure why we're here. If I remember right, Vhreho's parent registered him and Guhyeo for the appointment[5]. Their name is–"

Jo turned to Vhreho and whispered to him. "Which parent registered you and Guhyeo for the appointment? Or did both of your parents register you two together?"

Vhreho whispered back, and Jo told this information to the shark at the front desk. "Vhreho's father Phareegya Chinkchink registered him and Guhyeo for this appointment. Is he on your system?"

The shark at the front desk made a few clicks. "Yes, he is! Don't worry; you're not the first one to experience this situation. You're right on time. I'll inform Dr. Yaincala you're here. Dr. Yaincala will call for you when he's ready."

"Okay," Jo replied. "Thanks!"

---

[5] This is not possible on Earth. One person cannot register two people from separate families for one doctor's appointment. Also, it's probably not possible for two unrelated friends to go to a doctor's appointment together.

"Come," Vhreho told Guhyeo. "Let's look at the fish."

"Sure." Vhreho and Guhyeo walked to the fish tank, and I followed them. Tapping on the glass, Guhyeo examined the small rainbow fish; Vhreho observed an orange cichlid. The cichlid jumped back, scared.

Vhreho noticed how the fish jumped back when Guhyeo tapped the glass. "Guhyeo, you can't tap the glass. It scares the fish. Look, there's a sign here saying you can't."

Guhyeo was genuinely confused. "Why not?"

"Because it scares the fish," Vhreho re-stated.

"Fine." Guhyeo did not say more, but his face told me he wanted to.

Suddenly, Dr. Yaincala's booming voice was heard from one of the rooms. "Vhreho and Guhyeo! I'm ready! Come to Operation Room T, please!"

I expected Vhreho and Guhyeo to excitedly jump out of their chairs and run to Dr. Yaincala because they wanted new hearts, but the opposite happened. Both sharks planted themselves into their chairs more; Vhreho started trembling, while Guhyeo started crying.

"I'm scared," said trembling Vhreho.

"Me too," Guhyeo said through tears.

"It'll be fine! You'll live better lives after you get new hearts!" Jo said, trying to comfort Vhreho and Guhyeo. It did not work. Vhreho started shaking more, and Guhyeo cried harder. I whispered to Jo.

"What should we do? We need to get Vhreho and Guhyeo to Dr. Yaincala's office, but they're too scared to get up and walk on their own."

"We could try picking them up," Jo suggested.

I liked this idea. "Good idea! I'll take Guhyeo, and you can take Vhreho."

"Vhreho and Guhyeo! How would you like us to give you piggyback rides to the room? It'll be less scary that way!" Jo informed Vhreho and Guhyeo.

The sharks were hesitant, but they eventually agreed. "O– ok," Guhyeo stammered. Vhreho did not respond.

I stood in front of Guhyeo so he could wrap his fins around me. Jo did the same.

Operation Room T was not far away from the waiting area, but Vhreho and Guhyeo were both very heavy.

The room was large with two surgical chairs in the middle. A single desk touched the right wall, and a closed door led into a smaller room. Two long counters were in the corner to my right.

Dr. Yaincala greeted us and noticed Vhreho and Guhyeo on our backs. "That's an unusual method of transportation." We laughed. "Vhreho and Guhyeo, you'll be fine! You won't feel a thing."

Turns out, this was the exact reason why Guhyeo feared the operation. "That's exactly why we're so scared," he informed.

Dr. Yaincala did not respond to Guhyeo. Instead, he instructed the sharks to sit down: "You can sit in these chairs." Dr. Yaincala pointed to the two surgical chairs in the middle of the room.

Vhreho and Guhyeo got off our backs and slowly stumbled to the chairs. Vhreho almost fell over. "Jo and Max, I think Vhreho and Guhyeo would prefer you to stay here. Am I right, Vhreho and Guhyeo?"

Guhyeo did not hesitate before responding. "Stay here. PLEASE."

Neither Jo nor I expected a response like that. "Okay, okay. We'll stay here."

When Vhreho and Guhyeo reached the surgical chairs, they laid down on them and closed their eyes.

Dr. Yaincala continued. "Here is how I am going to do this procedure. It involves you swallowing your hearts, is where your hearts enter your body through a special kind of breathing, which I will show you how to do. Your recovery time will only be a few hours."

"Okay," Vhreho and Guhyeo agreed.

"Max and Jo, I need you to know Vhreho and Guhyeo are required to stay here for at least two hours to recover. You may pick them up anytime between four-thirty and when we close at seven o'clock; here is my business card, which has my address and phone number." Dr. Yaincala handed Jo the card.

"We can do that!" Jo agreed. "We'll pick them up as soon as we can."

Dr. Yaincala did not respond. Instead, he disappeared inside a smaller room for a minute or so, and he held two clear mason jars filled to the brim with a gross-looking red liquid that something else was floating in. Opening the jars, he pulled out two red, muscular balls of cells: the hearts.

Dr. Yaincala was unironically energetic. "Alright! Who would like to go first?"

"I— I— I—" Vhreho worried. He and Guhyeo both started trembling.

But Guhyeo eventually agreed; he wanted to just get it over with. "I guess I'll go first."

"Okay!" Dr. Yaincala exclaimed, grabbing a medium-sized plastic canister from the counter next to him. The canister was filled with bright red and neon yellow chewable tablets.

"What are those?" Guhyeo asked. The container had no label.

"These are medicine tablets that reduce the pain caused when you breathe your hearts in."

"Ew," Guhyeo complained. "I don't like medicine."

Dr. Yaincala was surprised. "Are you sure? Almost every other shark who has taken these said they taste almost exactly like fruity candy."

Vhreho regretted his decision to go second. "*No way.* I should have asked to go first."

"I love fruity candy!" Guhyeo screamed. He lunged for the plastic container, but Dr. Yaincala held it out of his reach.

"No, no," Dr. Yaincala responded. "You only get two. Would you like the cherry flavor or the lemon flavor?"

Guhyeo knew exactly how he felt. "I *hate* cherry."

Dr. Yaincala was surprised by such a strong response. "Oh-okay. I guess I'll give you the lemon flavor, then." He reached into the container and grabbed two neon yellow tablets. He handed them to Guhyeo, who gulped them up.

"I can't feel my fins!" Guhyeo exclaimed.

Dr. Yaincala wasn't surprised. "That's what the tablets do. They numb your body so you will feel less pain when you breathe the hearts in. Next, I'm going to show you how to inhale your hearts correctly."

Guhyeo did not respond. Instead, he nodded.

"Okay!" Dr. Yaincala said. He grabbed the jar with Guhyeo's heart. He started talking to Guhyeo about the heart-breathing process.

Suddenly, Guhyeo's head hit the table with a *thunk*. His eyes closed. "Egh."

Either Dr. Yaincala didn't care, or he expected this to happen after Guhyeo inhaled his new heart. "Vhreho, it's your turn!"

"Okay!" Vhreho reached for the container with the medicine.

"No, Vhreho. I have to give them to you because if you consume more than two, it could be deadly. But two is okay."

"Oh." Vhreho's expression turned horrified.

Dr. Yaincala removed the lid on the container. "Would you like lemon or cherry?"

Vhreho didn't hesitate. "Cherry."

Dr. Yaincala stuck his fin inside the jar and grabbed two bright red tablets. Vhreho gulped them up. "Blegh."

Now I needed to go. "Jo, I need to use the bathroom."

"Sure. Just come back when you're done," Jo stated. "Actually, now that I think about it, I need to go, too."

Later

Jo came running into my bedroom, interrupting the reading and relaxing I was doing on my bed. "Max! I almost forgot! We need to pick Vhreho and Guhyeo up from the doctor's appointment!"

I checked my clock. "It's only four o'clock! We don't need to be there until, like, 4:30."

Jo was matter-of-fact with her response. "Yeah, but it'll probably be longer because of traffic."

"Oh. Okay. I'll get my shoes on." And that is what I did. Jo already had her shoes on, and when I was finished, we walked to the living room together. "Are you ready to leave? I am."

"Yeah."

"Okay! I'll find my car keys." Jo ran to the kitchen and grabbed a metal keychain. "Here they are!"

Jo and I walked inside the medical building's entrance for the second time. We knew where to go, so we rode the elevator to the third floor and walked down the hallway to the correct office. Once we got there, we checked in at the front desk.

"Hello! We're here to pick up Vhreho Chinkchink and Guhyeo Skigamon," Jo told the person at the front desk.

"Alright! Vhreho and Guhyeo should be ready. It is 4:45 in the afternoon, after all. I'll inform Dr. Yaincala you're here."

"Thanks!" I said. The shark stood up and walked to Operation Room T. I heard the shark who worked at the front desk talking to Dr. Yaincala.

Suddenly, Vhreho and Guhyeo came running out of Operation Room T. They stood in front of me and jumped up and down, but they did not say anything.

"Hello," Jo said. "How was the surgery? Did you get your hearts?"

Once Jo said this, both sharks started talking at the same time, energy present in their voices. "Yes," Vhreho stated. "We got our hearts."

"Obviously," Guhyeo added. "We're going to Vhreho's house. Take us there now."

Wow, I thought. *No need to be rude.* "O-okay," Jo hesitantly agreed. "But please tell me your address first."

14

Grandma Mariohn

I slowly woke up the next morning—Saturday—to a dark room. It was exactly 7:15 in the morning.

Rapidly pulling my window shades open, I threw on my shark slippers and ran out of my bedroom. Not knowing if Jo was still asleep or not, I slowly cracked the door open and peeked inside, only to find Jo sitting up in bed. "Max! Good morning!"

Yay! She was awake! "Good morning!"

With her hopping out of bed and running to me, she seemed unusually energetic at this hour. Almost bouncing up and down in excitement, she asked, "Do you wanna know what's happening today?"

We were doing something different today? "Sure!"

"Grandma is coming over!" she exclaimed.

Wait, what? "I have a Sharkland grandma?" Now I was confused.

Thankfully, Jo had an explanation. "No. *My* grandma is coming over. Sorry for the confusion. I have two grandmas, Grandma Claise and Grandma Mariohn. Grandma Mariohn is the one who's coming over. She'll come after breakfast. I made pancakes!"

Suddenly, I heard a piercing ring cut through Jo and I's conversation. I dropped my fork on the table and ran to the door. Looking out the peephole, I noticed a shark wearing round glasses. It had to be Grandma Mariohn! I opened the door.

A faint scent of perfume filled my nostrils. "Jo!!" Grandma Mariohn exclaimed.

Jo responded not with words, but by running over to Grandma Mariohn and wrapping her into a hug. "Grandma Mariohn!! How are you??"

When Jo let go, Grandma Mariohn answered, "I'm doing well. What about you? Who's your friend here?"

Grandma Mariohn was talking about *me*! "Hi, Grandma Mariohn! I'm Max. It's a long story, but basically, I came here from a planet called Wah a few months ago. Jo's my best friend."

"Nice to meet you, Max!" Grandma Mariohn greeted me, grabbing my fin and giving me a fin-shake.

"Jo, I love your new house, by the way. It's– it's so big and modern! And that backsplash is so exquisite–"

"Thanks!" Jo thanked her, blushing. "You're taking us—err, me—to the deadly stote today, right?"

"Whenever you're done eating breakfast, that was the plan," Grandma Mariohn informed Jo. "And Max, I didn't know about you when Jo and I made plans, but I would love you to come, too!"

I couldn't help wondering why Grandma Mariohn made plans with Jo to go to a *deadly stote*—I didn't know many Sharkland words, but I did know "stote" meant "place of death". "Thank you for inviting me, Grandma Mariohn! But, just out of curiosity, why are you taking Jo and I to a place of death?"

Grandma Mariohn chuckled. "We're not! You must have just heard it wrong. We're going to the *deedly store*—
the plant shop."

"Oh." Oops! "Thanks."

"You're welcome, Max! Anyway, let's go to the car!"

It only took a few minutes to get to the deedly store.

Looking out the window, I noticed the car turning into a parking lot, ironically tiny compared to such a huge store. The light-up letters above the store read "The

Deedly Store", a very fitting name for, well, a deedly store.

After Grandma Mariohn parked, everybody unbuckled their seatbelts and exited the car. We all walked into the store together.

Walking into the store, the first thing I noticed were the many windows flooding the room with natural light; the small amount of wall space not taken up by windows was covered with nature-themed murals. The second thing I noticed was the scent: the entire store smelled like flowers, tomatoes, and soil with a hint of basil. The floor also was cement, and many plants were being displayed on large, circular tables around the store.

"Jo and Max, you can each pick one plant to take home," Grandma Mariohn informed us. "I would prefer it if it cost less than 20 SBucks, though." *$20? Woah, that's a lot for a plant!* I thought.

Looking around, I noticed the left wall had shelves with seasonal plants and herbs, such as mint and chili peppers—I realized this was why I smelled mint in the air. A tag reading "Mild" was attached to every chili plant.

Hmm. Suddenly, I felt an urge to sample a pepper off the plant. Feeling rebellious, I sneakily pried a pepper off one plant and popped it into my mouth. My mouth felt like it was going up in flames. So, I flipped the tag around, and I discovered why: the plant was actually an "Ultra-Spicy" plant disguised as a mild one!

Moving on from the seasonal plants and scanning the rest of the store, I saw something that caught my eye: a table at the front of the store with a sign labeled "Featured Plants". This table only had three plants: a plant called Purple, and two other flowers called Rainbow Rainbow flowers.

I examined the Rainbow Rainbow flower more closely and noticed it had eight petals: red, orange, yellow, green, blue, purple, pink, and white.

Suddenly, somebody behind me said something. "Do *you* know what that flower is?"

I spun around and saw it was Grandma Mariohn. "No," I replied truthfully.

"From what I have heard, the Rainbow Rainbow flower is a magical flower that can grant a certain number of wishes."

That made sense. "Oh, I see." But I noticed something strange: although the two flowers looked identical, the one on the right cost $20 more than the one on the left. "Grandma Mariohn, why does this one cost so much more?"

Grandma Mariohn did not hesitate to answer my question. "From what I understand, Rainbow Rainbow flowers have the ability to grant people's wishes. Perhaps the more expensive one can grant them more frequently."

I took this in and looked back at the plant. It seemed like a normal flower; did it really have the power to grant wishes? "Alright, thank you!"

"You're welcome, Max." She paused. "I just told Jo she may choose one item she wants from this store. Would you like me to buy this for you?"

Buying an expensive flower for someone you hadn't known for over twenty minutes took a certain level of kindness. And although I wasn't sure if it was true or not, I was intrigued by the thought that the Rainbow Rainbow flower might be able to grant wishes. I thanked Grandma Mariohn by saying, "I would love that!"

As Jo, Grandma Mariohn, and I walked through the store to leave, I held the Rainbow Flower, which Grandma Mariohn had bought for me, so tightly in my fins that I could've easily killed the plant if I had squeezed any tighter.

But an ear-splitting scream suddenly made me halt. *What was that?* "Jo! Grandma Mariohn! Did you hear that?"

"Hear what?" Jo asked.

"I didn't hear anything," Grandma Mariohn informed.

I whipped my head around in an attempt to find the source of the screaming. And I could not have been more surprised by who I saw. "Kay?! What are you doing here?!"

I blinked.

She vanished.

I was confused. Was I imagining things? That would make sense because neither Grandma Mariohn nor Jo heard the scream like I did. But Kay seemed *so real*—at least, she did before she vanished mysteriously.

Grandma Mariohn pulled me out of my head. "I bought Jo's plant, too. What would you like to do next? Would you like to go home?"

"I *would* like to go home, please," I said while rubbing the white petal. It looked fluffier than all the other petals, and I was correct.

But I never expected what happened next. All of a sudden, each of the flowers changed colors; the middle of each petal turned white and the outsides turned black. A quick electrical shock jolted from the flower's petal into my fin, causing me to jump back in backwards in shock. I tried to scream, but no sound came out.

I grabbed Grandma Mariohn and Jo.

Everything suddenly went pitch black.

I wasn't quite sure where I was, but it seemed familiar for a reason I couldn't quite put my fin on.

Then suddenly, almost as if by magic, a light appeared in the distance. The strange blob-like creature slowly made itself visible. *Now* I knew where I was...

The creature lifted the blobs that resembled its arms, almost in a godly way. I felt dizzy, almost like it was sending me into a trance. *"Max,"* it said to me in my mind.

I backed up in fear, only to find the voice was in my mind and backing up wouldn't help. What did it want from me, and why did it care about me so much? "What?"

But what the monster said next only made me more confused. *"I want you, Max,"* the creature coldly stated.

I did not hear more because the creature suddenly faded away and I became conscious again.

When I became conscious, I found myself on the floor in my room.

Looking up, I noticed Grandma Mariohn to my left on the floor, and Jo was on the bed to my left, about to fall off.

"That was fun!" Jo claimed, repositioning herself so she didn't fall. "Thank you, Grandma Mariohn!"

Grandma Mariohn sat up. "You're welcome!" After pausing, she added, "Okay, Max and Jo, it was awesome spending time with you, but I need to leave. I'll see you later!"

"Okay. Thank you for the Rainbow Rainbow flower!" It was a pleasure to have you here!" Jo added. Grandma Mariohn got up and exited the room.

Ten silent minutes passed without any talking, but Jo eventually spoke. "Max, I'm bored."

I agreed with Jo. "I am too."

And she had an idea. "I know we just went somewhere, but do you want to go to the Sharkland Zoo with me? I heard tickets are discounted today."

"I like that idea!! The Sharkland Zoo sounds fun."

"Yay!"

"Yep. There's the entrance." Jo pointed to a large arch above us with the words 'Sharkland Zoo.'

15

The Sharkland Zoo

Even though Jo and I were talking, we had been driving for a while, and I was getting bored.

But Jo said something that changed that. "Max, there's the entrance!!" Jo pointed to a large archway above us with the words "Sharkland Zoo".

I instantly started jittering with excitement, barely able to control myself. Yay!

Pulling into the parking lot, both of us noticed the Sharkland Zoo was not busy today; although the parking lot was ginormous, very few spaces were taken. Many spots in the front row were available.

Walking to the ticket counter, I noticed a large banner: "Last Day for Ticket Sale! All Tickets Are ₿1!" And Jo was excited about this. "OMG, Max! I knew there was a ticket sale today, but I forgot it was the biggest sale of the year!"

"That's great!" I replied. "Should we go buy our tickets?"

"Yeah!" Jo claimed. We walked to the ticket counter and paid for our tickets.

I took a moment to stop and look around after Jo and I bought our tickets. We were now in the main plaza area of the zoo, and I noticed multiple exhibits close to us, including the bison, Underwater World Building, lions, dolphins, Birds Building, spotted hyenas, and the Insects Building, as well as the gift shop and food court. I knew where I wanted to go first.

"Jo, I'm still hungry," I informed her. "Can we visit the food court?"

Jo looked in the direction I was looking to find the food court. "Of course, Max."

"Yay!" We started walking towards the food court.

The food court was nearly empty, like the parking lot. In the food court, I saw a quick-service restaurant, called the Roaring Tiger, and a café.

I wasn't hungry enough to eat at the restaurant, so I instead went to the café and looked at their menu.

Examining the menu, I was happy they had my favorite food, plant-based chicken wings—I was not vegetarian, but I preferred the texture of the plant-based variety. While the café offered multiple different sizes, I decided I wanted the small. "Jo, I think I want a small plant-based chicken wings. Do *you* want anything?"

Jo replied with a smirk, "I'll be fine. I'll just share with you." I laughed.

"That's funny. You can share with me." I walked up to the cashier. "May I have one small portion of plant-based chicken wings, please?"

"Okay. That will be ℬ5 SBucks, please."

I handed the cashier 5 SBucks; the cashier turned around and grabbed a small paper dish with six or seven nuggets from a ledge. The cashier handed the dish to me and stated, "Here you go."

"Thank you!" I replied. "May I have change?"

"Um... sure?" The cashier handed me a single penny, and I put it in my pocket.

Walking away from the café, all Jo and I needed to do now was find a table. "I got my nuggets, Jo."

"That's great," Jo replied. "Now let's find a table."

She looked around and found an empty table. "Let's sit here. Oh, and do you see the condiments? Do you think they would have pickle relish?"

Pickle relish? Why did Jo want pickle relish? "You like pickle relish with chicken wings??"

Jo was not hesitant. "Delish," Jo stated. "Oh, I see a condiments cart near the restaurant. I'll be right back."

She returned not a long time later holding two paper plates, one with a dollop of pickle relish on the side. Handing me a plate, she sat down and pushed the plant-based chicken nuggets toward where I was sitting. "Take what you want, and I'll have the rest." She grinned.

"Alright." Counting the nuggets, I picked up half—3 fried capsules of deliciousness—and put them on my plate.

Jo took the remaining three and dunked one into her relish, used the nugget to scoop a large amount, and ate it with a smile. "Max, you should try it. It's *so* good."

"No thanks," I replied. "Well... maybe I should." I used one of my nuggets to scoop a very small amount of Jo's relish, and I bit off a corner. Turns out, Jo was right—it was like a match made in heaven. "I'm going to go get my own portion of relish," I told Jo. "That is *so* good."

"I know, right." Jo grinned again.

Later, after Jo and I had finished our food, I asked Jo what she wanted to do next. "Where do you want to go next? Do you want to visit an exhibit?"

"I like birds," Jo claimed. "Let's go to the Birds Building."

We heard intense squawking before we even got inside—we were in the right place!

"I'm excited to see the birds!" I told Jo.

"I am too, Max!"

"Yay!"

The first birds that caught my eye were the crows. I walked to their enclosure, noticing their deep black feathers and harsh "caw" sounds. While some of them were asleep, most of the crows seemed to be awake. Wanting to take a photo, I asked Jo, "Did you bring a camera?"

"Yeah." Jo shrugged her black backpack off. Unzipping it, she dug through the contents until she found what she was looking for: a small silver-colored digital camera. She handed the camera to me.

We continued walking around the Birds Building and visiting exhibits of various kinds of birds for about ten minutes. After we had visited all the exhibits we wanted to see, we were ready to move on from the Birds Building.

"Jo, which building would you like to visit next?" I asked. "I want to see the bees in the Insects Building."

"I wanna go to the Insects Building, too," Jo agreed. "I wonder if it has stink bugs."

Jo wanted to see *stink bugs*? "You want to see the stink bugs? We see them all the time at home." It may have come across as slightly rude, although Jo hopefully knew what I meant.

Jo was adamant. "Stink bugs are awesome."

I decided not to question. Instead, I said, "Okay. Let's go to the Insects Building!"

The Insects Building was only a short walk away from the Birds Building. It was significantly smaller than the Birds Building

Jo changed her mind about what insects she wanted to see. "Nah, I changed my mind. I wanna see every exhibit."

Entering the Insects Building, I looked up at the signs for each enclosure. But I noticed something that looked wrong for some reason. *Ladybugs, Leaf Beetles, Stink Bugs, Springtails, Praying Mantises, Crickets, Boxelder Bugs, Honeybes, and Bumblebes.* "Jo!"

Jo spun around. "What?"

Pointing to the sign, I added, "Look. The signs for the bees are spelled wrong!"

Looking up at the sign I was looking at, Jo noticed the error too. "No way! You're right! Whoever painted the signs must have forgotten how to spell "Bee" or something, because that's super strange." She paused. "Let's go talk to an employee and ask." She walked up to one. "Excuse me?"

"Hello!" The employee turned around. "How can I help you?"

Jo pointed to the sign. "My friend and I just noticed that wherever the word 'Bee' appears on the signs over there, it's spelled wrong and only uses one 'E' instead of two."

Strangely, the employee seemed very surprised by this, almost as if she didn't notice the error. "What? No, I see two 'E's. You're probably just seeing things."

Strange. "Oh," I said. "Well, anyway, thank you."

"Anytime," the employee replied. We walked away.

Jo and I continued visiting insect enclosures and tried not to think about the misspelled signs. And I needed to use the restroom. "Jo, I need to use the restroom."

Jo nodded. "Actually, I do too. But where is it? Do you know where it is?"

I looked around. "No, I don't see a restroom. I'm going to ask the employee again."

Jo walked up to the employee and asked her where the closest restrooms were, and the employee responded by saying there weren't restrooms in the Insect Building, but there *were* some in the Underwater World Building. Jo and I agreed to leave the Insects Building and use the restrooms in the Underwater World Building.

The walk to the Underwater World Building was longer than we thought, but we eventually got there about ten minutes later.

From the moment I entered the building, I noticed it was different from the other buildings. It seemed like seeing the aquatic animals cost extra; three ticket counters blocked anybody from entering without a pass. Thankfully, the restrooms were on the right slightly past the ticket counters, so, hopefully, it wouldn't be too hard to get there. Jo and I tried cutting through the lines.

Turns out, another employee thought we were trying to get in without a pass. The employee stopped us and gave us a stern look. "Do you have tickets, young sharks?"

I put on my most innocent expression. "No, we don't. We came here to use the restroom," I matter-of-factly stated.

Jo joined in. "We promise we'll leave the building as soon as we finish."

The employee was *not* having it. "You want to go to the restroom together? *How sweet*," the employee mocked.

"No, we're not going in together. We just both need to go," I shot back.

This seemed to make the employee finally give up. "Fine. Just remember this building has security cameras for a reason."

"We know," Jo rolled her eyes and said. The employee walked away.

"Wow, that employee was *mean*, " I stated.

"I agree," Jo agreed. "Wait, why is this also wrong?"

"Wait, what?" Sure enough, the word on the sign was spelled 'restroms.'

Assuming that the spelling error was nothing major, I decided to not worry about it. "Oh, well," I stated. "It's probably just an error."

"That's true," Jo said. She left for the restroom.

But I had a realization in the stall. *The misspelling of the signs could just be a coincidence; maybe the zoo hired the wrong shark to make the signs. But why did the employee in the Insect Building not notice? Wouldn't she have noticed? Perhaps there is a greater reason why only Jo and I noticed the wrong spelling on the signs.*

No, Max. I'm probably just seeing things. But it was still strange. First, some voice in the castle made Mary and Anny its servants. I heard the same voice at Awesome Stuff For Less. And I saw Kay out of the window of the deedly stote, but she vanished when I blinked. Normal sharks can't do that. Lastly, the typos on signs here. All these events are related to each other; I just know it. What is going on?

After a few more hours of visiting various exhibits in various buildings, although the trip had been a ton of fun and I was super happy, I was tired and ready to go home. "Jo, it's been a lot of fun at the zoo with you. But I'm getting tired and am ready to go home."

Jo turned around and looked me in the eyes. "I agree with you, Max. I'm getting tired too. Let's go to the exit." She pointed to a gate close to the entrance that read "Exit".

I followed Jo's lead as she headed to the exit. But I felt like I was forgetting something. "Wait, Jo. I actually forgot to tell you something."

"What is it?" Jo asked curiously.

I sighed. "I realized something when I was in the restroom earlier. It's kind of hard to explain, but basically, I've noticed that the 'creepy voice' I've heard on multiple occasions has always been the same. For example, the voice I heard in the castle when Mary and Anny were captured, a naughty thing that I admit I did at Awesome Stuff For Less— I now realize it was a mistake, and I apologize—that caused me to go unconscious, and when I saw Kay at the Deedly Stote. I can tell you more about those later, but that's what I've noticed, and although I don't know why, I feel like they're all linked somehow."

Staring deep into my eyes as if trying to understand what I said, Jo realized, "I don't quite know what you mean, but now that you mention it, you've described that voice before and said they sound like they're all the same. Perhaps they *are* related somehow."

Jo grabbed my fin, passing buildings as we ran towards the exit. Until suddenly, we heard a surprising noise—it sounded a bit like a roar and a bit like a scream. We turned around. "Did you hear that?" I whispered.

"Hear what? The roar? Yeah, I did."

Being young sharks still and curious, we knew we had to check it out, so we followed the sound to its source. We never knew exactly where it was coming from, but the strangest part was how it seemed like we were the only ones who heard it. As Jo and I ran toward the sound, it started sounding more like words being chanted instead of screaming.

Ss-st-stee-steea-steal? Th-th-thei-their? H-hea-hearts?

Steal their hearts?

16

The Nightmare (The Vision)

Slowly, I decided it was time to get up and see Jo's progress on the pizza she was making for dinner.

I had been on my bed almost ever since I had come home from the Sharkland Zoo a few hours ago, and I had spent that time trying to process my new theory and writing what I found in a notebook. Yesterday, Jo had prepared homemade pizza dough, so today she got to turn it into delicious pizza for dinner. It smelled scrumptious.

I didn't even need a reason to stand up, because Jo suddenly gave me one. "Dinner's ready!" she called.

I sat up straight, adrenaline rushing through my veins. "Yay!" I exclaimed out loud. The amazing scent of melty cheese, herb-ified tomatoes, and whole-grain bread in the oven had dominated over all other usual house smells, making it unbearable to wait for dinner, and now it was time!

I raced down the stairs, almost tripping by accident. Jo was in the kitchen setting the table.

Sitting at the dinner table, I stared at my plate, nearly drooling—it looked *so* good. A pizza Jo had custom made for me, with four different flavors, rested on the plate. The pizza also had a thick and chewy crust dusted with flour, just the perfect amount of tomato sauce, and a thick layer of cheese. I couldn't resist any longer; I took a large, delicious bite out of one of the slices.

It was just as delicious as I thought—even better than, perhaps. But, after only coming out of the oven not too long before, it also burned my mouth. "Aah! It's hot! Hot! Hot!" I said. Jo laughed.

I wiped my mouth with my napkin and stared at my empty plate, still hungry for more. "Jo, that was *so good*!"

Jo looked at her plate, then looked at me and smiled. "Thank you! I liked it too!"

Standing up and bringing my dishes to the sink, I added, "Well, I think I'm going to get ready for bed now."

Jo liked my idea, but she had something to add. "I think that's a great idea. Now that you mention it, I think I'll get ready for bed too. But when you get into your room, please check that your window is closed."

Grabbing the sponge and dish soap, I stated, "Okay! I think it's closed, but I'm not sure. I'll wash my dishes first."

I finished my bedtime routine not too long later—my teeth were brushed, my face was washed, my pajamas were on, and I had said goodnight to Jo, who was also going to bed. Before I crawled into bed, I walked to my lamp and pulled the chain to turn it off, knowing I wouldn't need it.

Now that I was ready for bed, I should have been able to cuddle my stuffed animals inside the warm bedding and fall asleep, but I remembered something Jo had instructed me to do. Hearing car noises from outside, I realized the window was still open! Before I could relax, I had to close it. But as I started climbing back into my bed, I noticed an envelope on my nightstand under the window—it looked like it had blown in accidentally.

I examined the strange envelope to the best of my ability in the dim light. It had no return address, so I did not know who sent it, but the 'to' address read it was supposed to be delivered to somebody named "HifftYiz"—was this Linda? But I thought Linda had turned back into a shark! Maybe there was another HifftYiz in Sharkland, but whoever it was, it wasn't me, so now I was sure it had blown into my room accidentally. *Perhaps I should return it to the post office, I thought.*

But suddenly, I did not feel like returning it to the post office so it could be delivered to the correct recipient—I couldn't explain why, but I had developed a terrible feeling that this was something I needed to read. Grabbing a pair of scissors off my nightstand, I ripped the envelope open. Inside was a sheet of folded paper, printed with black ink.

I unfolded the paper inside the envelope, turned my bedside light on so I could see, and read the letter.

To HifftYiz,

As you already know too well, my goal is to gain 50 hearts from sharks so I can get the last magical Seashell of Power. That will make me immortal and invincible (my dream basically since I was born). I currently have 49 of the 50 hearts.

Recently, two male sharks named Vhreho Chinkchink and Guhyeo Skigmon gave me two of these 49. And when they did, I had expected them to die, which usually happens when sharks give me their hearts, but they didn't. Rather, they stayed alive even after I had the hearts in my possession. This leads me to believe that the hearts Vhreho and Guhyeo gave to me weren't truly *their* hearts. Of course, the hearts had to belong to somebody, and the hearts belonged to two sharks on the other side of the town. They died.

I asked Vhreho and Guhyeo about it and learned they got curious at the doctor's appointment the Friday before, so they looked in the fridge. The extra hearts from those two sharks' transplants are in that fridge. They found two jars and took them home. Because of this, I wonder why Vhreho and Guhyeo didn't just give me their own hearts; this would be much easier than getting hearts from somewhere else. Is it possible that they gave them to me already, but I forgot about it? I'm getting older, so that could be possible.

I hope you know this already, but when somebody is under my control, they cannot die since their brains have changed. But they drop dead as soon as I obtain their hearts. I may have to let Vhreho and Guhyeo go unless they give me their hearts right here in my sewer so I can see them. Not that they would be able to get in; it's so secret that any normal shark would not be able to detect it's there.

Do you remember Kay, my heart-retrieving servant? Since everybody knows she's nice, I *knew* she would be the perfect evil helper. I'm wondering if you remember her because there is one shark named Max who would be another great helper, and he and Kay are best friends. There is only one problem with that, though: Max is smart and will be very hard to control. I have attempted to communicate with him mentally before, but he does not listen.

I controlled Kay only a few months before Max arrived, by writing a letter to her at midnight on New Year's Eve. Only ten minutes later, she arrived at 1234 Help Street, a haunted house, and I possessed her very quickly. She was easy, but I know Max will be harder—*much* harder. Please give me support.

Yours Truly Evil, Gingashluckaquin

It didn't take me long to finish reading the letter. I was confused, worried, and angry, but somehow the letter had made the day's events much less confusing. It explained almost everything from Mary and Anny being captured to hearing the voice when I fell at Awesome Stuff For Less—the gingashluckaquin possessed Mary and Anny and turned them into sqwgamugurtz, and its voice was what I heard at the store. And perhaps the signs at the zoo were written by possessed sharks who had lost their ability to spell, but nobody knew because they were possessed!

Deciding I could think about it the next day, I wrote the new evidence in my notebook, turned my light off, and crawled under the covers.

The next thing I knew, I was asleep, and I appeared to be dreaming. I didn't quite know where I was, but I felt like I recognized it somehow—I stood in a black room with no walls, too dark to be able to see anything.

Then a creature appeared in the distance, standing over what appeared to be two sharks. Although it was so far away, I could see every detail, light illuminating the creature's outline and making it appear like it was glowing. And when I looked closely enough, I recognized the two sharks the creature stood over as Vhreho and Guhyeo. The creature standing over them was black and gray with red cylinder-shaped "bumps" around its edge, and it looked a bit like a shadow. Instead of a mouth, it had a strange black and white spiral-shaped sucker.

Vhreho and Guhyeo kneeled on the ground, holding large mason jars with unscrewed lids. Vhreho stuck his fin into his jar first, pulling out a red, slimy object dripping with thick liquid, and Guhyeo did the same. The objects looked a bit like hearts; perhaps these were the hearts from the doctor's office like the letter mentioned!

Next, the sharks held the hearts up to the sky as if they were worshiping them, the hearts defying all known laws of gravity and rising up to the creature, who seemed to be levitating. The creature snatched the red, dripping organs, growing in size like a cartoon. It was too much to handle, so I closed my eyes...

...and opened them again to reveal a bird's-eye view of the doctor's office I was at last Friday, still in the dream. From on top of the transparent ceiling, I could see nearly everything that happened that day, nearly screaming because I felt like I was about to fall. I noticed Vhreho and Guhyeo sat in the chairs while Dr. Yaincala was in the small room, grabbing two of the four jars. This was something that I did not notice when I was physically there: there were more— two more—jars of hearts in the fridge.

Next, I saw my past self talking to Jo; I couldn't hear what I said because all the sounds were blurred together, but when I saw Jo and I standing up, I realized we were leaving to use the bathroom. That's why I didn't remember what happened next. After Vhreho and Guhyeo had their new hearts, Dr. Yaincala walked back to the small room and washed his fins after taking his gloves off, and Vhreho and Guhyeo exchanged mischievous grins and whispered to each other. Were they planning something?

Then Jo and I returned from the bathroom, my memory coming back. This was right after recovery time had started and we no longer needed to be at the doctor's office, so Jo and I thanked Dr. Yaincala and left the room to go home.

I closed my eyes again, wondering if there was more to see. There was.

Now I was back in Operation Room T, but it was much later. Nobody was in the room except Dr. Yaincala and restless Vhreho and Guhyeo, but that changed when Jo and I entered, Vhreho and Guhyeo jumping up and down. I still saw everything from above.

After Vhreho told Jo and I his address, Jo, Dr. Yaincala, and I went outside to talk to the receptionist, but Vhreho and Guhyeo stayed in the room. This was when I noticed Vhreho and Guhyeo doing something *very* naughty: grabbing the two leftover jars from the fridge while grinning evilly. Quietly unzipping Jo's backpack, they snuck the jars inside and buried them under Jo's first-aid kit and rolled-up hoodie. When Jo returned, I saw—and remembered—her picking up the backpack and wondering why it was suddenly so much heavier, not bothering to open it and discover why.

Teleporting me somehow, I closed and opened my eyes again; now I was in a sewer, about to fall into the murky water. *Ew.* Behind me, the shadow-like monster from before was there delicately placing two hearts into a large metal box filled with many, many more hearts, each of them looking disgusting with their vein-filled red meat-like texture.

Next, something very strange started happening. My left eye saw one thing, and my right eye saw another. This should not have been possible, but I was dreaming, and I guess anything was possible in a dream!

Through my left eye, I saw what Vhreho and Guhyeo did after we dropped them off. While Guhyeo gave Jo and I a tour of his house, Vhreho sneakily unzipped Jo's backpack and lifted the jars out. Later, once Jo and I were gone, the troublemakers sat down in worshiping positions on the floor in Guhyeo's bedroom and let the hearts lift through the air and the ceiling to a creature I could only see part of. *So that was what I was seeing earlier!* I realized. Meanwhile, through my right eye, I saw two random sharks in a bedroom giving hearts to the creature. Once the creature had what it wanted, the sharks dropped to the floor, dead.

Suddenly, I could no longer see that scene, and all I was seeing were Vhreho and Guhyeo. It had now been about some time since they had given their hearts to the monster, yet they were still alive. Remembering the letter, I knew the creature was called the "gingashluckaquin", and Vhreho and Guhyeo didn't die because the hearts they gave weren't their own hearts.

When I closed and reopened my eyes again, I saw a different monster. This creature looked like Linda in her HifftYiz form, but it was much, much older, and it spoke to the other monster—the gingashluckaquin. I couldn't explain how, but the gingashluckaquin looked younger, almost.

The HifftYiz spoke in a formal, yet vaguely warm, tone. "Gingashluckaquin, I offer you an opportunity to gain the last Seashell of Power, which you have seeked for a long time. If you give me fifty shark's hearts, I will give you the last Seashell of Power in exchange."

The gingashluckaquin did not respond, but it seemed to light up a bit "HifftYiz, thank you for giving me the chance to take over Sharkland and become its new ruler. I gladly accept."

The HifftYiz responded without emotion. "You have exactly four months." While it didn't appear to have feet, acid came out the ends of its legs.

I blinked again, hoping to see another scene so it would all make sense, but instead, I woke up, the sun shining through the curtains. I knew it was a dream, but the strange thing was that I seemed to remember it all.

16½

Kay

Earlier That Year

Kay awoke to a strange sound coming from the main level. It was midnight on New Year's Eve at Kay's house in Sharkland, and she had been asleep for only a few hours. The sound sounded like a loud knock, but Kay was unsure.

Extremely tired and feeling vaguely like a zombie, Kay reached for the flashlight she always kept on her bedside table. Next, she slipped into her fuzzy slippers and silently opened the door to her room, revealing a staircase to the main level. Staying quiet so she wouldn't wake her parents, she crept down the steps.

That's when she heard the noise again. This time, it was more defined. It was a knock, and it was coming from the door a few yards away. *Who could be knocking at this hour?* Kay thought.

Wondering who was there, Kay slowly opened the door to reveal a mailshark with a large bag full of letters, her vehicle parked on the street. *What could the postman want at this hour?* Kay thought, checking the clock next to the door. *It's almost midnight!*

"So sorry to interrupt your sleep at this time of night, but I received this letter that claims to be very urgent in huge red letters," the mailshark whispered.

Kay stared down at the letter in her fins. "Uh... thanks, I guess," she whispered back.

She grabbed her flashlight and the letter, then walked back to her bedroom. The mailshark drove away.

Wow, the mailshark was right—this seems to be very urgent. But what could make this letter so *urgent that it needed to be delivered at midnight?* Kay removed the letter from the envelope, which had no return address. *Besides, I thought the post office wasn't open!*

Kay pulled the blankets above her head and read the letter to herself, whispering so nobody would hear her.

"Hello, Kay Kallyn! We are excited to inform you that we have recognized all of the good deeds you did over the years and will present you with a reward tonight at 1234 Help Street. This reward is a once-in-a-lifetime opportunity. You should not overlook it. Thank you, and goodbye!"

What a strange letter, Kay thought when she finished reading it. *I think I know where Help Street is, but no such address with 1234 as the zip code exists, at least not on that street.*

Is it just me, or does something about this letter seem off? I know I've done many good deeds over the years, but why am I getting a reward for it—an 'urgent' award? Although she didn't want to break her parent's trust, Kay knew she should probably go anyway, in case the letter was not telling lies. *It's not like anything bad will happen if I go and see if the letter is correct,* she thought.

Opening her closet, she grabbed her faux-fur winter boots and thick aqua-colored puffer jacket. She reached for a bin on the top shelf and grabbed a pair of gloves from inside. She also grabbed an energy bar from a different bin and stashed it and the flashlight inside her coat pocket.

She was about to leave her room but remembered she had forgotten something. She snatched the letter off her bed and a neighborhood map from her closet. Then she quietly tiptoed to the kitchen, where she grabbed the emergency pocket knife from a drawer to the right of the stove.

She opened the door and walked out into the blazing cold. *Alright, Kay. You can do this. All you have to do is find 1234 Help Street, claim the reward, and get out of there as fast as possible. Then you can get back to sleep and pretend that none of this ever happened. Assuming the reward they promised is real.*

Unzipping her coat pocket, Kay grabbed her flashlight and map from her pocket. Turning the flashlight on, Kay examined the map, locating her house and Help Street. Tracing a route to Help Street with her fin, she learned how to get where she needed to go and started moving.

It took about ten minutes, an energy bar, and a few breaks to get to Help Street. But when she got there, she was proud of herself.

Kay assumed she would have to look around to find 1234 Help Street, but she didn't need to; a large banner was on one of the houses—number 1234—that read "Welcome Kay Kallyn!". Thinking she was in the right place, she opened the front door and walked inside.

The house was dim inside, but Kay could still vaguely see where she was going. In front of her, she saw a set of stairs leading down into what appeared to be infinite darkness, but it was blocked off, so although she had no intention of doing that, Kay couldn't investigate.

Before she could decide to continue or run away, a strange blob-like shadow-colored creature appeared at the end of the hallway. It had no mouth, so it spoke to Kay in her mind. *"Why hello there, little female shark. Do you want a hug? Come to me."*

Now Kay knew she was not here for an award. This monster was large and creepy, and it levitated a foot or so off the ground, defying all known laws of gravity. And the voice the monster used was probably the coldest Kay had ever heard. Besides, who would ask you to come to their house because you were giving an award, but ask for a hug after you arrive?

Not knowing what to think, Kay spun around to see if she could still escape, but she couldn't—another animal with tiny legs, giant eyes, and a claw instead of a nose blocked the door. Kay started panicking. Thinking quicker than ever, she forcefully removed the rope blocking the stairs and started down without hesitation. Even with her flashlight on, she could only see a few steps in front of her. Not knowing what was at the bottom, she feared she would never come back.

There were many, many more stairs than Kay expected, and it felt like it took an eternity to arrive at the bottom of the stairs. But when she did reach the bottom, she stumbled onto the ground, thinking there would be another step. Kay was surprised neither monster tried to stop her.

In the middle of the large, dark, damp-smelling concrete room, Kay saw a glowing machine at the bottom of the stairs. Not wanting to die but also being curious, she poked her head into the blue-colored light streams the machine emitted. *Ow... What is happening? It feels like my brain is being played with like putty.* She removed her head from the machine's lights, but it was no use. The machine had finished doing what it had done.

The machine started changing Kay's thoughts. Her beautiful ocean-blue eyes turned a glamorous shade of emerald green. *If I help the gingashluckaquin get what it deserves, Sharkland will finally be how it was meant to be.*

17

The HifftYiz, Part 2

When I woke up the next day, I found myself sweating all over. I learned *so* much information during my dream—or was it a vision?

Not opening my eyes yet, I pulled the covers down to cool myself off. After a few minutes of lying in bed, I gathered the energy to get out of bed even though I was still groggy. I rushed downstairs to the kitchen, excited to tell Jo about my vision, which was still vividly playing in my brain even though I was awake. Jo was pouring milk from a carton into a bowl of cereal for her breakfast.

"Good morning, Max!" she exclaimed.

I was impatient, but I still tried to speak slowly. "Good morning, Jo!"

"How did you sleep?"

"I had a vision last night," I replied, getting impatient.

"WOAH!" Jo exclaimed. "Tell me about it! When did it happen? Why? How?"

"It was last night at bedtime," I said. I could hear my speech rate increasing. "A letter blew in through a window, so I read it."

"What happened in the vision??" Jo asked with a tone that screamed *Give me answers now. Please.*

I drew in a large amount of air, preparing to tell Jo. "Therearethesefourmagicalseashellsthatgrantimmor tallityandpowerandtheHifftYizhasoneofthemandtheging ashluckaquinwantsitandTheHifftYizistrading50sharkshe artsfortheseashell-"

Jo looked at me, clearly confused. "Hold on there. I would like to learn what you learned *and* be able to understand it," Jo said.

"Sorry," I said, embarrassed. I started over. "Basically, I read a letter before I fell asleep that blew in from my window, and it introduced me to much of what I learned during the vision. The vision showed these four magical seashells called the Seashells of Power—whoever gains possession of all four seashells will be granted immortality and invincibility forever. A shadow-colored monster covered with strange bump-like things that has a sucker instead of a mouth and levitates off the ground has three of the four seashells, and it wants the last seashell. The monster is called the gingashluckaquin.

"And do you remember the HifftYiz from that day at school? I also saw another HifftYiz in the vision. It was much older than Linda from Sharkschool, and it was making a deal with the gingashluckaquin. If the gingashluckaquin gives the HifftYiz fifty hearts from sharks, the HifftYiz will give the gingashluckaquin the last Seashell of Power, which will give the gingashluckaquin immortality and invincibility."

Jo paused. "Oh gosh. That's scary. I didn't have a vision too, but the gingashluckaquin sounds evil."

"Yeah. I also heard the gingashluckaquin wanted to use the powers from the seashells to take Sharkland over."

"That's terrible!" Jo exclaimed.

"I agree," I replied. "I also saw Vhreho and Guhyeo from the Friday appointment. Do you remember how your backpack was so heavy when we left? And do you remember Guhyeo giving us a tour of Vhreho's house? There was a reason for that. The backpack was heavy because of two jars with shark's hearts inside that Vhreho and Guhyeo put in there when we were talking to Dr. Yaincala, and when Guhyeo gave us a tour of his house, Vhreho was secretly unzipping your backpack and taking two jars out. They stole these jars from the back room in Dr. Yaincala's office."

"So *that's* why my backpack seemed so much heavier than normal," Jo observed. "How dare they!"

"Seriously," I replied. "How dare they."

"Err, sorry for interrupting," Jo realized.

"It's okay," I replied. "After Vhreho took the jars to his room, he waited for Guhyeo to finish his tour so we would leave, then he walked to Vhreho's room to join him in what he was about to do. After Guhyeo was in the room, they took the hearts out of the jars, kneeled in a worshiping position, and held their hearts up to the gingashluckaquin, who was levitating above them. I learned in the letter I read before I had the vision that sharks are supposed to die once they give the gingashluckaquin their hearts. That's why I also saw two random sharks somewhere else in the town dropping dead. Also, do you remember Kay?"

"Yes," Jo replied. "Your girlfriend?"

"No! We're just friends," I shot back, annoyed with Jo.

"I'm kidding," Jo commented. "But I do remember Kay."

"I read in the letter before I had the vision that Kay was controlled by the gingashluckaquin. According to the letter, the gingashluckaquin says Kay is its 'personal servant in helping retrieve the hearts' and 'the perfect evil helper.' I don't know much about that, but I learned that the gingashluckaquin wants me to also be its servant because it thinks I would be a 'good helper,' and now I'm scared."

Jo did not say anything for a few moments while she scribbled something on the back of her napkin with a pencil. When she wrote her last word, she looked up at me with worried eyes for a few seconds, and instead of responding, she stood up and hugged me tightly. "Max, I'm worried!"

I looked back at her. "I am too, Jo!"

But after a few moments of awkward silence, Jo changed the subject. "It's impressive how you remembered everything that happened in your vision, Max."

"Thank you. I think so too. Wait! Isn't that the mail truck?"

"It is! I forgot, it's Saturday!"

"But I thought the mail came on Sunday," I wondered.

"You would be correct if it was any week before this week. The schedule has changed and the mail now comes on Saturday. I'm not sure why."

"Oh."

"I'll go outside and retrieve the mail before we forget." Jo put on her blue-and-yellow canvas high-tops painted with sharks and opened the door. When she returned from the mailbox, I noticed all the mail Jo had was junk mail except for one letter, which was addressed to me.

Jo noticed this too. "You got a letter from somebody!" She handed me the letter. "And it's addressed to you, not a strange monster."

I examined the letter. The "to" address read "Max Alderin," and the return address read "HifftYiz—1234 Help Street" in loopy, neat writing. "The HifftYiz? Why would the HifftYiz send me a letter?"

"I'm not sure," Jo replied. "The HifftYiz was the monster who had the deal with the gingashluckaquin, right?"

"Yes. Do you think I should read it?"

Jo did think I should read the letter. "I think you should read it, in case the HifftYiz has something important to say. What if this letter mentions that other letter you received by the wind?"

I considered Jo's opinion. "You're right." Using a pair of scissors to open the envelope, I gently pulled out the carefully written note inside and started reading.

Max Alderin,

Hello. I'm the HifftYiz. I'm assuming you know about the deal I had with the gingashluckaquin since it informed me its letter to me blew into your window by accident. I know this might seem surprising, but while this is true, it's not the full story. I don't believe I'm evil at heart.

You can choose to believe me or not, but my deal with the gingashluckaquin is fake. What I mean by this is that even if the gingashluckaquin gave me fifty shark hearts, I would never give it the last Seashell of Power. The gingashluckaquin's horrendous enough already! It doesn't need to rule Sharkland!

The main reason I offered the deal was because the gingashluckaquin threatened to kill me if I didn't give it what it wanted—it gives me awful threats like this all the time. But I hoped the deal would give me a bit more time to decide what to do. The last thing I want is for it to gain the power it would get by collecting all four Seashells Of Power. If I remember right, the gingashluckaquin has forty-nine out of fifty hearts, and I'm getting worried.

I think you should know the gingashluckaquin wants to possess you. (You might know this already.) Although it has done this for many sharks, the catch is that the gingashluckaquin doesn't want to possess you to make you a servant—instead, it wants to so it will be easier to obtain your heart. According to the gingashluckaquin, you are "very hard to possess because you are so smart,'" but with enough time, it will figure out a way. The reason the gingashluckaquin wanted to control you is because it claimed no survivors in Sharkland had the right kind of hearts, and you are the only currently living shark who had the right kind. As you can see, I have few options here. I want to make sure you stay alive because something tells me that is important for the fate of Sharkland.

Im sure you've noticed the smaller population. This is because many sharks were sacrificed because they didn't have the right kinds of hearts. I did some thinking, and I came up with an idea. You should be the keeper of the last Seashell of Power.

The gingashluckaquin does not know anything about you besides you have the heart it wants and that the letter blew into your window. (I have no idea how the gingashluckaquin knows these things.) If I give the seashell to you, we will all be safer.

Please come to my house on 1234 Help Street as soon as you can. I have included a map so you know where 1234 Help Street is. Just be sure not to go into the basement as that is where the gingashluckaquin keeps its possession machine. (I have drafted a plan to disassemble it, but if I get too close, the machine

"Oh gosh," I commented after reading the letter.

"What?" Jo asked.

I didn't know how to explain it, so I could only say one thing. "Read it," I instructed her. I handed the letter to Jo and she examined it. I also gave her the letter I had received the previous night.

It only took a few minutes for Jo to read the letters and learn about my struggles. While she was reading the letters, I unfolded the map included inside the envelope, which showed a very close-up view of Help Street. I had been on Help Street before, so I recognized most of the houses on the street, but there was one I didn't—I realized this was number 1234. "Jo, do you think I should go?"

Jo did not hesitate. "Yes. Yes. Go as fast as you can. This is a big responsibility and we both know that, but it might save your life, if everything in these letters is true. I do think you should bring this, though." Jo handed me a small device on a key ring.

"What's this?" I asked.

"It's a GPS tracker. Hide it in your pocket. It'll tell me where you are, although the reason I bought these is because it also has a calling function."

"Okay," I replied. I grabbed the device out of Jo's fin, put my shoes on, and ran out the front door.

I didn't stop running until I reached Help Street, which was not far away, and when I was there, I looked at the map again. The map claimed house number 1234 was between house number 7632 and house number 7633, which was strange, but I decided to ignore it.

I found 1234 and knocked on the door quietly, wondering who or what would answer. Much to my relief, The HifftYiz, not the gingashluckaquin, opened the door. The HifftYiz was a wide, hairy creature with huge eyes and a claw instead of a nose. "Hi! Are you Max?" he asked.

"Yes, I am Max. May I come in?"

"Of course. Feel free to take off your shoes, although I think you should keep them on. Let's go upstairs to my bedroom, and we can 'hang out'." Whispering, the HiffYiz added, "I know you're not here to "hang out"; I barely know you. But the gingashluckaquin will return from the School of Evil soon, and it might be here already. We better hurry."

The HifftYiz was old, so he used an elevator to change floors. He pressed the button to the second floor, and when it got there, the elevator doors opened. We got off the elevator.

When we were on the second floor, the HifftYiz opened the door to the house's only bedroom. It was unlike any other bedroom I had seen: a long piece of blue tape divided the two sides of the room: the gingashluckaquin's and the HifftYiz's. The HifftYiz's side of the room was neat and tidy, while the gingashluckaquin's looked like a disaster.

The HifftYiz walked to his desk and opened a drawer. "What are you looking for?" I asked.

"My seashell collection. Last summer, I vacationed at a beach and returned with a bucket full of seashells. The gingashluckaquin never thought much of it since it knows all of these seashells are important to me, and that is completely true. But little does it know that I have added an extra shell since my trip..." The HifftYiz dumped the contents of the bucket on his bed.

"Do you mean the magical seashell it wants so badly?" I asked.

"Yes. Not long ago, the seashell was in a safe in my closet, but one day, I discovered that the combination part of the lock-and-key safe was unlocked, which made me think the gingashluckaquin learned the code. That's why I moved the magical shell to my seashell collection and replaced the shell that was originally in the safe with an almost-identical ordinary shell. The gingashluckaquin has no idea the magical shell was moved and is still looking for the key."

Now I knew the HifftYiz was *smart*! "That's a great idea. Now there's a higher chance we'll all stay safe!"

After a bit of time spent searching through the shells on the bed, the HifftYiz found the fourth Seashell of Power.

"Max," the HifftYiz said. "It's time for you to have the seashell. I'm getting old, and my time is running out. It is time for you to get the fourth Seashell of Power. I haven't known you for more than a half-day, but something tells me the fate of Sharkland depends on you."

He handed it to me. I cupped my fins to receive it, and when I had it, I stared at it, not knowing what to do with such a powerful object.

"Thank you. I promise I will try as hard as I can to keep this away from the gingashluckaquin. I won't let you down, HifftYiz."

"Thank you so much, Max," the HifftYiz responded with a mellow tone. "Now, please leave. It won't be long before the gingashluckaquin will come home and see you."

I got home only a few minutes later, the Seashell of Power never leaving my fin. Jo was excited when I got home. "Max! You're alive!!"

I had to catch my breath before responding. "Yes, I *am* alive. It went great. I got the last Seashell of Power and promised to keep it away from the gingashluckaquin."

"The way you said that makes it sound like the thing you're holding *isn't* the object that will mean the difference between life and death," Jo remarked.

I paused. "Is it really *that* powerful?"

"Well, you were there, not me," Jo said. "But I read both letters multiple times, and these Seashells of Power seem extremely strong."

For the first time since the vision, I realized how powerful the shells were. "Gosh. You're right, Jo. I will put my heart and soul into guarding this."

Meanwhile

Point Of View: Third Person Omniscient

The gingashluckaquin floated into the house at 1234 Help Street. It was tired from a long day at an 'evil refreshment session,' which was held at the School of Evil. It went upstairs to the bedroom it shared with the HifftYiz, being careful to not cross the blue-tape line on the floor into the HifftYiz's side of the room.

The HifftYiz was not there since he was busy working hard downstairs, cleaning the gingashluckaquin's breakfast dishes, tidying the mess in the living room, taking the trash out, and preparing to mow the lawn. Meanwhile, the gingashluckaquin lay down on its round-shaped bed, feeling much more relaxed. But it remembered something, which caused it to hesitantly sit up. *The key to the safe. I need to keep looking for it.*

The gingashluckaquin quietly opened the HifftYiz's desk drawers in order, even though it knew it would not find the key in any of them. It had already checked each drawer many times before, and the only key that he could find was one that was too small to fit in the safe's lock.

And then it saw something shiny on the desk's writing surface—another key. The HifftYiz had taken it out when he was looking for his seashell collection and had forgotten to return it. Now the gingashluckaquin was bubbling with excitement and nervousness; it had no idea what to expect once it had the seashells' magic.

It carefully opened the HifftYiz's closet and looked inside for the safe, which was behind a stack of blankets— blankets were the only thing in the HifftYiz's closet since he didn't need clothes. The gingashluckaquin carefully turned each number dial to match the combination it suspected was correct, and when it unlocked, the gingashluckaquin turned the key in the lock beneath the number dials.

The safe opened with a *squeak*, revealing the seashell inside. *Finally, I've got what I've deserved all along— immortality and invincibility! Now, I should return to my sewer to activate the shells.* The gingashluckaquin silently floated out of the house without being seen and went back to its sewer. The gingashluckaquin normally went to the sewer to sleep and stayed at 1234 Help Street in the daytime so the HifftYiz would do the gingashluckaquin's chores, but this was a special occasion!

When it was in the sewer, it floated to the exact middle. It had been planned for this day for many years, so a big red X was marked on the floor where the middle of the sewer was.

The gingashluckaquin placed one shell each on each of the X's points. It followed the ceremonial pattern of touching the shells needed to activate them: top left, top right, bottom left, bottom right, etcetera. When it finished, it drew a large circle around all the shells with a stick and waited for the magic to happen.

The reality of what actually happened suddenly came crashing down on the gingashluckaquin. Three shells glowed, but nothing else happened.

The gingashluckaquin jumped so high with surprise that the top of its body hit the sewer's ceiling. If the spell had worked, it would not have gotten hurt because the shells would have made the gingashluckaquin invincible. Instead, it felt a surge of pain. *Ouch, that hurt. Why did this not work? Did I do the taps wrong? But why didn't all the shells glow the way I envisioned it?*

The gingashluckaquin repeated the taps. Three shells glowed again, but the bottom left shell stayed dark—nothing different happened. The gingashluckaquin was about to give up until it realized something.

Wait. That was the shell from the HifftYiz's safe. Now the gingashluckaquin was getting angry. *Was the Seashell of Power FAKE? When I see the HifftYiz next, I will give him what he deserves: death.*

I now have no clue where the real shell is, so I need to find it before the HifftYiz gives it to somebody else. He now knows his life is in danger, so it would make perfect sense how he gave it to somebody else, but who? It can't be Kay. I possessed her already. There are other HifftYizes around here, but the HifftYiz I live with doesn't trust them. Who took the last Seashell of Power, and how will I get it back?

18

The Last Seashell of Power

Two days later, close to midnight

The gingashluckaquin laid awake on the cold cement ground, trying to think of who could have taken the seashell. It had not slept for multiple days, yet it did not feel tired, just angry and confused.

Who took the seashell? I know it wasn't Kay; possessed sharks don't do things like that. The HifftYiz may still have it, but it is unlikely...

Wait! I remember that young shark he mentioned once, the one who saw the letter I sent to the

Earlier that afternoon

The gingashluckaquin burst the door open to the bedroom at 1234 Help Street. It was clearly in a rush to get answers. "HifftYiz. Tell me now. Where does Max live?" the gingashluckaquin asked.

The HifftYiz, who was taking his midday nap, jolted awake, sitting up straight in his bed. "M-Max? Max who?" He was starting to get suspicious of the gingashluckaquin because it usually only went to the sewer to sleep; it had gone there for something. But he decided not to question it. "I have no idea. Go ask someone else." Thankfully, it didn't seem to know about the letter the HifftYiz sent to Max.

"Fine. I guess I'll have to release spiders in the bathroom when you're in there and lock the door." The gingashluckaquin had the worst way of getting what he wanted: threats. It knew that the HifftYiz had a *very* strong fear for spiders.

A strong chemical smell suddenly filled the air. Screaming, a puddle of acid formed around The HifftYiz, tinting the air purple. "Fine! Fine! I'll tell you. He lives on—" The HifftYiz whispered something in the gingashluckaquin's ear, which resembled a lizard's ears in the sense that they were only a hollow part of the gingashluckaquin's skull.

The gingashluckaquin grinned, instantly making the HifftYiz realize he shouldn't have given it Max's address.

The HifftYiz suddenly realized what he had done. *Oh no, Max. I spoiled our secret. I wish you luck—you'll need it.*

Present time

In the gingashluckaquin's sewer

Grabbing a small GPS device from the mess on the cold, stone ground, the gingashluckaquin grabbed a handheld GPS device and ran out of the sewer. It imputed Max's house address into the GPS and morphed into a human-like shape with legs so it could run. Following the address the GPS gave it, the gingashluckaquin ran to the house Max and Jo lived in.

The gingashluckaquin struggled to catch its breath after running so hard. Max's house was large, and it had a porch; the gingashluckaquin stepped onto it as stealthily as it could. But when it did, a board squeaked. "Sssh," the gingashluckaquin whispered to the board. "If Max knows I'm breaking into his house, who knows what he will do?"

The gingashluckaquin opened the door to the house, which was unlocked. Jo had forgotten to lock the door since she and Max had a 'family game night' late into the night and were exhausted by the time 9:00 came, having only bedtime on their minds and nothing else.

The kitchen was surprisingly tidy; Jo and Max were generally messy sharks, but the kitchen was the one thing they tried to keep clean. A carpeted staircase was forward and to the right, and the gingashluckaquin crept up the steps to reveal an upper level with two bedrooms and a bathroom. Jo and Max shared the large bedroom, and Jo used the smaller bedroom as her homework station—sadly, seventh grade meant more homework. The bathroom was on the other side of the hallway.

The gingashluckaquin opened the door to Max and Jo's bedroom, which was easy to spot because the door to their room was labeled with a sign that the sharks had colored with crayons. It assumed if Max had the seashell, the seashell would be in his room.

Jo slept in the bed closest to the air conditioning vent on the left wall, and Max slept in the bed on the right. The gingashluckaquin quietly crept inside the room, making sure to not wake either of the young sharks.

A nightstand was next to Max's bed. His entire body was under the covers except for his head.

The nightstand was relatively tidy, and its surface only had three things: a tissue box, a small light, and a CD player with a CD by the band *The Sqwgamugurtz* next to it. Opening the nightstand's one drawer, which was used to hold a journal, a pencil, and the two letters Max received from the gingashluckaquin and the HifftYiz, the shapeless shadow creature almost gasped out loud. The HifftYiz had sent Max a letter?!

Since the shell was not on or in Max's nightstand, the gingashluckaquin thought it might be in his dresser. It opened the top dresser drawer, which contained Max's socks, underwear, and accessories; the fourth Seashell of Power was not in the first drawer.

The second drawer contained Max's shirts. The gingashluckaquin moved to the third and final drawer, not seeing the last Seashell of Power. It could not see a seashell in the third drawer, even with some rummaging. Now the gingashluckaquin was about to give up.

But before it could do that, the gingashluckaquin noticed something shiny under Max's covers—pulling back the covers, the creature noticed Max was clutching it as he slept. But was it the Seashell of Power?

No way. It's the final Seashell of Power.

Trying to pry out the shell without waking Max up, the gingashluckaquin got a grip on the Seashell of Power and slowly pulled it out. And it almost jumped when it heard Max talking in his sleep, saying something about Jo.

"Jo... why... are... you... awake... this... late... at... night..."

Max's point of view

Suddenly, my eyes opened faster than I thought I had ever opened them before. When I saw what stood above me, I screamed. "WHAT ARE YOU DOING HERE?!?"

"You have something that is mine," the gingashluckaquin replied calmly. It tried to snatch the shell out of my fin, but I slapped it before it could.

My scream must have also woken Jo up, because out of the corner of my eye, I saw her sneakily grab the camera on the bookshelf.

But my attention was shortly diverted back to the gingashluckaquin. "All I need is the last Seashell of Power, and I'll get out of your house," it hissed.

My mood turned stubborn the moment the gingashluckaquin said that. "No. The HifftYiz told me that I should never let you have this. I promised I wouldn't. You're evil, and never getting this Seashell of Power, so you should leave before I get angrier. Besides, why are you even in my house anyway?"

The gingashluckaquin was now also getting stubborn. "Like I said, I'm not getting out until I have that seashell."

"It's the middle of the night. I'm tired, and you probably are too. What about you leave, and I get back to sleep? It's a win-win: I get to go back to sleep, and you get... Well, nothing. But it's still a great idea."

That angered the gingashluckaquin. It rambled on and on about its lifelong obsession with power and the many things it had to do on the grueling quest before showing up in my room randomly when all I wanted to do was to sleep. "Immortality and invincibility have been my dream almost since I was born. Not too many decades ago, I learned about these objects called the Seashells of Power. If a creature had activated all four of them at once, the shells would grant the creature immortality and invincibility.

"I started searching for the seashells, and I found three out of the four after many years of exhausting effort. Later in life, I met the HifftYiz and learned he had the last shell. I tried to steal it, but he resisted, claiming I could only get it by giving him 50 hearts from sharks.

"As soon as I learned this, I tried to collect hearts from not-so-intelligent sharks with the right kinds of hearts. I almost succeeded, but I didn't, and it was very hard to gain the hearts I did have. As you may know, sharks dominate Sharkland for a reason. They could always figure out a way to avoid losing a body part to a poor thing like me. After many months with no success, I was about to give up, but I remembered I could possess someone... err, hire a helper. I chose this ten-year-old shark named Kay. She helped me by convincing sharks that giving their hearts was right.

"Soon, my number of hearts increased to 49—I only needed one more! Soon the last shell would finally be mine! The heart would come from you, Max. The only thing that got in the way was that I could not figure out how to possess you; you are too intelligent. I searched the rest of Sharkland for sharks with the right type of heart and found nothing. I wanted to roam the rest of Dennisatroy for hearts from sharks, but sharks only live on Sharkland.

"But I eventually learned the HifftYiz was lying the whole time—he *never* would have given me the last seashell. I think I beat him up a little too hard-"

I didn't even need to internalize the rest of the speech; the last sentence truly fired me up. "YOU DID WHAT?!?" I screamed so loudly it probably woke up the entire neighborhood.

I shoved the gingashluckaquin off the bed, and it fell onto what would have been its back if it were truly human. I winced but felt no emotion otherwise, except for the anger rising in the pit of my stomach. I stood above the gingashluckaquin, experiencing a feeling of domination as it laid on the floor, complaining about the pain and clutching what would have been its stomach if it were truly human. "Gingashluckaquin, guess what? You don't even deserve the seashell. Sharkland would fall to ruins almost as soon as you came to power. The HifftYiz is doing the right thing ."

"No. I will never give up. What you are holding is mine, and I know you know that deep down. Do you actually believe you, a weak, young shark, can keep the shell from me forever?" The gingashluckaquin stood up. It reached for the seashell but banged what would have been its head if it were truly human against the door instead and let out a shriek.

Knowing it could still do serious damage to me, I rapidly grabbed my pillow from my bed so I could use the pillowcase to carry my things. Under the pillow was a flashlight, which I always kept under the pillow. I also snatched a paper bag by the side of my bed, which bore the words "survival kit"—this contained things such as a few emergency SBucks and my government-issued ID Jo bought for me after the house closed. I had never used the bag before because I had never been in a dangerous situation like this, but now it seemed necessary. I emptied the contents of the "survival kit" into the pillowcase as well as the Seashell of Power and the flashlight.

I knew it would be a terrible—and possibly life-threatening—decision to stay in the room, but the gingashluckaquin blocked the door, so my only possible escape was the window. The screens on the windows were in the process of being replaced, meaning the window had no screen. With only a bit of hesitation, still wearing my pajamas, I opened the window and jumped out, falling for only a few moments until I landed, checking to make sure my pillow was under me. It was a hard landing, but I got back up quickly.

Because I now took the place of a runaway, I now had to figure out where to run to—I decided to run to 1234 Help Street where I hoped the HifftYiz would be, as there was no better place to run to. I had to leave Jo behind, but I hoped the gingashluckaquin wouldn't go after her because I had the seashell, not her.

1234 Help Street was now visible; the HifftYiz had never removed my ability to see it. When I got there, I instantly started running toward the back door—the HifftYiz had said to me he locked only the front door on most occasions. But when I ran over to the door and tested the door handle to see if the door was unlocked, it did not budge.

Before I knew what to do next, I saw Kay walking down the hill toward me, her emerald-green eyes shining in the darkness like a diamond in a sea of slate rocks. I started panicking.

Kay started talking when she reached the door where I was. Her words just sounded *so smooth*, every syllable flowing into the next, reminding me of a creek, but the actual words she spoke reminded me this was not true. "Max, please. Everybody knows the last Seashell of

Power belongs to the gingashluckaquin. If you give it to me, we can be friends again." For a moment, I seemed to have fallen under her spell, but I snapped out of it shortly. *That's NOT how friendship works,* I mentally corrected her.

I was scared, yet I knew Kay would still be possessed even if I gave her the last Seashell of Power. But I also felt bad for the poor shark; this had done so much damage to her brain. As I considered what to do next, I thought about the seashells and how I should get them away from the gingashluckaquin. *I could crush the seashell, but all of the seashells are linked magically, and destroying them might cause damage. The best option is to go inside somehow and grab the rest of the seashells—I don't know exactly where they are, but they're probably in the bedroom somewhere. But how should I get inside, and how should I keep Kay from stopping me?*

Oh, I know! If I gave her a fake Seashell of Power, she would be distracted trying to find the gingashluckaquin, at least for a little while. The HifftYiz gave me the fake today after I came to his house for a second time. I reached inside the pillowcase to find the fake Seashell of Power. Making sure to hide the real shell, I found the fake shell in the pillowcase; Kay would become suspicious if she saw me holding two almost identical seashells.

"Fine. You win. Here is the last Seashell of Power. Take it to the gingashluckaquin."

Kay's eyes rapidly changed color from an emerald green to a fiery red—although Kay did not know it was the fake seashell, she thought it was real. *How can eyes even change color like that? I thought genetics controlled eye color.* Kay ran up the hill.

I continued trying to open the door. I pushed, and...

...the door opened. The door's mechanism was simply jammed.

When I shined my flashlight inside, I saw a set of stairs leading to the HifftYiz's and gingashluckaquin's bedroom. Creeping up the stairs, I noticed that the HifftYiz wasn't there, nor were many of his things—where had he gone? Like I had seen before, a piece of tape divided the two sides of the room, but I also noticed a nightstand was next to the gingashluckaquin's bed. A safe was on that nightstand.

Because the safe had three glass windows, I saw three seashells inside the safe—not only were they in a locked safe, there were three of them. I could easily open the safe by breaking the glass. *What a bad design for a safe. Not only can I see inside it, but I can open it super easily by smashing it with something—maybe a knife. Wait! I have a knife!* I located my multitool from inside the pillowcase, and I unfolded the sharpest blade I had, which was still not very sharp, but I hoped it would work for the moment.

I considered myself nice, so I hesitated to break the safe open, but I quickly solved that problem by reminding myself of how much the gingashluckaquin angered me and how evil it was. Feeling the rage and hate bubbling up inside me like a bomb that was about to explode, I seized the knife in my right fin and thrust it into the glass like a remodeler tearing down a wall with a sledgehammer. The glass shattered instantly, awarding me easy access to the Seashells of Power that were inside. *The gingashluckaquin can deal with this mess later, but for now, I need to focus on making sure it isn't able to access these seashells anymore.*

I snatched the three seashells that were inside the safe. All three had a red dot on the back, proving they were the real deal. I dropped them into my pillowcase, making sure to separate them so they wouldn't activate themselves— I didn't want to live forever! I tied the pillowcase closed with the twine in my survival kit so the shells would stay inside.

I was now ready to leave the gingashluckaquin's room, but first I needed to look out the window and check that no shark was outside the door, especially Kay. If she or anybody else caught me trespassing, I would be in *big* trouble! I saw the stairs leading from the upper level to the main level. Nobody was on the stairs.

Somebody was in the kitchen, though. It appeared they had red eyes. It was Kay. *Oh no. I need to leave quickly, and without Kay noticing me.*

I could always jump out the window, but I'm not too excited to do that again. That was painful. I need to escape via the bedroom's main door, but how should I do that without Kay noticing? She's in the kitchen right now.

Kay *was*, in fact, in the kitchen. Squinting in an attempt to see what Kay was doing, it appeared like she was spreading peanut butter on graham crackers while sipping an energy drink. *Wait, what?? Kay stole my favorite after-school snack!!* But I knew she would finish eating soon. I silently opened the door to the gingashluckaquin's bedroom, not bothering to close it since it was open when I first walked in, and tip-finned down the first stair step.

Suddenly, I stepped on the wrong part of the stair, and it squeaked. *Uh oh.* Kay turned around. Her bright red eyes shone in the dark. "What was that?" she mouthed.

I ducked underneath the railing. Kay would see me if it was daytime, but it was past midnight and very dark—Kay didn't see me! She turned around, stuck the knife back into the peanut butter jar, and spreaded a dollop of peanut butter onto her second graham cracker, not knowing I was there.

Kay took the last bite out of her second graham cracker a few minutes later. Rinsing the plate in the sink and putting it inside the dishwasher, she was done and probably about to come up the stairs. I panicked.

Taking advantage of the louder noise caused by the running water, I sneaked down the rest of the stairs and hid behind a stack of blankets. When Kay started going up the stairs to the gingashluckaquin's and HifftYiz's bedroom, I ran out of the house as fast as possible.

When I reached the backyard, I quietly opened the door to the basement, grabbed a blanket from the bin as sneakily as possible, exited the house, and laid it on the ground.

While a while had passed since I had last seen the gingashluckaquin, I did not know if it was still in my room. Therefore, I decided it was best to sleep outside, just to be safe. And while I was angry how I even needed to sleep outside in the first place (if the gingashluckaquin hadn't come, I could have been lying in my comfy bed!), which I had never done before, I reminded myself of all the things that *could have* happened, but didn't.

I could have died.

I could have accidentally given the real *seashell to Kay instead of the fake one.*

I could have given up and gave the Seashell of Power to the gingashluckaquin.

I could have not survived the fall.
But I didn't.

Since I was so tired, I fell asleep within a few minutes.

Part 3

Returning to Wah

19

What I've Done So Far

I awoke the morning after to Jo's whispering in my ear. "Wake up, Max. It's nine o'clock, and we have an appointment with the museum in less than an hour."

I was still groggy, so I didn't quite know what Jo was talking about. *Nine o'clock? Appointment with the museum? Huh? I should have gone to Sharkschool by now!* I thought. "What? It's Monday! And we should be at Sharkschool right now! We're late! Also, what museum appointment? I'm confused."

Jo stayed calm. "I will explain. When I woke up this morning around seven thirty, I called Sharkschool to fill out a late arrival request after receiving a letter from the museum, so we won't be marked as late for school today. The letter wondered if the museum could create an exhibit for the Seashells of Power, and they wanted a response as quick as possible so I scheduled an appointment. I probably should have asked you first, but I knew you went through a lot last night, so I decided to let you sleep. I also overheard you saying yesterday that you wanted to get rid of the Seashells Of Power without causing trouble."

This made sense to me. "Yeah, I did say that. You made the right decision, but how does the museum know about the Seashells of Power?" I asked. "Yesterday, I saw you grabbing your video camera off your shelf; does it have something to do with that? Did you take a video?"

"Yes, I did," Jo replied. "Shortly after I woke up this morning, a neighbor knocked on the door. She asked me what all the noise the previous night was about, so I showed her the video and gave her a copy of it. I think she shared the video with more sharks, because we sort of literally became famous overnight. Also, I think the gingashluckaquin died last night."

I didn't know what to say. So Jo responded for me. "You're welcome."

"Wait, did the gingashluckaquin *actually* die?" I wondered.

"Come with me," Jo simply stated. She opened the door to the basement and walked inside, and I followed her.

She was right. A pool of blood was on the carpet in my and Jo's bedroom, right next to my bed. It was *disgusting*, yet I felt so relieved and safe now that the gingashluckaquin wasn't around anymore, and I knew the blood would come out of the carpet if Jo and I worked hard enough to clean it up. "Jo, what happened when I left? Were you attacked by the gingashluckaquin? Did you stay safe? I didn't mean to put you in danger by leaving."

Jo thought for a moment. "Don't worry, Max. Although the gingashluckaquin attacked me at first and tried to make me say where you were going, I think I did a good job making it believe I genuinely had no idea. Of course, I assumed you were going to 1234 Help Street to look for the HifftYiz, but the gingashluckaquin didn't know that. So, after a while, it left. And Max, don't worry. That's what you needed to do to stay alive. Besides, the gingashluckaquin's dead now, right? You did what was necessary."

"Thanks, Jo." I was relieved how the evil shadow monster didn't torture Jo *too* much.

Jo went back downstairs and started preparing breakfast. Meanwhile, I stayed in the room, opening my drawer and grabbing my day clothes. I changed, then walked downstairs to the kitchen, where Jo prepared cereal with berries for herself.

When I got to the kitchen, she handed me a bowl of peanut butter oatmeal topped with banana slices. "Here you go, Max! I made your favorite breakfast!"

"Oh my gosh, Jo! Thank you so much!" Peanut butter and banana had recently become my favorite food combo, especially when it was in oatmeal.

It took us about twenty minutes to finish eating breakfast, brushing our teeth, and getting out the door, plus an extra ten-ish minutes to arrive at the museum's entrance we were supposed to enter. A guard stood by the door. "What do you want?" the guard asked grumpily.

Jo's tone was bright and cheery, completely opposite to the guard's tone. "Hi! I'm Josephene Brime, and this is Maxamil Alderin."

"Hello. You had an appointment scheduled for nine thirty, right?" The guard checked a device he held. "Do you have identification? You cannot enter without it."

Thankfully, Jo already had the IDs ready. "Yeah, we do. Here they are."

The guard examined the IDs. "Thank you. You may enter."

"Hello, Max Alderin and Jo Brime!" one staff member exclaimed when we got inside.

"Hi!" I expressed.

"Hello!" Jo added.

"We're very pleased you're here. We have already chosen a display case for those four magical seashells," the staff member informed, pointing to a glass display case that was big for the seashells' small size. It consisted of a glass box set atop a wooden stand. "What do you think? Is it a good fit?"

"I like it!" Jo and I exclaimed in unison. We placed the shells inside the case. "It looks good!"

The staff member continued. "Now, the team and I are considering making a sign telling visitors what makes these different from normal seashells found at the beach. Would you mind giving me a brief summary of what these are, what they do, and maybe some of their history?"

I thought for a moment. "Hmm... I honestly don't know much about these. Would you mind if I just told you the whole story?"

"Not at all."

"Thanks." I started my "brief" summary. "Alright, put simply, these seashells are unique because whoever has all four of them is granted immortality and invincibility. A shadow-like creature called the gingashluckaquin had obtained three of the four. The gingashluckaquin lived with another creature part-time, called the HifftYiz—nobody knows why they lived together since they both hated each other to death, quite literally, but they still did.

"The gingashluckaquin thought the HifftYiz had made a deal with it. If the gingashluckaquin gave the HifftYiz 50 shark hearts, it would get the last Seashell of Power. Well, the HifftYiz was storing the Seashell of Power in a safe in his closet, but the HifftYiz had replaced the shell with a one that looked like it and put the real shell somewhere else. To open the safe, one needed a key and a combination.

"The gingashluckaquin eventually learned the safe's combination. And one day, it found the safe's key, too. So it was able to access the fake Seashell of Power. Now that the gingashluckaquin thought it had all four, it tried to activate them using a series of taps.

"The taps did not work, so the gingashluckaquin tried to figure out a way to locate the real Seashell of Power. It somehow knew my address, so it snuck into my room yesterday in the middle of the night to find the shell. Noticing I was holding the shell while I slept, it tried to pry the shell out of my fins, but thankfully, I woke up. I ended up escaping through my bedroom window and running to the HifftYiz's and gingashluckaquin's house. The HifftYiz had become my friend, and I wanted to see if he was there—he wasn't—but I also went to the house to collect the other three Seashells of Power.

"The only thing keeping me from entering the house was a shark named Kay, who knew what I was trying to do. The gingashluckaquin had possessed Kay earlier in the year and turned her into its servant. She stopped me and demanded I give her the shell, so I took out the fake one and gave it to her. She was distracted with it, meaning I could go inside and grab the shells.

"In the bedroom, I broke the safe with a knife, grabbed the other three Seashells of Power, and tried to get out of the house, but Kay was back by then. So when she wasn't looking, I crept out of the house and ran back to my house. Then I fell asleep on the grass in the backyard."

Kay's point of view

When Kay woke up earlier that morning

I woke up from a light sleep. Looking around, I realized I was lying in an open field near a playground. *How did I get here?* I wondered.

That's when I remembered.

Something felt very different, but in a good way. The gingashluckaquin was dead. That meant all the sharks it possessed were free, including me. All the sharks who died from no hearts were living again. Magic can't kill you completely; it can kill your body, but never your soul.

The night before, I never found the gingashluckaquin. Every day when I was possessed, I fell asleep when the gingashluckaquin did and woke up when it woke up. It had not slept for a few days, so I had not either.

I eventually realized the seashell was fake at about one o'clock in the morning when I examined it again. By that time early in the morning, I had switched my focus to finding Max and punishing him, but that never happened because I suddenly collapsed. It was the moment the gingashluckaquin died. And now that I had woken up, I felt a lot happier. My eyes were blue again. I would no longer follow every command the gingashluckaquin gave me. It never should have lived. I cannot believe it managed to control me for that long. What a waste of time.

I was going to get up, find Max, and apologize to him, but I had only slept for five hours. I laid back down and slipped into a deep sleep.

20

The HifftYiz, Part 3

Opening my eyes the next morning, I saw Jo standing over me and felt her rubbing my belly to wake me up. She didn't normally have to do this, but I was so tired this morning that she had to. It was about 7:30 AM. "Max, it's time to wake up! Please get dressed quickly, because we're going to be late for Sharkschool if we don't go fast."

"Okay," I responded, still groggy.

I was dressed and in the kitchen less than two minutes later. Jo was already downstairs at the table eating SharkBites cereal. She seemed to be sorting

through a stack of letters, and she was reading one.
"Max!" Jo suddenly said. She sounded sad.

"What?" I asked, curious.

"Read this," she replied. She handed me a letter,
which only used a half-sheet of paper. This one was
typed out instead of hand-written. I read the paper.

Dear Max Alderin,

I am aware you and the HifftYiz have formed a strong
friendship. Right now, I am writing with a heavy heart to tell
you that he has sadly passed away. When he gave you the
Seashell of Power, he lost ownership of a powerful,
magic-filled object, and when that happens, sometimes
HifftYizes, or any creatures on Sharkland, can die because of
the sudden loss of the body's magic. I invite you to his funeral
on Thursday at noon. It will take place at his house at 1234
Help Street.

With grief, Mother of the HifftYiz.

After reading the letter, I felt a strange feeling,
one I had never felt before. It was a mix of loneliness,
grief, and this other feeling that could only be described
as a question ("Is reincarnation real? If so, what will the
HifftYiz come back as?"). Since Sunday the previous
week, the HifftYiz and I had become great friends—we
trusted each other and helped each other with our
struggles.

Strangely, though, there was this one feeling I had not expected to feel: relief.

I hadn't known the HifftYiz for long, but it seemed like he had to endure a lot of suffering just to get by. With the gingashluckaquin constantly abusing and threatening him, and with the gingashluckaquin making the HifftYiz do its chores even at his very old age, the HifftYiz seemed to live a very hard life. It was damaging to my emotions and his heart. Sadly, letting go of life may have been best for him.

Jo got me out of my head with a question. "I'm so sorry your friend passed away! Are you thinking of going to his funeral on Thursday?"

"Thank you, Jo. Yeah, I'd really like to go to his funeral on Thursday. Wait... isn't *today* Thursday??"

Jo thought for a moment. "Oh, my gosh. Yeah, today IS Thursday! We better get going! I'll call Sharkschool to fill out a request to leave school at 11:45. In the meantime, please find an outfit to wear to change into after school. It should be somewhat formal, meaning no T-shirts and sweatpants. If you have a suit, that would look great."

"Okay." I ran upstairs and grabbed my nicest black suit, then folded it and placed it in my backpack.

The funeral was one of the saddest, most beautiful funerals I'd ever attended.

21

Jo Reunites With Her Mom

Approximately three days later

I was watching TV on the couch with Jo when I suddenly heard a knock on the door, causing me to jump.

I stood up and walked to the door. In the past few days, *so* many journalist and sales-sharks had knocked on that door, and if yet another shark was trying to get info on how I defeated the gingashluckaquin—

But I didn't even need to think about journalists or sales-sharks, because the shark who stood outside looked like neither of those. She wasn't holding any microphones or cameras, and only a minivan was parked in the street. She looked friendly overall.

"I think it's fine if we open the door," Jo suggested, who had randomly appeared behind me. She opened the door, and much to my surprise, the shark came in, dropped to her knees, and sobbed.

Jo's eyes widened. "Mom?! What are you doing here?!" Jo said with an annoyed tone of voice. Getting a better look at the sobbing female shark, I noticed she was covered with cuts and scrapes, her clothing was shabby and covered with dirt, and she desperately needed a shower. And apparently, she was Jo's mom. Questions bubbling up inside me, I couldn't help wondering what happened to her.

But even though this shark was apparently Jo's mom, Jo did *not* seem happy to see her, and she was angry, and I did not see her angry very often. "Would you please mind explaining why you ABANDONED ME when I was only FOUR YEARS OLD?"

"Please. Just let me explain," the shark said in between sobs. "There was a reason I had been acting strange the week before I disappeared. I received this letter from this suspicious address—1234 Help Street—describing this job opportunity for many SBucks. I can't remember since it was so long ago, but I think it was ℬ50 SBucks per hour, which you may know is *a lot* of money. I hesitantly called the number listed at the bottom of the letter.

"I was kidnapped when I went to that house the next night, and somebody explained that this meanie monster called the gingashluckaquin lived in a stinky sewer. When the gingashluckaquin learned that a creature called The HifftYiz was living in a house at 1234 Help Street, it decided to move in because it figured it could make the HifftYiz like its personal servant, and the HifftYiz would buy everything for the gingashluckaquin such as groceries and the house loan. Besides, the HifftYiz acted evil, just like the gingashluckaquin. They could become good friends.

"Little did the gingashluckaquin know that the HifftYiz only *acted* like he was evil—he secretly helped me escape from that awful place that was like a prison. I had almost no money, and I had no home, but I immediately started searching for you, Jo. I was living in my car for the next year and a half. I eventually learned where you lived, but I was too nervous to return to your house because I didn't know how I would apologize.

"Yesterday, there was a newspaper on somebody's doorstep with you in the headline, Max, and the story mentioned you, Jo. It caught my attention, so I read the story on the front page since it did not appear that anybody was home—I wish my future self luck apologizing to them if they ask why I stole their newspaper. After I finished reading the article, I decided it was finally time to come and apologize.

"That is also why I had disappeared from the house, but my things were still there. I remember thinking it was just a normal job, so I left everything at home except for my laptop and savings money, which the gingashluckaquin took. But the HifftYiz found the laptop and its charger and gave them to me as I escaped. Even though the model is now very old, I thought you should have it, Jo. It might be helpful for your day-to-day life."

Tears welled up in Jo's eyes. She ran over and hugged her mom. "Well, I forgive you, Mom. I'm so sorry the gingashluckaquin treated you so badly."

When they finished hugging, which took a while, Jo suddenly ran upstairs to the attic, returning with a heavy- looking stack of boxes. "By the way, I saved your things, not knowing if you would return home."

Jo's mom stared at the boxes, not knowing what to think. "I— I don't know what to say." Jo blushed. An awkward silence fell over the room.

And Jo's next question was vaguely unexpected. "Do you think you could live with us?"

Jo's mom did not expect Jo to ask a question like this. "I— I— I— I would love that!!"

"Well, Max, what do you think?" Jo asked me.

I thought for a moment. "Well, I'm not the best shark to ask right now since I have to return to Wah tomorrow."

As soon as I finished my sentence, Jo started crying again. We all sat in silence until I broke the silence by asking Jo what was wrong.

"Jo, are you okay?"

Jo said nothing. Tears welled in her eyes, and she wrapped her arms around me. "Max. I'll miss you so, so much!"

This made me start crying, too. "I'll miss you so much too, Jo!" I paused. "If only there were some way I could contact you from Wah, or even better, if there was some device that would make me able to visit again…"

Jo interrupted me. "Wait! I might have something that could help solve those problems. I'm not quite sure if I still have it, but I remember I was once given this magical phone device for my birthday that allowed two sharks worlds apart to call each other, and it even could let one shark teleport. It might be broken, but I'm going to go see if I still have it. I never used it—I never needed it."

After Jo ran upstairs, I noticed Jo's mom was awkwardly standing by the door.

She knew I was looking at her, so she introduced herself. "Hi, Max. I'm Katrina."

Oh, so Katrina was her name! "Hi, Katrina! Did you hear what Jo went upstairs for? She was talking *really* fast."

"I think she said she's going upstairs to grab a device. I think she also said it was something that would let you return here whenever you like..."

I still didn't know quite what Jo was grabbing, but now I was *excited*! "Thank you!" I said to a confused Katrina, not even looking back.

I ran up the stairs to the top floor, where the ladder to the attic was. When I realized I had just left Jo's mom downstairs by herself, I climbed back down a few steps. "Sorry if we didn't make it clear enough, but you're very welcome here! You can sit on the couch if you like. We also have snacks in the kitchen if you're hungry."

"Thanks!" Katrina replied. Before I ran back up the stairs, I saw her walk to the kitchen and grab a bag of freeze-dried strawberries off the counter, then walk to the couch and collapse on it.

I continued up the stairs to the attic, but suddenly, I heard a bang, which made me halt. "Jo! Are you okay?"

Since the door to the attic was closed, I could not see Jo, but I could hear her. "Better than I've been since my mom left!" Jo shouted. "I mean, Max, you're awesome, and I'm not trying to say you're not, and you've made my life a lot better since you came. It's just that it's extremely difficult to be unsure whether your mom is alive or not for eight years."

Now I felt terrible for Jo—I had no idea she'd been without a mom for eight years. "Thank you Jo for saying I've made your life better—that means a lot to me. But I will never begin to know how painful it must have been. It's great how you feel better now!"

I opened the door to the very dusty and odd-smelling attic and looked around.

22

The Sleepover

I saw Jo bent over a box. She did not seem to notice me, so I called out to her. "Jo!"

It took a few seconds for her to respond. "What?"

"Do you need help?"

Now Jo turned around to look at me. "That would be great. I would love it if you could help look in these boxes." She pointed to a stack of about three or four small cardboard boxes.

"Okay," I replied, sorting through the first box. I did not know what this device looked like, but I figured I would know if I found it.

All of a sudden, we heard a snort. I couldn't tell where it was coming from, but it sounded *very* familiar...

"Jo, what was that?" I whispered.

Jo looked around the room as if she was trying to find the source of the noise. The thing snorted again—now I could tell it was coming from the back of the attic, inside the closet.

"I'm not sure, but it's coming from the closet," Jo noticed. "I'm going to check it out, what about you?"

"Sure..." I was a bit scared, but I followed Jo as she quietly walked to the closet. "SNORT!" went the noise again; I told myself I was brave and slowly opened the door.

When I opened the door, I was so surprised that I actually jumped back in surprise. Mary and Anny were inside the closet, and I couldn't believe it. "MARY?! ANNY?! You're still alive?! And you're still in sqwgamugurtz form?!" The sqwgamugurtz both snorted.

While I was surprised and *very* confused, I told myself I was brave again after a few seconds of awkward silence, which helped me feel less scared. Walking up to the large animals, I put my left fin on Mary and my right fin on Anny. I prepared myself to ask them how they'd been, but a bright flash of light stopped me—the light was so bright that closing my eyes didn't even help.

Everything was blurry when the light faded, and all I could see were blurry outlines of three sharks. "Jo? Are you still here?"

"Yeah, I'm here," Jo responded. "But what happened? How did you turn Mary and Anny back into sharks like that? That's so cool!"

Wait, what? "I turned Mary and Anny into—OMG! Woah, I can't believe I just did that! I guess touching them must have turned them back."

Jo stared at me, in awe. "Woah. That's *so cool.*"

"Thanks."

Because Mary and Anny probably hadn't had fins for a few months by now, they almost fell over, but Jo helped steady them. While they stared at each other in shock about their new shark bodies, I continued searching through the boxes until I suddenly found something. I wasn't sure what it was, but because it was small and had a piece of paper taped to the back, I had a feeling it was the device Jo was talking about. "Jo, is this what you were looking for?"

Jo examined the device. "Yay, thank you, Max! This is the right thing! I guess I *didn't* get rid of it, after all, but it hasn't ever been used, and there are some things we'll need to do before we can use it. But we can use the mini-workshop over there and the manual! Mary and Anny could help, too."

Anny, who had forgotten she now had the power of speech, snorted in agreement. When she remembered how to speak, though, she translated, "Err... cool!!!"

"Thanks!" Mary added, learning from Anny.

"You're welcome!" Jo exclaimed and giggled. She walked to the back of the attic and found a table with five ancient-looking chairs and many different tools, such as a drill, screwdrivers, bins of nails and screws, and a few types of glues. Jo, who was looking at the table, stated, "Wow. I remember seeing this table when Max and I moved in a few weeks ago, but I forgot the old owners left all this here!"

"Well, this is AWESOME, so I'm happy the old owners left it all," Anny added, pulling out one of the chairs. But when she tried to sit down, the chair collapsed.

"Oops, I guess the chairs are older than I thought," Jo noticed. "Well, I guess you might have to stand, Anny. But anyway, the manual says the first step is to remove the plastic tab on the back of the device."

After Jo tightened the last screw, I assembled the last part, and Mary spoke the last word of encouragement, we were finally finished with all ten steps of the process. "Yay! We're done!" Jo exclaimed.

"Wow, that's great!" Anny replied. "What time is it?"

Jo checked her watch. "Wow. It's 7:06. I'm sorry, but I usually start getting ready for bed around this time, and I think we should put the tools away and go back downstairs."

"I like that idea," I responded.

When we were done putting the tools away, Jo opened the door to the attic, and everybody climbed down the ladder.

Katrina was asleep on the couch with an almost-empty bag of freeze-dried strawberries and empty glass of water by her side. Her fingers were coated with red strawberry powder. She had changed her clothes using what she had found in the box that Jo brought downstairs. *Wow, Katrina must have been hungry. I'm pretty sure the bag of freeze-dried strawberries was unopened before she arrived.* "Mary and Anny, it's time for Max and I to get ready for bed. Do you two have somewhere to go?" Jo asked.

Anny jumped in so quickly she almost interrupted Jo. "Wait! Can Mary and I stay here for the night? We were previously under the gingashluckaquin's control, but it died. Being the small-minded sqwgamugurtz that we were, our instinct was just to get out of there, and we somehow ended up here. We now have nowhere to stay!!"

"Wow, Anny. You make it sound like being homeless is the best thing ever," Mary said with an annoyed tone of voice.

"Yeah, it would be alright for you two to stay here. We can set up the two-person air mattress in the guest bedroom. The only problem is that the guest bedroom is currently my homework station. I never expected it, but there is a lot of homework in seventh grade."

"Thank you! You're the best!" Anny squealed in delight.

I told the twins about bedtime. "Well, let's get ready for bed. Jo and I have a few extra toothbrushes you two can use. We don't have any pajamas that would fit you, Mary and Anny, so you might have to sleep in your clothes, unless you see any pajamas in the donation pile downstairs that fit you. You're welcome to wear those for tonight if they fit. We have extra bedding, and you two can use it, and if you get cold, we have a stack of extra blankets in the basement family room. We'll bring those up, too."

"Okay! Thank you so much for letting us stay the night!" Mary exclaimed.

"You're welcome!" Jo and I said in unison. Jo disappeared down the stairs to the basement, returning a bit later with a stack of fuzzy blankets. "I'll go bring these blankets to the guest bedroom," she informed me.

"Wait!" I interrupted.

"What?" Jo asked.

"Instead of Mary and Anny *just* staying the night, I think it would be awesome to turn this into a sleepover. Just letting Mary and Anny sleep here is *boring*, and we haven't seen Mary and Anny in a long time, so it might be a good opportunity for us to hang out and catch up on life."

Jo considered this. "I like that idea! Mary and Anny, what do you think?"

"Now that you mention it, a sleepover sounds fun," Anny thought out loud.

"I'm excited already!" Mary exclaimed.

I considered ways to make it work. "Are you two okay sharing a bed? Jo and I can share a bed so you two can sleep in the other. I'll put the bedding back since there's already bedding on my bed."

"That sounds great!" Anny said. "Mary and I used to share a bed, like, every day before we turned into sqwgamugurtz." I walked up the stairs to the large bedroom. Jo, Mary, and Anny followed me.

"Okay, let's all get ready for bed first—since it'll be a sleepover, we'll probably stay up later than usual. I'll get two extra toothbrushes from the closet. Max, it would be great if you helped set up Mary and Anny's bed for tonight."

I agreed. "Okay, I'll do that."

Jo walked over to the closet. I walked over to the bedroom that Jo and I shared, and the twins followed me. "Which bed do you want to use?" I asked them.

"Which bed would you recommend we choose?" Mary asked.

I thought about this. "If I were you, I would choose the bed on the right; Jo's bed gets kind of cold sometimes because of the air-conditioning vent next to it."

"That's a valid reason. I agree with Max. Do you agree?" Anny asked Mary.

"I agree too."

"Alright. How many blankets should we put on the bed? Two, maybe?"

"That's a good idea," Mary replied. "We can pull one blanket up and leave the other two at the end of the bed."

"I like that idea too," Anny agreed.

Mary placed two of the blankets on the bed and the extra blankets on the ground next to the bed.

Suddenly, Jo emerged from the bathroom. "Hi, y'all! "Once you're done discussing the placements of the blankets, it's time to get ready for bed." She noticed that the time was now approaching 7:30. "Would anybody like snacks, like popcorn or candy?"

Mary didn't hesitate. "Ooh, I just *love* Galaxy Bars!" she exclaimed.

"Buttered movie-theater-style popcorn is *the best*," Anny added.

"Great! I'll make popcorn. I think we might have Galaxy Bars in the cupboard downstairs, too. Mary and Anny, do you want to go to the game closet in the basement to see if there are any games you would like to play?"

"You have games?! That's awesome!" Mary stated. "Anny, let's go look for games in the basement!"

I wondered what Galaxy Bars were, but I decided not to question because they sounded delicious. Following Jo downstairs, I opened a cupboard to the right of me—sure enough, inside the cupboard, there was a cardboard box with many candy bars inside.

Mary, who stopped at the kitchen before going to the game closet downstairs, read the box: "'Six-Inch Long Bars! Perfect For Sleepovers!'" She paused. "Sounds disgusting," she said sarcastically. Everybody laughed because Mary said she loved Galaxy Bars.

Before I could even grab the box from the cupboard, Mary beat me to it and snatched two of the bars inside. She sniffed the bars, forgetting that there was a wrapper that made it harder to smell the heaven-like food, and sighed. "Six inches of gooey caramel and melt-in-your-mouth milk chocolate. Not something you eat every day. Say, why do you even have these in the first place? I mean, it's not a bad thing. I LOVE these. But why do you have so many of them?"

Jo knew the answer. "I originally bought them for Max, but I remember wondering if Max was allergic to dairy, and I forgot to ask, so I put them in the cupboard instead. I guess you could say that we just forgot about them," Jo replied from the other end of the kitchen.

"Oh," Mary realized. "Anyway, Mary and I should go choose games."

"Alright!" Jo acknowledged. "I'll make your popcorn, Anny. Do you like a little butter or a lot of butter?"

Before following Mary and disappearing down the basement stairs, Anny told Jo, "As much as possible. I

LOVE butter!! Err, please." When Jo nodded in response, she went to the basement with Mary.

Meanwhile, I stayed in the kitchen with Jo and watched her making Anny's popcorn. I took in the amazing smells of corn kernels being heated in a small amount of oil and rapidly expanding when they reached the right temperatures. It smelled *so good.*

Mary and Anny returned only a few minutes later holding a heavy-looking stack of twenty or so board games. Jo wasn't quite done with Anny's popcorn yet, but I could tell she was getting close. "Wow, Mary. You and Anny sure like a lot of games!" I observed.

Mary laughed. "Oh, yeah. Before Anny and I were possessed, we would play board games at least once a week, so we quickly knew which ones our favorites were."

"Should we bring all of them upstairs, just to have options?' Anny wondered.

Jo thought this was a good idea. "That would be great! I'm excited to play them tonight."

Mary and Anny had just returned from multiple trips to bring the games upstairs. And almost at the same time, Katrina, who had just woken up, appeared in the kitchen. "Hello," she said groggily.

Jo's eyes brightened. "Hi! How did you sleep?"

"It was the best sleep I've had in a very long time— your couch is *so* comfortable! Wait, what are *your* names?" Katrina was talking to Anny and Mary.

Anny answered first. "We're Mary and Anny, and we're both ten years old. Actually, we're twins. We're friends with Jo and Max, and to make a long story *much* shorter, we appeared in a closet, and Max found us because we were honking, I guess."

Katrina laughed. "That's funny."

Anny introduced herself. "I'm Anny. I like the band The Sqwgamugurtz. I can also be crazy sometimes."

Wait, Anny liked The Sqwgamugurtz too? "No way! They're my favorite band!! What's your favorite song from them?" I chimed in.

Anny thought for a moment. "Hmm. I honestly love all their songs, but I think Dance Your Fins Off from their first album is my favorite!" she informed me.

Wow, Anny and I were more alike than I thought! "That's so cool! I think Dance Your Fins Off is my favorite song, too. I had no idea you liked The Sqwgamugurtz too!"

"Thanks," Anny said, smiling.

Mary introduced herself next. "I'm Mary. A fun fact about me is that my favorite color is light blue." Mary paused. "And *my* favorite band is Bad Roaming Animals. Anny and I argue a lot about the best band."

"That's cool! I haven't heard of either one, but I'm sure they're both great. Nice to meet you, Anny!" Katrina shook Anny's fin. "And nice to meet you too, Mary!

"Thank you!" Mary replied.

"Oh, hello!" Anny remarked.

"By the way, I'm Katrina, and I'm Jo's mom. It's cool how you, Mary, Max, and Jo are having a sleepover!"

I chimed in. "Thanks! Yeah, I'm not meaning to brag, but Mary and Anny have nowhere to stay, so I had the idea to make it fun and turn it into a sleepover. Since this sleepover is about seeing old friends again, it would be cool if you could join, too! Well, if Jo says yes—besides you, she's the oldest one here, so she's kind of like a parent figure to us."

"That would be awesome! Thanks, Max!"

Next, I asked the others what they thought of my idea. "Mary, Anny, and Jo, what do you think of Katrina joining the sleepover?"

"That would be amazing!! Oh my gosh, why didn't I think of that before?" Anny exclaimed.

Jo didn't respond to the question, but she changed the subject. "Anny, your popcorn is ready! I followed your request and used as much butter as possible. And we will have a ton of extras, so you can get some if you want it. Katrina, if you want anything, there's popcorn, or I can get you something else."

"Nah, I think I'll be okay. Those freeze-dried strawberries are *so* good," Katrina said. Everybody laughed.

"So *that's* how so much of the bag managed to disappear," I joked. Everybody laughed.

Looking down at her bowl of popcorn, Anny noticed how it had turned a bright yellow from all the butter. "Wow. That's a lot of butter."

"Well, you *did* ask for as much butter as possible," Jo reminded Anny.

Anny tasted a piece. "But it's the best popcorn I've ever tasted, though—*mmm*. Thank you."

"You're welcome!" Jo replied.

"Anyway, should we go upstairs and play some of the awesome games Mary and Anny brought up?" I asked.

"Yeah!!" Jo exclaimed.

"I agree with Jo," Katrina added.

So did Anny. "Me three."

"Me four," Mary commented.

It didn't take long for all of us, the games, and the food to sprawl across the floor in Jo and I's bedroom. And once everybody was settled in, we were faced with the question about what game to play. "Which game should we play first?" I asked. "I want to play 'Sinking Ships'."

"I want to play 'Squirrel Mania!'" Anny suggested, stealing a handful of Anny's popcorn.

"But I want to play 'Tabasha,'" Mary requested.

"I think we should play 'Frying Frenzy' first," Jo politely mentioned.

"I don't have a preference over what game we play first," Katrina commented. "I do want to play Hide Starter sometime, though."

Anny thought for a moment. "Oh, yeah! I like Hide Starter too."

"Beginning with Hide Starter is fine with me," Mary changed her mind.

"I agree," Anny replied after she finished chewing.

I shared my opinion after Anny. "As for me, well, I have no idea what Hide Starter is, so somebody will have to explain it to me, but I think it sounds like a fun game."

"Yay!" said Katrina. "I'm excited."

"I can explain," Jo informed me. "The goal of this game is to find the hidden object, but the seeker will walk around, and if they see you, you're eliminated. The shark who finds the object first wins the game. I'll start as the seeker so Max can learn how the game works."

I understood this. "Oh. So it's kind of like hide 'n seek, but with an object we need to find?"

"Well, I never lived on Wah, but if that sounds right, it probably is," Katrina mentioned.

"Okay," Jo said. "Everybody, close your eyes. I'm going to hide the object. This is what the object looks like. It glows, and it is colored blue." Everybody nodded in understanding. "I believe the boundaries should be every room on the main and upper levels; do you all agree?"

"Those boundaries seem reasonable to me!" Katrina agreed. Everybody nodded in agreement.

I closed my eyes and pictured the object in my mind. Meanwhile, Jo ran out of the room—she was going to another room to hide the object.

She returned in a very short amount of time. "All right, everybody, the object has been hidden. You may hide. I'll give you 20 seconds to hide. 1, 2, 3, 4, 5..." Jo continued counting.

Everybody instantly ran out of the room, including me—I ran downstairs to the mud closet and hid between two coats. Meanwhile, I heard Jo run into the kitchen.

When her caudal fin-steps became inaudible, I emerged from the mud closet and ran into the living room. But there was Jo! Thankfully, she was facing the other way, and I darted behind the couch just in time.

I quickly scanned the room for the hidden object. Not seeing it, I waited until Jo's fin-steps became inaudible, then ran to the kitchen and hid under the sink.

Then I heard more fin-steps. But looking out the crack of light between the sink doors, I learned it was Anny, not Jo. Perhaps she had become another seeker!

And when she was gone, I crawled out of the small space and looked for the object; there was no object. Now I knew it had to be hidden on the upper floor since I had checked all of the main story.

So, when the coast was clear, I darted up the stairs and quickly hid behind a chair before anybody saw me. But something I saw excited me, and it wasn't the chair. I noticed a tiny cardboard box next to its leg, but there seemed to be a blue glow shining through the box's walls. Impatient, I lifted the box, revealing the object underneath. I won!

"I found the object!" I shouted. Everybody came running towards me. Surprisingly, Mary was almost finished with her candy bar, and Anny was about half done with her popcorn.

"Congratulations! That's correct!" Jo paused. "Great job, Max! Sorry to change the topic, but it's now 8:15. Is anyone tired, or do you want to play more games?"

Mary had bit into her candy bar, which had gotten much shorter, so she could not answer. "Well, *I'm* not very tired," Katrina stated.

"Me neither! At the gingashluckaquin's place back when we were sqwgamugurtz, we got very little sleep because we were doing hard work all day!" Anny said in an ironically cheery tone of voice.

"You make it sound like being possessed by the gingashluckaquin and doing torturous work was the best thing that you ever experienced," Mary said.

"I know, right? It was the most terrible thing that has happened to me at this point in my life!!" Mary sighed and rolled her eyes.

"What's a sqwgamugurtz? Did the gingashluckaquin possess you?" Katrina asked.

Mary stared at her blankly. "Well, a sqwgamugurtz is this super-weird monster with three heads and a door on its feet. And one bad day—which was actually going really good up until then because Max had arrived—last summer, the gingashluckaquin—probably the same one who kidnapped you—thought we would be great servants even though we're only ten and can't legally work yet—"

"And we did tortuous work for many months until Max finally killed the gingashluckaquin, so we escaped and ended up here," Anny finished the sentence.

"Oh, wow. Well, it's good the gingashluckaquin is dead now!" Katrina said.

"Yeah..." I started. After the awful encounter with the evil monster, simply thinking of the gingashluckaquin brought back memories—*terrible* memories. I sighed. To change the topic, I quickly added, "Anyway, what game should we play next?"

We didn't stop playing games until much later, a few minutes past 10:00. Everybody was happy, but tired. It was time to go to bed.

"Katrina, would you like to sleep in this room with the rest of us, or somewhere else? It would be *totally awesome* if you slept in here with the rest of us, but you'll need an air mattress. What do you think?"

"I'm fine with that; it's better than the back of a car!"

"That's very true," Jo said. She paused. "I'm so sorry you had to live in your car for so long because you were scared to apologize to me. I know it's hard to apologize when you are worried that your child thinks you abandoned them."

Katrina sighed. "Jo, I can't put how sorry I am into words. I should have come and apologized, but I didn't."

Jo looked Katrina in the eyes. "Aww, Mom... it's okay. I'm not kidding. I forgive you." She hugged her mom.

Anny joined in, too. "We're sorry too, Max. I feel bad how we were acting so strange when you first arrived at Sharkland. It's just because we both had this awful gut feeling that was about to happen."

I looked Annny in the eyes too. "Anny. There's no need to apologize. You didn't do anything wrong. The gingashluckaquin decided to possess you; you didn't want to be possessed. It wasn't your fault. I mean who would *want* to be possessed?" And I meant it.

Everybody started hugging and apologizing to each other. Turns out, everybody was sorry for something.

And when it was over, a dead silence fell over the room. Mary interrupted that silence by noticing, "Well, it's past 10:00 at night. That's *hours* after many of us usually go to bed. We better continue getting ready for bed."

"Oh, right." Jo laughed. "Sorry, I forgot to remind everybody to get ready for bed before we played all those games. Let's brush our teeth."

"It's okay," Anny reassured Jo. "I was eating that delicious popcorn you made."

In the bathroom, Jo had already laid out two extra toothbrushes for Mary and Anny. Because I did not know how often Katrina was able to brush her teeth while she was living in her car, I replaced the head on my electric toothbrush and gave it to her. Therefore, I had no toothbrush to use, so I grabbed a new one from the box.

Jo next started passing the toothpaste around. She squeezed some of the cyan paste on her brush head, then passed it to the rest of us. After starting the mini sand timer on the wall, we all brushed our teeth for two minutes, then we spat into the sink when we were done.

Mary, Anny, and Jo went back to the bedroom to put their pajamas on, but Katrina and I stayed to floss our teeth. And when we were done, which did not take long, we joined Jo and the twins in the bedroom.

I noticed Mary, Anny, and Jo were wearing different clothes than they were before. "Oh, Mary and Anny! Did you find pajamas in the donation pile that fit you?" I asked.

"Yes, we did! They're comfortable, and they're even our favorite colors!" Mary exclaimed. It was true. Mary's pair were bright blue, and Anny's pair were pink.

Suddenly, a familiar, yet muffled, voice came out of seemingly nowhere. "I think you and Katrina should get changed, Max," somebody said.

I looked around, but I could not figure out who was talking. "Woah. Who said that?"

"Oh, sorry. I was in the closet." It was Jo. Everybody laughed.

"Okay, everybody. Let's get into bed now. We're all tired," said Anny.

"Wait! We still need to blow up the air mattress!" Mary interrupted.

"Oh, right. I'll grab it from the basement."

It took about ten minutes, but we finally got Katrina's air mattress set up, complete with blankets and a pillow. "Thank you! You all are so kind!" Katrina exclaimed, testing the mattress, and liking it.

"Well, we wouldn't just make you sleep on the floor, that's mean!" I reacted.

But Jo interrupted our discussion of the air mattress. "You guys, I'm, like, so tired that I feel like a zombie. I think it's time for us all to go to bed."

I looked around the room, expecting a response, but Jo got none. Surprisingly, Mary and Anny were already curled up in my bed, and Anny looked like she was asleep already.

Following their lead, I let Katrina and Jo crawl into their beds, and I flipped the light switch when they were settled. When the lights turned off, I pulled the cover of Jo's bed back and crawled inside, clutching my shark plushie.

It only took a few minutes for me to fall asleep.

23

Max Goes Home

I appeared to be the last one to wake up the next morning—nobody else was still in bed. And when I woke up, the first thing I noticed was a sweet smell wafting in from the kitchen. I didn't know what it was, but it smelled *delicious*.

Wanting to investigate, I jumped out of bed and peered over the railing outside. And there were Anny, Mary, Katrina, and Jo, making peanut butter-banana pancakes— my *favorite*! Bubbling with excitement, I ran down the stairs so fast I almost tripped.

"OMG, pancakes!" I said, forgetting to say hello.

Jo turned around, and when she saw me, her smile grew. "Hi, Max! How are you doing on this fine morning?"

I thought for a moment—I didn't quite know how to answer the question. "Well, I'm a bit tired, but I slept well! But since there's no school today even though it's Tuesday, it was nice to sleep in. Thanks for making pancakes, though!"

Mary, who stood across the room chopping bananas, replied to me. "Of course. It's your last day in Sharkland." I could see tears welling in her eyes.

That's when I realized the *true* reason why everybody was making pancakes for me aside from the fact that it was a sleepover, and a tear rolled down my cheek, too. "Mary, it's okay. I will never forget you. Or any of you. Instead of feeling sad that I'm leaving tonight, I'd say let's try to make the most of my last day."

But before anybody could respond, Katrina called from the other end of the kitchen, telling us the pancakes were ready. "Max! Your pancakes are ready! How do you want?"

"Hmm. Once you have made all the pancakes, please divide them equally so everybody gets the same amount. I don't want more than everybody else."

"That's nice of you! I'll finish cooking the pancakes, and I'll divide them equally," Katrina replied.

"Thanks."

Meanwhile, Jo asked Mary to help her set the table. "Mary, can you help me set the table with enough settings for five sharks?"

"Five? Sure," Mary responded.

"Yeah. Me, Max, Anny, you, and Katrina."

"Oh, right." Katrina's cheeks turned red. "My apologies, Katrina. You've only been here since yesterday afternoon, so I'm still getting used to you being here."

"It's okay," she assured Mary.

Later, the pancakes were finally ready. Everybody sat down at the table and started eating.

Excited from the delicious scent of the peanut butter and banana mixed with the butteriness of the fluffy bread, I grabbed my fork and dug it into the edge of one pancake. "*Woah*. These are *so good*," I told the "chefs".

"Thanks, Max!" Anny responded, beaming.

The pancakes were so good that everybody finished rapidly. When we were done, we all needed to brush our teeth, and Anny needed to shower. After washing her dishes, Anny told us she would do that. "I'll get started with my shower," Anny said.

"That's a good idea. I'll bring our toothbrushing supplies downstairs so you can shower in peace," I replied.

"Good idea," Anny remarked.

Anny was almost finished with her shower, and Jo, Mary, and I were all done brushing our teeth. So we all headed back upstairs to get dressed and make our beds. The time was about 10:40 in the morning.

And when we were done with those things, Anny, fully dressed in her clothes she wore yesterday, emerged from the bathroom. "Hi, everybody! I finished my shower! Gosh, I feel *so* much better now." Her breath smelled minty fresh, so I assumed she also brushed her teeth."

Jo agreed. "Yeah, showers always make *me* feel so much better."

Mary suddenly changed the subject. "Hey, would anybody like to play another round of 'Sinking Ships'? Everybody loved that game when we played it yesterday."

"I want to!" I declared.

"Me too!" Anny added.

"Me three!" Katrina mentioned.

"Me four!" Jo stated.

"Okay then, let's play!" Mary grabbed the game's box from the side of her bed. "I'll set the game board up."

Mary's idea had really stuck—it was past noon, and we were still playing games. But when a loud sound that sounded like either a doorbell or a knock suddenly came from downstairs, I dropped my piece in shock.

"What was that?" Mary whispered, suddenly becoming alert.

"It sounded like somebody was ringing the doorbell," I thought out loud. "But I also heard a knock."

Anny didn't think of the sound as creepy like the rest of us. "Let's go downstairs and investigate!" Anny exclaimed, standing up and running down the stairs so fast she almost tripped.

"Woah! Slow down! We don't even know who's on the other side of the door!" Mary mentioned.

I was the last one to get there, but I was still looking out the peephole only a few seconds after Mary finished her sentence. Out of the peephole, I noticed many familiar shark faces on the other side of the door.

Opening the door gave me a better look at the sharks outside. I saw Lachenz, Kay, ZY, and Linda, and even Vhreho and Guhyeo were in the crowd. Almost as soon as the door was opened, a delicious meat smell wafted towards Jo, the twins, Katrina, and I.

"MAX!!!" they all screamed. Unexpectedly, Kay came over and hugged me, and everybody else followed her lead. I noticed Kay's eyes were no longer fiery-red or emerald green; they were a beautiful shade of blue.

Lachenz made a very mature-sounding comment. "We're to say goodbye. But it's not over yet."

Kay spoke next. "I'm so sorry, Max, for the way I treated you when I was possessed by the gingashluckaquin. I didn't know how to apologize, though, so I threw a surprise party for you on your last day at Sharkland! ZY brought, like, *a ton of* food, and he assumed you guys have a grill, so he'll grill hamburgers, hot dogs, bratwursts, and a vegetarian option—plant-based chicken tenders—for lunch! And we didn't know if you guys had a pool, so we all brought our swimsuits, just in case you did."

"Just so you know, bratwursts are these long sausages that are eaten with buns like hotdogs," ZY added.

The only thing I could think of to say was a lame "Wow! Thank you, everybody!"

I didn't do anything except standing there and staring into space, trying to ponder how someone who was once a rebellious rule-breaker had organized a goodbye party for me and invited many of the sharks I met at Sharkschool. And that was Kay, the previously naughty female shark who previously didn't seem to care about me. And Vhreho and Guhyeo came! These were all surprising to me, but I remembered they wouldn't have happened if they were still possessed by the gingashluckaquin. "Here, everybody, let's go to the backyard!" I led all the sharks to the fenced-in grassy area at the back of the house.

Jo and I had gotten lucky with our house's backyard. Not only was it large and spacious, but it had a pool, too, which was rectangular with a 6-foot deep end. A wrought iron fence strung with fairy lights separated our backyard from the neighbors', and a tall tree with a swing stood in the corner. Kay, noticing the pool, wondered, "OMG, you guys *do* have a pool!! Can we use it??"

I walked to the pool's edge and started peeling the tarp off. "Of course! Just let me take the tarp off first."

Stepping out of her shorts and pulling her shirt off, Kay claimed, "Don't worry, I have my swimsuit on under my clothes." And, while walking to the pool's deep end, she yelled, "CANNONBALL!!!"

"Since you *do* have a pool, I'm going to go into the bathroom and change into *my* swimsuit," Lachenz said. "If you would be okay with me using your bathroom."

"Yeah, that's okay with me!" Jo informed him. "It's to the right of the stairs."

When Jo gave Lachenz permission to change in the bathroom, everybody else followed his lead and asked to use the bathroom too, starting with ZY. But not everybody could change in one bathroom at the same time, though. "Why doesn't somebody change in the bathroom on the upper level? Not all of you can change in one bathroom at once!"

"Well, if it helps, I'm probably not going to change because I will be grilling most of the time," ZY thought out loud.

I didn't believe that. "I think you should change, ZY, or at least put your swimsuit on underneath your clothes. There'll probably be a time when everybody gets full and you can stop grilling, ZY."

"That's a good idea! I'll do that."

Everybody was either off changing in the bathroom or waiting for their turn in the bathroom, and Jo decided it was a good time to start the jets. "Well, now that everybody's off changing, I think I'll start the jets in the pool," Jo stated. Jo was not only the oldest out of the group at twelve years old, but she was like the family's handyshark—she could fix anything, regardless of how broken or damaged it was, and she knew how to do many things others did not when it came to getting things to operate or assembling products.

She walked to the pool's edge and turned a dial I didn't even know was used to control the jets. Meanwhile, I walked upstairs to my bedroom to change into *my* swimsuit.

Surprisingly, everybody had finished taking turns changing in the bathrooms when I came back from my room. Linda stood next to my and Jo's huge outdoor speaker. "Do y'all want some music?" she asked.

I nodded. "Sure!" Linda pressed a few buttons to turn on the radio. A dance-style beat started playing. Recognizing the song, Anny and I exchanged glances.

"NO WAY!!!" we shouted in unison. We started jumping up and down in delight.

Everybody else looked at us, confused. "What?" Vhreho asked.

"It's Anny's and my favorite song, *Dance Your Fins Off* by The Sqwgamugurtz!!" I squealed. I could not be happier that this song was on the radio!

"That's awesome!" Kay said. "I like this song, too!"

Before I could ask Kay if she was a fan of The Sqwgamugurtz too, Guhyeo asked if we wanted to go to the pool. "Well, how about we all go into the pool?" he asked. "It's hot."

"You're right. I'm also hot. CANNONBALL!!!" Vhreho jumped into the pool's deep end, making my entire right side wet. Everybody laughed.

With the exception of ZY, who was grilling, everybody else got into the pool too. ZY asked, "What do you all want for lunch?

Everybody responded to ZY's question, and ZY noted what people wanted. But Guhyeo's answer was especially funny.

"I want 2 hamburgers with a side of 3 plant-based chicken tenders, please—Swiss cheese on one of the hamburgers and Cheddar cheese on the other," Guhyeo stated.

Everybody's attention turned to Guhyeo. "Why so much food?" Katrina wondered.

"I'm still growing," was Guhyeo's response. He paused. "It also helps that I didn't eat breakfast this morning since I woke up late." Everybody laughed again.

Suddenly, Lachenz felt something touching him from under the pool's surface. "Woah, what's that? Who's touching my tailfin?"

Taking a big breath, Kay emerged out of the water. Everybody laughed. "Is lunch ready yet?" she asked.

After about ten or twenty minutes of dancing, chatting, and swimming, ZY finally announced that everything had finished cooking. "All right, everybody. Your food is off the grill!" ZY reached into the meat bag and grabbed condiments, plus a can of chili beans.

"Max, would you like to go first? You're the entire reason why we're here."

I sighed. I knew too well that I would go back to Wah tonight. "Sure, thanks! This looks delicious!" On my plate, I saw delicious-looking plant-based chicken tenders and a scrumptious hamburger, all with grill marks.

Before I started eating, I squirted a dollop of ketchup on half the burger and mustard on the other. I also squirted a generous amount of pickle relish on the plate for the chicken tenders—Jo had taught me at the Sharkland Zoo that this was a delicious combo.

I let everybody else get their food before I started eating mine, just to be polite. ZY pulled his shirt off, ready to chill in the pool after the meal.

Later

About 8:30 PM

The party had been over for a few hours by now. I was lying in my bed, satisfied I had finished my bedtime routine, clutching all my favorite plushies and memorabilia from my stay at Sharkland. Jo, Anny, Mary, and Katrina were all sitting at the edge of my bed, and everybody was crying, except for Mary, but she looked like she would burst into tears at any moment.

"Max, I haven't really known you for more than a day, but I know I'll miss you!" Katrina sobbed.

Mary and Anny joined in. "We'll miss you too!"

"I'll miss you so, so much!" Jo said as soon as she could speak.

"I'll miss every one of you, too!" I murmured. I wasn't crying physically, but mentally, I was weeping.

My eyes were starting to feel heavy and tired, so I closed them. As I felt myself drifting to sleep, I tightened my grip on all my things: the Rainbow Rainbow flower from the Deedly Store and my ID from Sharkland. The dirty, creased "sqwgamugurtz advertisement" I ripped off the pole at the creepy castle was tucked in my

297

waistband, and the phone device Jo had given me was in my pajama shorts pocket.

I only heard one thing before I slipped into the sleep realm, and it was Jo saying, "Max, I have one last thing before you go. If Sharkland is ever in danger, if it needs your help, I will call you back here."

Point of View: Third Person

Slowly, Max's sleeping body faded away from the bed as he returned to Wah. The "sqwgamugurtz advertisement" and phone device were the only things that went with Max; everything else was still in the bed.

"Too bad his things got left behind," Anny said in a silly voice, lightening the mood a bit.

The End

Wah (Epilogue)

Exactly five months before on Wah: Around June 20.

Point of View: First Person

Before I even opened my eyes the next morning, I knew something had changed. The smell was different, the room was brighter, and the bedding was thicker. Strangely, I recognized the room, but I couldn't figure out why.

Other sharks must have been in the house because I suddenly heard fast-paced caudal fin-steps, increasing in volume as they moved toward my room. Finally, they were so loud that I could tell the shark owning the caudal fin-steps was directly outside my door. I watched as the door opened at rapid speed.

"MAX!!!" the shark practically shouted.

But there was no shark. Rather, it was my human mom, Clara. *Now* I remembered; I wasn't on Sharkland, but Wah, and I had just arrived that morning.

Peeling back the covers with the long limbs I remembered were called "arms", I got out of bed and stood on what I remembered were called "feet" and "legs". My mom ran over to me and hugged me. I tried to say hello, but I couldn't find the words. But when I *did* find words, I shouted, "Hi, Mom!! I missed you so, so much!!" into her arms.

We finally let go of each other. She responded, "I missed you so, so much too!"

"Where's Dad? Is he at work?" I wondered.

"Nope. He's downstairs," Mom informed me. She walked to the door and shouted out. "JUSTIN!!!"

"What?" I heard from downstairs.

"Max is home!!"

"No way!!" Justin came running up the stairs and bounded into my room. He attacked me with a big hug. "Max! I'm so happy you're home!"

Before either of us could say much more, I heard a knock on the door from downstairs.

Wondering who it was, I looked out my bedroom window—it was my best friend Sebastian, wearing a bike helmet. He must have heard I was coming home and wanted to greet me.

"Max! Do you see Sebastian? He must have come to greet you after your trip to Sharkland! You should go see him!" Mom advised me.

"Alright!" I replied. Excited that my friend was here, I ran downstairs to meet him at the front door.

Sebastian was out of breath. "Max!! How are you? How was Sharkland? When I heard you were back on Wah, I raced here—sorry if I interrupted anything. I've just been so excited to see you again! Can we hang out?"

I had no idea Sebastian would be coming over, but I was excited! "I also missed you so much! I'd love to hang out! Can I bike over to your house?"

"Of course!" Sebastian said. "We might be able to swim, too, so I suggest you bring your swimsuit."

It took me about twenty minutes or so to get ready to leave: get permission from my parents, gather my swim gear, dress myself, eat breakfast, put my shoes on, and get my bike ready. But when I was, it was finally time to leave!

"Let's roll!" Sebastian exclaimed, getting off the couch and following me outside.

"Hold on," I said. "I haven't had legs for five months. It'll take a bit to re-learn how to ride this thing."

"Oh, right," Sebastian said, embarrassed. He parked his bike on the street and walked over to me while I tried to climb onto my bike without losing my balance. "Don't worry, Max. If you fall, I will catch you."

It didn't take us long to arrive at Sebastian's house—I was surprised at how easily I was able to adjust to riding my bike with legs. Once we put our bikes in the garage, Sebastian took me to his gamer-style bedroom with LED lights and a desk with multiple monitors.

We did many things in our time together, including chatting, playing video games, baking cookies, building forts, watching movies, and playing outside, and after lunch, we biked to the indoor pool and swam for a while. But the time to go home came shortly—6:00 was here before I knew it!

"Max, I think it's sadly time to go home," Sebastian said with a sad tone of voice.

I was sad to go! "But I don't want to leave!"

"I know; I don't want you to leave either! Your parents did say to be home by six, though."

"That's true." I ran to Sebastian and hugged him. "Well, I guess I'll see you later."

"See you later!" Sebastian responded.

I exited Sebastian's house and got my bike out of the garage, and then I started biking home.

The first thing I did when I got home was to park my bike inside the garage and take off my helmet. After that, I entered the house through the door in the garage and took my shoes off.

Immediately as I walked through the threshold, I was hit with a strong, delicious smell—it smelled like juicy beef was cooking in the oven. Not able to see into the kitchen from where I stood, I settled on the idea that Mom and Dad were making their favorite frozen meat pasta dish for dinner.

I would have peered into the kitchen to see if I was correct, but before I could do that, I noticed my relatives sitting on the sofa and talking to each other. On top of that, the house looked different, too: shark-themed decorations were plastered all over the walls. I didn't know what to say; why were all my family members here? "Hi, guys! How have you been? But just out of curiosity, why are you all here?" I wondered.

"MAX!!" everybody exclaimed. At least ten of my favorite people were in the living room, and more were in the kitchen helping cook the meal.

It smelled *scrumptious*, but I still didn't know what it was. "What's cooking?"

Justin called from the kitchen. "Would you like to know now, or would you like to wait until everything is on the table in about five minutes?" he asked.

I thought for a moment. "Hmm. I'll wait."

"I'd love to hear what Sharkland was like!" Grandma Brooklyn exclaimed.

I thought again; how was I supposed to describe such an amazing, yet complicated, trip? Sharkland was hard to describe in words. "Gosh, I don't know where to start! I guess I woke up in Sharkland on a hot June day—this was probably January second for you, since Sharkland is 5 months ahead. Overnight, I turned into a human-shark hybrid. And I met three other sharks after I exited my room: Mary, Anny, and Jo.

"Well, they offered to take me on a gold hunt. During that gold hunt, I plunged into a frigid lake while sitting in a moving car, witnessed a fake emerald steal Mary away, was trapped in a glass hallway, saw a royal palace, touched red-hot laser beams, and went into a trance while hearing a voice inside my head."

"Woah! Are you okay?" Grandpa Rufus worried.

"Yeah, I'm fine," I replied. "But anyway, Mary and Anny disappeared at different times during that gold hunt. The map we were using told us to go to a royal palace to find the gold, and when we got there, we found them again, but they were not sharks; rather, they were these animals called sqwgamugurtz. In fact, I have this." I grabbed the dirty, torn "sqwgamugurtz drawing" from my pocket and started talking again. This is the drawing of a sqwgamugurtz I found in the royal palace." Everybody examined the drawing, confused—a sqwgamugurtz was a strange-looking creature.

I continued explaining my journey. "Not much happened in the two months that followed. Jo and I bought a house, but not many other exciting things happened in those first two months, except for when my friend and caretaker Jo and I registered for Sharkschool.

On the first day of school, I met this other young shark named Kay Kallyn. We quickly became friends.”

“That’s nice,” Aunt Lola responded. “It’s amazing how you made friends in Sharkschool.”

“Yes,” I said, annoyed that my relatives were interrupting me. But I continued anyway.

“On the last day of the third week of school, an animal called a HifftYiz got onto Sharkschool’s property. But the HifftYiz was actually my classmate Linda, who had turned into the monster. I remember using a product called Monster Bottle to change it back into Linda. Nobody was hurt.

“But after the incident with the HifftYiz, Jo took Kay and I to a store called Awesome Stuff For Less. Well, I admit that I made a terrible decision when I was there and accidentally fell off a metal bar while trying to impress Kay. I ended up going unconscious, and I heard the same creepy voice again that I had heard on the gold hunt. “

“Just use it as a learning opportunity,” my cousin Riley stated. “You’re still growing.”

“One day, two classmates, Vhreho and Guhyeo, were called to an appointment to get new hearts—Jo and I had to come, and we had no idea why. Apparently their hearts were knocked out one day in a forest. But the same day, Jo’s grandma, Grandma Mariohn, took Jo and me to a deedly store, also known as a plant shop. But when I was there, I realized Kay was not just a normal shark: she was there one moment, but I blinked, and she vanished.

"Next, on the Saturday after the second week of school, Jo took me to the Sharkland Zoo. It was fun, and I could see more animals than I expected, but another strange thing happened there. The spelling on some of the signs for the enclosures was wrong, like "bes" instead of "bees" and "restrom" instead of "restroom". It felt like it was more than bad spelling.

"And before I fell asleep that night, I noticed a letter on my nightstand that had blown in from the window. The most surprising thing about the letter wasn't how it blew in from the window, but the recipient was named "HifftYiz", just like the HifftYiz I saw at Sharkschool!

"But this HifftYiz was different. The letter was sent from another monster called the "gingashluckaquin", and when I opened the letter, I was informed that it was trying to obtain the last of the four Seashells of Power, which could grant whoever had all four immortality and invincibility. And the gingashluckaquin had a deal with the HifftYiz, which I later learned was Linda's grandfather. The HifftYiz would give the gingashluckaquin the last Seashell of Power if it gave him fifty hearts from sharks. The letter also read that the gingashluckaquin possessed Kay and turned her into a servant, and it wanted to do the same for me, too."

"Did the gingashluckaquin possess you?" Uncle Daniel asked.

I sighed. "I'll get to it eventually."

"Sorry," Uncle Daniel replied.

I continued. "After I fell asleep that night, I had a vision—a vision, not a dream. I saw Vhreho and Guhyeo stealing hearts after their doctor's appointment. I won't go into detail about the vision since it was long, but I learned that Vhreho and Guhyeo actually stole hearts from the doctor's office and gave them to the gingashluckaquin.

"The next day, I received a letter from the HifftYiz. It mentioned I was the only survivor in Sharkland with the right kind of heart, and it would do whatever it could to get mine. It also wanted me to be the keeper of the Seashell of Power and stop the gingashluckaquin from getting it. It asked me to come to its house at 1234 Help Street.

"Three days later, the gingashluckaquin broke into Jo's and my house around midnight. It knew I had the Seashell of Power—I don't know how it learned that. The gingashluckaquin blocked the door, but I had to escape, so I grabbed my pillow and the fake Seashell of Power the HifftYiz gave me and jumped out the window—"

"Max. I know it's rude to interrupt, but that is very unsafe," my cautious Grandma Prudence stated.

"I know. I wouldn't have done it if my life was not in danger," I replied. I continued, "I ran to 1234 Help Street, where the HifftYiz lived and the gingashluckaquin lived part of the time, and broke its safe to access the other three Seashells of Power. Then I ran back home—it was around one o'clock in the morning, and I was very tired—and slept outside because I did not know if the gingashluckaquin was still in my bedroom.

"The next day, which was Monday, Jo and I arrived at Sharkschool late because we met with the local museum. They wanted to create an exhibit for the Seashells of Power. The day after that, the HifftYiz died because the Seashell of Power transferred possessions, and the loss of such a magical object can kill sharks sometimes. We left Sharkschool early because we attended The HifftYiz's funeral." I tried to hold back tears. "Shortly after getting home after the funeral and changing clothes, Jo and I heard a knock on the door—it was Jo's mom, Katrina. When Jo was four, the gingashluckaquin kidnapped Katrina, but at the time, Jo thought Katrina abandoned her, and Katrina came to apologize.

"Later, Mary and Anny randomly appeared in a closet in the attic. They were still sqwgamugurtz, but they turned back into sharks when I touched them. And I had a super-fun sleepover with Jo, Mary, Anny, and Katrina to celebrate seeing old friends again. I woke up the morning after to a delicious breakfast of peanut butter banana pancakes. Later that day, some of my classmates, Lachenz, Kay, ZY, Linda, Vhreho, and Guhyeo came to our house! And the awesome thing was that many of them were previously possessed, but they had become free, and they all seemed so much happier. We had a party in the backyard, and ZY grilled.”

“Woah! That is *so* cool!” my cousin Ella said.

“I’m so happy you made so many friends!” Aunt Lola reminded me. When she noticed everybody looking at her, she added, “But your entire trip sounded amazing.”

Everybody continued commenting on my Sharkland trip summary, but they were interrupted by Mom’s shouting. “Dinner’s ready!”

Now I was *excited*; the smells in the house smelled so delicious, it was driving me crazy how I couldn’t eat yet. And now I finally could! And all the food looked *so good*. As I sat down at my seat, I read all the cards labeling the dishes: Caesar salad, cheesy potatoes, steak, green beans, fruit salad, dinner rolls, mac n’ cheese. All on my favorite foods list.

I stared at the food, nearly drooling because it looked so *good*. “Wow. Did you make this all just for me?” I asked.

“Well, duh! You were just in Sharkland for five months and we missed you! Of course you deserve a big party!” Mom exclaimed.

"Thank you!"

I loaded my plate with a bit of every dish on the table and poured myself a glass of milk from the fridge. The meal was just as, if not even more, delicious than I thought it would be.

I had finished my dinner, and now it was time for dessert. "Max, are you ready for cake?" Justin asked.

Cake? "OMG, there's cake?! Yay!!"

Instead of responding, Mom and Dad walked to the fridge and grabbed a round vanilla cake in a box with a see-through lid. Through the box, I noticed the cake read *Welcome Home, Max!* in large, red frosting letters.

I couldn't help smiling as Mom cut the cake into equal slices, missing my friends in Sharkland but being happy to be back home on Wah. She gave me a plate with a slice of cake and chocolate ice cream on the side. Just like the dinner, everything smelled delicious. I dug into the cake with my fork, my mouth covered with delicious frosting.

That night

I lay in bed, waiting for sleep to come. While I knew I would miss Sharkland, I felt happy to be home. I had another life outside Sharkland, after all. And the party was awesome! It was unexpected, but super fun!

It only took me a few minutes to fall asleep.

Pronunciations of Names in Sharkland

Sharks (Main Characters)

- Maxamil Alderin (max-uh-MUHL all-derr-IN)
- Anny Calida-Yif (ANN-ee call-EYE-duh-YIHF)
- Mary Calida-Yif (MARE-ee call-EYE-duh-YIHF)
- Jo Brime (JO brr-EYE-mm)
- Kay Kallyn (K KAA-lynn)
- Katrina Brime (kuh-TREEN-uh brr-EYE-mm)

Sharks (Sharkschool)

- Guhyeo Skigamon (GUH-yee-oh / guh-YOU ss-KIG-a-MON)
- Vhreho Chinkchink (vuh-REE-who CHINKCHINK)
- Zing-Yang (zing-YANG), shortened to ZY (ZY)
- Lachenz (luh-CHENZ or LAA-chenz)
- Lindang (lin-DANG), shortened to Linda (LIN-duh)
- Mr. Kennager (KEN-uh-grr)
- Mr. Schakss (sh-CACKS)
- Ms. Hagger (Katarine) (CAT-uh-rihn HAGG-err)
- Ms. Gingashnugger (GING-uh-SSHNUGG-er)
- Mr. Klongei (klaahn-gee)

Sharks (Adults/Other)

- Moe (mm-OH)
- Grandma Mariohn (MARE-ee-own)
- Shan (sh-ANN)
- Phareegya Chinkchink (fuh-REEG-yuh ch-INK-ch-INK)

Monster Names

- Sqwgamugurtz (SQUIG-uh-muh-grr-tz)
- HifftYiz / HifftYuez (HIFF-tuh-yiz or HIFF-tuh-youz)
- Gingashluckaquin (ging-uh-ssh-luck-uh-QUING)

People on Wah

- Max's mom Clara (cul-AIR-uh)
- Max's dad Justin (JUST-in)
- Mr. and Mrs. Istruugabon (is-TROOG-uh-bahn)
- Sebastian (see-BAAS-chin)

Other Names

- Dr. Yaincala's Family Care (YAH-EE-in-call-uh)
- Skicks (pronounced like "sticks", but with a "k" sound instead of a "t")
- Wah (Waah with an "aah" sound you might make when the doctor asks you to open wide)

Dennisatroy's Countries

- **Dennisatroy (den-ISS-uh-troy)**
- Sharkland (SHARK-lind)
- Impood (ihm-POOD)
- Hile-Backa (HIH-lee-BAAH-kuh)
- Hacoshof (HAA-coah-shoff)
- Genevail (JEN-uh-vay-ll)
- Achebail (AA-kuh-bay-ll)
- Wilderbang (WIHLDER-bang)
- Fikasi (FEE-kuh-see)
- The Scar (The Scar)
- Quinsiching (QUIN-see-ching)

Other (Sharks)

- Caudal fin (KAH-dull)
- Pectoral fin (peck-TORE-uhl)

Glossary of Sharkland Terms

- **Shark-human hybrid ("shark"):** What Max turns into when he wakes up in Sharkland. Note that Sharkland sharks are different from sharks on Earth; they walk with their long caudal ("tail") fins, have both lungs *and* gills, and sleep with their eyes closed.

- **Sqwgamugurtz:** A sqwgamugurtz is a large, strange looking creature with three legs, three heads, and three eyes with triangular, square, and rectangular pupils. Legend states that if you are desperate and need a home, a sqwgamugurtz can act as a temporary shelter.

- **Wah:** Wah is the planet Max lives on before he goes to Sharkland. It is very much like Earth, but it is not the same.

- **Caudal fin on a shark:** This is also known as the tailfin. This helps sharks on Earth swim, and Sharkland sharks use it to walk.

- **Pectoral fin on a shark:** Like sharks on Earth, Sharkland sharks have two of these. Sharkland sharks use their pectoral fins like hands for grabbing objects, and sharks on Earth use them to steer themselves in the water.

- **Sharkland:** Sharkland is the place Max goes to for Go Anywhere Day. It is on the planet Dennisatroy, which is so far away you can only get to it by teleportation. Sharkland has shark-human hybrids instead of humans. Max stays here for five months before returning back to Wah.
- **Go Anywhere Day:** Go Anywhere Day is a day when nine-year-old kids choose a place they want to visit and stay at for exactly five months. It happens on New Year's Eve. The place the kid chooses to go to is almost always imaginary.
- **Dennisatroy:** Dennisatroy is a planet. It is so far away that you have to teleport there. It is the planet that holds dreamlands and imaginary worlds. Time there is five months ahead of Wah, and that is why Max arrives when it is June on Sharkland but January on Wah.
- **Sharkland, Impood, Hile-Backa, Hacoshof, Genevail, Achebail, Wilderbang, Fikasi, The Scar, Quinsiching:** Countries on the planet of Dennisatroy.
  - **Sharkland** *(SHARK-lind)*: The "shark world". One of the three main countries.
  - **Impood** *(ihm-POOD)*: The "land of devices". One of the three main countries.

- o **Hile-Backa** *(HIH-lee-BAH-kuh)*: The "land of nothing". One of the three main countries.
  - o **Hacoshof** *(HAA-coah-shawf)*: The "land of dogs".
  - o **Genevail** *(JEN-uh-vay-ll)*: The "land of witches".
  - o **Achebail** *(AA-key-bay-ll)*: The "land of labyrinths", also known as the "land of mazes".
  - o **Wilderbang** *(WIHLDER-bang)*: The "water world".
  - o **Fikasi** *(FEE-kuh-see)*: The "land of pink".
  - o **The Scar** *(The Scar)*: The "land of revenge".
  - o **Quinsiching** *(QUIN-see-ching)*: The "land of magic".
- **SharkBites and SharkTadlets:** Common foods Sharkland sharks like to eat. SharkBites is the name of a cereal, and SharkTadlets are granola bar-like foods made of dried fish.
- **SBucks ($):** The currency on Sharkland.

Part 2

- **Sharkschool:** Sharkschool is one of the few schools on Sharkland, and it is the largest. It is also a private school. Sharkschool is divided into four buildings: the Low Building for kindergarten–5th graders, the Middle Building for 6–8th graders, the High Building for 9–12th graders, and the Preschool Building for preschoolers and pre-K students, 3 of which are connected via a long hallway.

- **Nuggings:** The currency used in a game called *Be Mean: When Hurt Feelings Mean Winning.*
- **Skicks:** A game with a ball that youth on Sharkland like to play. Not much is described about Skicks.
- **Hot Potato:** A game Max plays in gym class during the first week of school. In comparison to games on Earth, Hot Potato is most like kickball.
- **Monster bottles:** Types of liquids that turn monsters back into sharks. Monsters were almost always born sharks but changed into monsters somehow.
- **HifftYiz/HifftYuez:** A HifftYiz is an animal with very large eyes and tiny legs with a claw replacing the place where the nose would go. When HifftYizes are scared, acid comes out the ends of its legs. In Sharkland, Max meets two HifftYizes: Linda (chapter 9), and Linda's grandfather (chapters 14–17). The spelling *HifftYuez* is used in some parts of Sharkland, and the spelling *HifftYiz* is used in the other parts, including where Max lives.
- **Stote:** A Sharkland word meaning "place where death happens" or "murder scene".
- **Deedly:** A Sharkland word meaning "plants".
- **Gingashluckaquin:** A blob-like creature colored like a shadow that levitates off the ground and has a sucker

instead of a mouth. Not all gingashluckaquins are evil, but the one Max meets *is*. Since gingashluckaquins do not have mouths, they cannot speak in the normal way, so they communicate with people mentally. Gingashluckaquins do not have genders, which is why the gingashluckaquin is described as an "it".

- **Seashells of Power:** There are four of these. According to legend, if a living being gains all four of these and activates them in a certain way, they or it will become immortal and invincible. The gingashluckaquin wants to use these to take over Sharkland.
- **Mailshark:** A Sharkland word for "mail carrier".

About The Authors

Morgan and Carissa (Sam) Goldstein are siblings. Morgan is on the left and Carissa is on the right.

Morgan is an aspiring author. While I have yet to win special recognition, math, along with writing, are my passions, and I plan to be a mathematician when I grow up. I live in Minnesota with my family and dog Josie. Sharkland is my first novel.

Carissa (Sam) is also an aspiring author. While I like many things, such as playing viola, writing is one of my favorite things to do, and I plan to be an author when I grow up. Like my brother, I live in Minnesota with my family and dog.

Acknowledgements

First, both of us would like to hugely thank our parents, Joanna and Matt, for being so supportive of us throughout our writing and publishing journey. They supported us with all our random questions—the house closing process, curfew times, etcetera—read the entire book and make suggestions, and as well as supporting us with the money part of publishing a book, they were very supportive of us in general.

Huge thanks to Carissa's best friend Island, too. They motivated us to get our book published. On top of that, they made comments on various paragraphs and excerpts from Sharkland, and overall, they were a very supportive friend.

And thank you to everybody else who supported us along our publishing journey!